A FOX INSIDE

A Fox Inside

DAVID STACTON

faber and faber

This edition first published in 2012
by Faber and Faber Ltd
Bloomsbury House, 74–77 Great Russell Street
London WC1B 3DA

Printed by Books on Demand GmbH, Norderstedt

All rights reserved
© David Stacton, 1955

The right of David Stacton to be identified as author of this work
has been asserted in accordance with Section 77 of the
Copyright, Designs and Patents Act 1988

This book is sold subject to the condition that it shall not, by way of
trade or otherwise, be lent, resold, hired out or otherwise circulated
without the publisher's prior consent in any form of binding or cover other
than that in which it is published and without a similar condition including this
condition being imposed on the subsequent purchaser

A CIP record for this book is available from the British Library

ISBN 978–0–571–29466–4

Our authorised representative in the EU for product safety is
Easy Access System Europe, Mustamäe tee 50, 10621 Tallinn, Estonia
gpsr.requests@easproject.com

Introduction

The Case of David Stacton

Might David Stacton (1923–68) be the most unjustly neglected American novelist of the post-World War II era? There is a case to be made – beginning, perhaps, with a simple inductive process.

In its issue dated 1 February 1963 *Time* magazine offered an article that placed Stacton amid ten writers whom the magazine rated as the best to have emerged in American fiction during the previous decade: the others being Richard Condon, Ralph Ellison, Joseph Heller, H. L. Humes, John Knowles, Bernard Malamud, Walker Percy, Philip Roth, and John Updike. It would be fair to say that, over the intervening fifty years, seven of those ten authors have remained solidly in print and in high-level critical regard. As for the other three: the case of H. L. Humes is complex, since after 1963 he never added to the pair of novels he had already published; while John Knowles, though he continued to publish steadily, was always best known for *A Separate Peace* (1959), which was twice adapted for the screen.

By this accounting, then, I believe we can survey the *Time* list today and conclude that the stand-out figure is David Stacton – a hugely productive, prodigiously gifted, still regrettably little-known talent and, yes, arguably more deserving of revived attention than any US novelist since 1945.

Across a published career of fifteen years or so Stacton put out fourteen novels (under his name, that is – plus a further raft of pseudonymous genre fiction); many short stories; several collections of poetry; and three compendious works of non-fiction. He was first 'discovered' in England, and had to wait several years before making it into print in his homeland. Assessing Stacton's career at the time of what proved to be his last published novel *People of the Book* (1965), Dennis Powers of the *Oakland Tribune* ruefully concluded that Stacton's was very much 'the old story of literary virtue unrewarded'. Three years later Stacton was dead.

The rest has been a prolonged silence punctuated by occasional tributes and testaments in learned journals, by fellow writers, and around the literary blogosphere. But in 2011 New York Review Books reissued Stacton's *The Judges of the Secret Court,* his eleventh novel and the second in what he saw as a trilogy on American themes. (History, and sequences of titles, were Stacton's abiding passions.) Now in 2012 Faber Finds is reissuing a selection of seven of Stacton's novels.

Readers new to the Stacton *oeuvre* will encounter a novelist of quite phenomenal ambition. The landscapes and epochs into which he transplanted his creative imagination spanned vast distances, and yet the finely wrought Stacton prose style remained fairly distinctive throughout. His deft and delicate gifts of physical description were those of a rare aesthete, but the cumulative effect is both vivid and foursquare. He was, perhaps, less committed to strong narrative through-lines than to erecting a sense of a spiritual universe around his characters; yet he undoubtedly had the power to carry the reader with him from page to page. His protagonists are quite often haunted – if not fixated – figures, temperamentally estranged from their societies. But whether or not we may find elements of Stacton himself within said protagonists, for sure his own presence is in the books – not least by dint of his incorrigible fondness for apercus, epigrams, pontifications of all kinds.

*

He was born Lionel Kingsley Evans on 27 May 1923, in San Francisco. (His parents had met and married in Dublin then emigrated after the war.) Undoubtedly Northern California shaped his aesthetic sense, though in later years he would disdain the place as an 'overbuilt sump', lamenting what he felt had been lost in tones of wistful conservatism. ('We had founding families, and a few traditions and habits of our own . . . Above all we had our sensuous and then unspoilt landscape, whose loss has made my generation and sort of westerner a race of restless wanderers.') Stacton was certainly an exile, but arguably he made himself so, even before California, in his estimation, went to the dogs. In any case his fiction would range far away from his place of birth, for all that his early novels were much informed by it.

Precociously bright, the young Lionel Evans was composing poetry and short stories by his mid-teens, and entered Stanford University in 1941, his studies interrupted by the war (during which he was a conscientious objector). Tall and good-looking, elegant in person as in prose, Evans had by 1942 begun to call himself David Stacton. Stanford was also the place where, as far as we know, he acknowledged his homosexuality – to himself and, to the degree possible in that time, to his peers. He would complete his tertiary education at UC Berkeley, where he met and moved in with a man who became his long-time companion, John Mann Rucker. By 1950 his stories had begun to appear in print, and he toured Europe (what he called 'the standard year's travel after college').

London (which Stacton considered 'such a touching city') was one of the favoured stops on his itinerary and there he made the acquaintance of Basil 'Sholto' Mackenzie, the second Baron Amulree, a Liberal peer and distinguished physician. In 1953 Amulree introduced Stacton to Charles Monteith, the brilliant Northern Irish-born editor and director at Faber and Faber. The impression made was clearly favourable, for in 1954 Faber published *Dolores,* Stacton's first novel, which *Time and Tide* would describe as 'a charming idyll, set in Hollywood, Paris and Rome'.

A Fox Inside followed in 1955, *The Self-Enchanted* in 1956: *noir*-inflected Californian tales about money, power and influence; and neurotic men and women locked into marriages made for many complex reasons other than love. In retrospect either novel could conceivably have been a Hollywood film in its day, directed by Nicholas Ray, say, or Douglas Sirk. Though neither book sold spectacularly, together they proved Stacton had a voice worth hearing. In their correspondence Charles Monteith urged Stacton to consider himself 'a novelist of contemporary society', and suggested he turn his hand to outright 'thriller writing'. But Stacton had set upon a different course. 'These are the last contemporary books I intend to write for several years', he wrote to Monteith. 'After them I shall dive into the historical . . .'

In 1956 Stacton made good on his intimation by delivering to Monteith a long-promised novel about Ludwig II of Bavaria, entitled *Remember Me.* Monteith had been excited by the prospect of the work, and he admired the ambition of the first draft, but considered it unpublishable at its initial extent. With considerable application Stacton winnowed *Remember Me* down to a polished form that Faber could work with. Monteith duly renewed his campaign to persuade Stacton toward present-day subject matter. There would be much talk of re-jigging and substituting one proposed book for another already-delivered manuscript, of strategies for 'building a career'. Stacton was amenable (to a degree) at first, but in the end he made his position clear to Monteith:

> I just flatly don't intend to write any more contemporary books, for several reasons . . . [M]y talents are melodramatic and a mite grandiose, and this goes down better with historical sauce . . . I just can't write about the present any more, that's all. I haven't the heart . . . [F]or those of conservative stamp, this age is the end of everything we have loved . . . There is nothing to do but hang up more lights. And for me the lights are all in the past.

Monteith, for all his efforts to direct Stacton's *oeuvre*, could see he was dealing with an intractable talent; and in April 1957 he wrote to Stacton affirming Faber's 'deep and unshaken confidence in your own gift and in your future as a novelist'.

The two novels that followed hard upon *Remember Me* were highly impressive proofs of Stacton's intent and accomplishment, which enhanced his reputation both inside Faber and in wider literary-critical circles. *On a Balcony* told of Akhenaten and Nefertiti in the Egypt of the Eighteenth Dynasty, and *Segaki* concerned a monk in fourteenth-century Japan. Stacton took the view that these two and the Ludwig novel were in fact a trilogy ('concerned with various aspects of the religious experience') which by 1958 he was calling 'The Invincible Questions'.

And this was but the dawning of a theme: in the following years, as his body of work expanded, Stacton came to characterise it as 'a series of novels in which history is used to explain the way we live now' – a series with an 'order' and 'pattern', for all that each entry was 'designed to stand independent of the others if need be'. (In 1964 he went so far as to tell Charles Monteith that his entire oeuvre was 'really one book'.)

Readers discovering this work today might be less persuaded that the interrelation of the novels is as obviously coherent as Stacton contended. There's an argument that Stacton's claims say more for the way in which his brilliant mind was just temperamentally inclined toward bold patterns and designs. (A small but telling example of same: in 1954 at the very outset of his relationship with Faber Stacton sent the firm a logotype he had drawn, an artful entwining of his initials, and asked that it be included as standard in the prelims of his novels ('Can I be humoured about my colophon as a regular practice?'). Faber did indeed oblige him.)

But perhaps Stacton's most convincing explanation for a connective tissue in his work – given in respect of those first three historical novels but, I think, more broadly applicable – was his admission that the three lives fascinated him on account of his identification with 'their plight':

> Fellow-feeling would be the proper phrase. Such people are comforting, simply because they have gone before us down the same endless road . . . [T]hough these people have an answer for us, it is an answer we can discover only by leading parallel lives. Anyone with a taste for history has found himself doing this from time to time . . .

Perhaps we might say that – just as the celebrated and

contemporaneous American acting teacher Lee Strasberg taught students a 'Method' to immerse themselves in the imagined emotional and physical lives of scripted characters – Stacton was engaged in a kind of 'Method writing' that immersed him by turn in the lives of some of recorded history's rarest figures.

*

Stacton was nurtured as a writer by Faber and Faber, and he was glad of the firm's and Charles Monteith's efforts on his behalf, though his concerns were many, perhaps even more so than the usual novelist. Stacton understood he was a special case: not the model of a 'smart popular writer' for as long as he lacked prominent critical support and/or decent sales. He posed Faber other challenges, too – being such a peripatetic but extraordinarily productive writer, the business of submission, acquisition and scheduling of his work was a complicated, near-perpetual issue for Monteith. Stacton had the very common writer's self-delusion that his next project would be relatively 'short' and delivered to schedule, but his ambitions simply didn't tend that way. In January 1956 Monteith mentioned to Stacton's agent Michael Horniman about his author's 'tendency to over-produce'. Faber did not declare an interest in the Western novels Stacton wrote as 'Carse Boyd' or in the somewhat lurid stories of aggressive youth (*The Power Gods, D For Delinquent, Muscle Boy*) for which his *nom de plume* was 'Bud Clifton'. But amazingly, even in the midst of these purely commercial undertakings, Stacton always kept one or more grand and enthralling projects on his horizon simultaneously. (In 1963 he mentioned almost off-handedly to Monteith, 'I thought recently it would be fun to take the Popes on whole, and do a big book about their personal eccentricities . . .')

In 1960 Stacton was awarded a Guggenheim fellowship, which he used to travel to Europe before resettling in the US. In 1963 the *Time* magazine article mentioned above much improved the attention paid to him in his homeland. The books kept coming, each dazzlingly different to what came before, whatever inter-connection Stacton claimed: *A Signal Victory, A Dancer in Darkness, The Judges of the Secret Court, Tom Fool, Old Acquaintance, The World on the Last Day, Kali-Yuga, People of the Book.*

By the mid-1960s Stacton had begun what he may well have considered his potential *magnum opus*: *Restless Sleep,* a manuscript that grew to a million words, concerned in part with Samuel Pepys but above all with the life of Charles II from restoration to death. On paper the 'Merrie Monarch' did seem an even better subject for Stacton than the celebrated diarist: as a shrewd and lonely man of complicated emotions holding a seat of contested authority. But this work was never to be truly completed.

In 1966 Stacton's life was beset by crisis. He was in Copenhagen, Denmark, when he discovered that he had colon cancer, and was hospitalised for several months, undergoing a number of gruelling procedures. (He wrote feelingly to Charles Monteith, '[A]fter 48 hours of it (and six weeks of it) I am tired of watching my own intestines on closed circuit TV.') Recuperating, he returned to the US and moved in once more with John Mann Rucker, their relations having broken down in previous years. But he and Rucker were to break again, and in 1968 Stacton returned to Denmark – to Fredensborg, a town beloved of the Danish royal family – there renting a cottage from Helle Bruhn, a magistrate's wife whom he had befriended in 1966. It was Mrs Bruhn who, on 20 January 1968, called at Stacton's cottage after she could get no answer from him by telephone, and there found him dead in his bed. The local medical examiner signed off the opinion that Stacton died of a heart attack – unquestionably young, at forty-four, though he had been a heavy smoker, was on medication to assist sleeping, and had been much debilitated by the treatment for his cancer. His body was cremated in Denmark, and the ashes sent to his mother in California, who had them interred in Woodlawn Cemetery, Colma.

From our vantage in 2012, just as many years have passed since Stacton's untimely death as he enjoyed of life. It is a moment, surely, for a reappraisal that is worthy of the size, scope and attainment of his work. I asked the American novelist, poet and translator David Slavitt – an avowed admirer of Stacton's – how he would evaluate the legacy, and he wrote to me with the following:

> David Stacton is a prime candidate for prominent space in the Tomb of the Unknown Writers. His witty and accomplished novels failed to find an audience even in England, where readers are not put off by dazzle. Had he been British and had he been part of the London literary scene, he might have won some attention for himself and his work in an environment that is more centralised and more coherent than that of the US where it is even easier to fall through the cracks and where success is much more haphazard. I am delighted by these flickers of attention to the wonderful flora of his hothouse talents.

*

In 1955 Faber had a pair of novels by Stacton in manuscript for their publishing consideration, and on reflection they decided to take them as a pair. '[B]oth books', Sir Geoffrey

Faber wrote to Stacton, 'are evidences of your imaginative power and wide range.'

Stacton was to develop a yet wider range in the years ahead, and *A Fox Inside* and its successor *The Self-Enchanted* might be considered as a diptych of sorts. Both novels draw their strength from Stacton's assured evocations of the landscape and ambience of the western United States. Both feature brooding self-invented men with shadowy pasts, complex private schemes, and obsessively guarded weaknesses. Both of these men marry women they consider passive and pliable, though in this they are mistaken. Both books feature a mother who is monstrous and domineering, a 'boss lady' who has an almost vampiric effect on her offspring. And both also have a sort of Nick Carraway figure: one who is implicated in the main drama yet somehow forced to watch it from one remove, unable to wholly influence events or prevent bad things from happening.

Sir Geoffrey Faber did express a couple of small concerns to Stacton in respect of *A Fox Inside*: firstly that 'there isn't a single character in it whom I could bring myself to like' and secondly that there was 'perhaps too much promiscuity for our puritanical [English] taste'. Stacton didn't counter the second objection, perhaps thinking, quite reasonably, that English tastes were in the process of changing; but his response to the second was assured, indeed jaded by experience: 'The people in *A Fox Inside* are, alas, the people around me in my teens, and very tiresome they all were too, though not without a certain charm . . . [But] *A Fox Inside* does indeed explain why I don't care for California . . .'

If the novel does indeed propose that a touch of evil lurks behind the pleasing façades of the San Francisco Bay area, then this is only one of its accomplishments. Reviewing it in 1954 V. S. Pritchett found *A Fox Inside* 'mysterious and absorbing', and asserted that 'as a mystery story with marked psychological perceptions this one grips and pleases'. It is only the first of Faber Finds' 2012 Stacton reissues; and mystery stories would be only one of the forms through which Stacton expressed his restless, protean gift. But we hope the reading of it will encourage you to delve deeper inside this quite extraordinary body of work.

Richard T. Kelly
Editor, Faber Finds
April 2012

Sources and Acknowledgements

This introduction was prepared with kind assistance from Robert Brown, archivist at Faber and Faber, from Robert Nedelkoff, who has done more than anyone to encourage a renewed appreciation of Stacton, and from David R. Slavitt. It was much aided by reference to a biographical article written about Stacton by Joy Martin, his first cousin.

To J. McC.

who taught me much as a friend

and more as a teacher

*What we steal destroys us. Thus the Spartan boy,
proper without, but with a fox inside.*
                                        GERTRUDE BELL

I

SAN FRANCISCO, CALIFORNIA, 15TH March 1953. The clouds had begun to part, as the louvres of an observatory slowly part, to reveal a cold and sparkling sky. There was a crisp snap in the air, so that if you were at a great height you would have seen the world in its separate compartments. Far to the south, beyond the last barrier hills that protected the city, lay the more opulent suburbs, quiet under their trees. The city itself was a drenched grid of red and yellow lights, inimical and strange. North of the city, across the black waters of the bay, and at the other end of the high-swinging red lacquer bridge, rose the sullen bulk of Mount Tamalpais, a little legendary in that air. Its foothills fell sheer to the dangerous water.

The city seemed to sleep. Only the angry electric eye of the prison island of Alcatraz patrolled the darkness. But to the north, on the other and ocean side of the mountains, the long coastal sandbars were cluttered with week-end shacks. There it was less quiet. Even so, there was merely the restless sobbing of the sea and a few noisy drunks loitering outside the shanty dance pavilions at Stinson Beach. Stinson Beach was lower middle class and sometimes wild.

Farther north, and much more respectable, was the

brackish lagoon of Bolinas, the ocean swirling through a breach in its spit to snap at a dissolving cliff which rose from the surrounding marshes. It was a place that seemed somnolent and forgotten. It had the quiet of old age.

As a township Bolinas was small, being a cluster of weathered wooden villas sprawled along two vacant streets. On the top of the bluff that protected the town from the sea mangy pines contended with the spray. On the land side grey eucalyptus trees rustled, swayed, and dripped with a steady precipitation of ocean fog that fell always on the same disintegrating, knife-shaped leaves, rotten in the heavy suffocation of damp eucalyptus oil. The red and yellow blossoms, like ragged sea anemones, lay wilted on the ground.

An outsider named Shannon had built a summer house along the edge of the cliff, to the right of where the arroyo sloped down to the beach proper. He never bothered to speak to the townspeople, and since he had thrown a high brick wall round the town front of his property, there wasn't much they could find out about him. He never gave parties and his house was always idle. Only the cold glow of the floodlights in his garden shone over the top of the wall. And those were out now, for it was late at night.

That is what you would have seen if you were at a great height, but Maggie was not at a great height.

She was at Bolinas. She turned and went swiftly out into the yard. The gravel path cracked and exploded underfoot, and over that sound she could hear now the steady drip of water from the trees and the snarl of the surf as it lashed at the lagoon on the other side of the cliff. She did not know anything about Bolinas, and that made these noises ominous to her. She heard them all too well. She went down the drive, whose gravel hurt her bare feet, and stepped over the low chain that held the entrance driveway private.

She did not look round, for she knew that the house lay low and quiet behind her. It seemed to sleep, like the rest of the town. Only on the beach the faint patterns cast by the dimly lighted windows trickled out across the sand. But she did not think that there would be anybody on the beach. Of course she should not have left the lights on, but she had no intention of forcing herself to go back to turn them off, either. She did not dare to push herself that far.

Because the arroyo was narrow and she would have made too much noise backing the car, she had left it up the road a piece, parked in a clump of bushes under the trees. The street she had to walk up was banked by closed-up Victorian cottages, their wood blistered ash-grey by the corrosion of the ocean air. She went by them rapidly, having no way of knowing whether or not, from behind their windows, someone might be watching her. She hunched slightly forward, ducking her head, concentrating on getting to the car. By the time she reached the clump of bushes she was fighting down the panic to run. As it was she overshot the mark and had some difficulty in finding the car. It was an open convertible and even while she had been away a few of the scythe-shaped eucalyptus leaves had dwindled down into the front seat. Cautiously she threw them over the side, and then, closing the door softly, she leaned back in the driver's seat and tried to pull herself together.

At last she turned on the engine and eased the car out of the shrubs towards the highway. In the silence of the night the sound of the engine was frighteningly loud, but to her surprise nobody stopped her and the car was built for quiet speed. Speed was something that luxury could understand.

She raced down the deserted road beside the lagoon, in a hurry to get safely past Stinson Beach. She need not have worried. The town was quiet now. Only one or two lights in a kitchen window shone out across the sand. Stinson Beach was a temporary town: anyone might come and go there, and yet not be observed.

As she climbed the mountain she rattled over a cattle guard. At the top, before the last pull, the road reversed so that she could look down through the darkness far into the distance. Even in bright sunshine there was something eerie and inhuman about that strip of shore. It was too savage and too dry. At night it was all the worse. It had been like Charles to go hide himself there. She could only hope that he would remain hidden a while longer.

It did not occur to her to wonder where she was going. She was too eager to get away for that. She wanted to become lost in the back roads and suburban alleys of the mountain, under the steady drip of the pines and the redwood trees. It seemed to her that every moment she lingered was a bit of her future in jeopardy. She put her head into the wind, to let the fog-laden air clear it, but nothing seemed to clear it.

When she came out of the yellow adobe tunnel, lined with concrete, and faced the approach to the Golden Gate Bridge, she was doing fifty. It was a windy night and high above the water, under the criminal glare of the vapour lamps, the bridge swayed alarmingly. She had to stop while her toll money was taken. It was another danger of being identified. Resentfully, afraid to turn her face away, but also afraid to show it, she drew the car up and fumbled in her purse for a dollar bill. Beside her, on the floor, she could see a paper bag.

The attendant wore a black leather jacket with a fur collar, breeches and boots and a visored cap. He creaked as he moved, and the fog made the stench of leather all the stronger. He took the bill and said good night, but the car had stalled. She got it started again soon enough, but by that time she was shaking. She began to realize she could not get through with this alone. Even if the attendants, huddled up against the fog and impersonal and bored, noticed nothing, she would have to get help before someone did notice something. And she did not know where or how to get it. Charles had always shut her off from any help.

Before going down the wide, barricaded ramp and through the military Presidio, under more of those glaring yellow lights, she stared helpless at the shadowy and silent city, closed against her on its hills. She had had friends once. She did not have them now. She had lived here most of her life, but there was no one left for her to turn to. She did not know, she never had known, she now thought bitterly, anyone that she could trust.

From force of habit she turned the car up the Vallejo street hill, angrily shifting gears when the car stalled half-way, and stopped in front of the Barnes-Shannon house. She even started bleakly to get out of the car. But there was no point in going in. She looked at the shaded windows. She could not use the telephone there, for telephone calls could be traced. And worse than that, the servants had all been chosen by Charles. If they were loyal to anybody, it was not to her. She had not so clearly realized before how even this house was not really hers.

She swung the car down through the wet spaces of the Italian district and into the deserted financial section of the city. In front of the building in which Charles had his office she passed a water truck, slowly spraying the street and sidewalk with a constant hissing of dirty water. There was an all-night Western Union office down there. It was not until she drew up near it that she remembered that if telephones could be traced, a telegram was that much worse. Nor could she linger where she was, for cars were rare in that district at night and a patrolman might stop to ask her questions. She shivered in the fog that smelled of dust and iodine. It was then she thought of Lily. There was no affection between them, but at least Lily was her mother. She always did have to go back to Lily in the end, and Lily, she knew, preferred that it should be that way and liked it so. This time, she thought grimly, she might not like it so much.

With a crooked smile she swung out of the canyon of high buildings and over the slough bridges of the factory districts to get on to the express highway going south, which was the quickest, if also the most dangerous, means of reaching her mother, who lived forty miles away, in the suburbs of Atherton.

It was only then, because of the smell of heated rubber and of hot dust near the tubes behind the instrument panel, rather than because she heard anything, that she realized that all this time the radio had been going full blast. She could not remember having turned it on. It was playing the national anthem as the station closed down for the night. She did not turn it off, not even after the three long dots that were followed by a crackling, troubled silence on the disused air. Playing the radio full blast in the car had been Charles's trick. He liked to turn the radio on full and then go about sixty or seventy, on those rare occasions when they had driven together in her car. And it was her car. After two years of marriage it was the only thing she owned outright, and it was five years old. She had lied to her mother to buy it. She had had to have some means of escaping and had known that even in those days.

Escaping in cars ran in the family. Their cars were their life line. Lily had the station wagon and the Cadillac, and Charles had a grey Jaguar, because it was smart; and she had the Ford with the Mercury engine. She had it because when she was at college that was the car to buy. She had bought it second-hand out of her trousseau money and now it had to save her neck.

II

LILY BARNES LIVED IN ATHERTON. She always had, or at any rate so she pretended. She felt there was magic in that name and for that reason she lived there. Of all the suburbs of any city that ebb and flow through fashion, there is always one that manages to hold its own through pride of place. For San Francisco, Atherton was that suburb. Through the years its grandeur may have been whittled down to ostentation, but it was grandeur all the same, if you so considered it. And Lily Barnes did so consider it, deliberately.

Once it had been nothing but a sandy waste of tidal land, yellow with straw and brown with dusty oaks. But in the 1850s, when the city had grown rich on fraudulent merchandise, those people who elsewhere were to be called robber barons had built for themselves to the south of San Francisco great wooden houses furnished from France and set in gardens which were without a fountain, despite the dry heat. That was Atherton and it was not without its glamour.

Lily Barnes was born and raised a snob, but she had few illusions about her own status. Magic to her had always been glamour in the next room. Perhaps this was because she had been born in the Palace Hotel, had spent her childhood in hotels, and when she married, had married out of an hotel, in that luxurious and squalid way of the American transient rich. Even as a child, far below her, six stories down in the palm-clogged carriage court, she must have heard the dancing and the laughter. And that was how she always heard it.

To marry Jerome Barnes and move to his house was the closest she could get to reality. But the suburb changed. The houses built in her time became discreetly smaller, if no less expensive, just as the site of her own house had been carved out of the old Flood estate. She did not remove. She never thought of removing. Atherton was her ambition, and to live there was her accomplishment. It was what she had married to achieve. To leave it would have been to leave herself. She enjoyed it. There was nothing about it that she did not know. She felt safe there.

Maggie did not.

Now, as she drove rapidly through the unobservant streets, she felt that old heavy dread of appearances that had always been her emotion there. She also felt a sense of safety, however, in the defensive discretion of the rich, who know just how much they should not see and so have a mutual agreement to go through the world unwatched. She was grateful for that.

But if what was behind her bothered her, it did not bother her half so much as the thought of the next half hour. She circled the block once, and then went slowly up the drive, afraid of the gravel popping under the tyres in that still air. The moon had gone down but the stars were bright. They were too bright. She stopped the car and sat for a moment in the cool air, gazing across the lawn towards the to her somehow dangerous bulk of the house. She had always dreaded coming back to it, and she did not dread it any the less now. Somewhere up there Lily was asleep, and she had reason to know that the night thoughts of her mother were sometimes treacherous. She knew this house and this garden with the clarity of childhood. She knew it too well. And of course she had been married from this house; she was self-possessed enough to know the irony in that.

She got out of the car and stood waiting. She was afraid that the sound of the shutting car door would make a light spring up in the servants' attic. Then, slim and furtive, she slipped out of the night and into the shadows of the *porte-cochère*. She got the door unlatched, but was baffled by the night chain being on. It took her a moment to remember the trick of that chain; sliding one hand painfully through the opening, she found, as she recalled, that it was just possible to loosen the fastening by lengthening her fingers. The chain fell with a rusty clank. She closed the door behind her and stood in the cluttered darkness of the hall.

It was difficult to see. The downstairs doors, open on each side of her, gave into shadowy wastes haunted by furniture, with dim light from windows in the distance. The floor was wood, it smelled of too much polish, and it cracked underfoot. More from knowing where it was than from being able to see it she made her way to the foot of the stairs and began to mount them, keeping, as she had done in childhood, to the outer edge of each tread, where the noise would be least. It took her a long time to go up that way, but she did not want to rouse anybody. Lily's maid on the floor above was deaf, but she was not that deaf. She pretended to herself that once she reached her mother she would be safe. She had pretended it before when anything went wrong. She knew it wasn't true, but it helped.

She gained the landing. The transverse corridor was open to the hall for the length of the far wall, protected from space by a thin ornamental balustrade. In front of her was the room, almost never used unless someone important was staying in the house, in which her father had once slept. To her it had always been a mysterious, sad place that seemed to be waiting for someone. Behind the other doors were rooms almost as empty, for Lily no longer had any love of guests. She did not like to be seen too constantly or too close.

Lily's rooms were to the left. Hesitantly Maggie turned the knob and let herself into the small sitting-room. She stood there, just inside the door, blinking and somehow wishing she had not come. Feeling her way across the rug she passed under the open archway into Lily's bedroom and faced what she imagined to be the place where the bed was.

"Mother," she called. The act of speech somehow destroyed that false calm that had held her together. "Mother."

There was no answer and she could not bring herself to speak again. She did not like to call Lily "Mother". But as she stood there Lily, sensing someone in the room, moved uneasily in the darkness and with a heavy rustle of bedclothes came up to consciousness. The room smelled heavily of powder and perfume. The air was thick with it and had an uneasy odour. At first she did not speak. When she did speak her voice was calm and level, the fear in it kept under, as the fear in it always was. She did not seem surprised and she did not ask who it was. She asked, "What is it?" as though her daughter's voice was unfamiliar to her. Probably she knew perfectly well who it was, but she always treated her daughter like that, as a matter of policy.

Maggie cleared her throat. "It's me," she said. "Don't turn on the light."

"Why on earth shouldn't I?" demanded Lily. She was using her sensible voice, the one she always used to make objections, as though making an objection tied the situation down. She sat up in bed. Maggie could hear her doing it, but couldn't yet see her. She did not, however, turn on the light. She was silent and then asked again, "What is it?" in a voice that was curiously low, as though she knew what it was.

Maggie could not speak.

"Well," said Lily. Her voice was drowsy and slightly unpleasant. It was also vigilant. She reached out, a barely definable bulk, and Maggie caught sight of her pale face in the glow of the lighter, as she lit a cigarette. She saw her mother's eyes, staring inquisitively into the darkness, and knew that Lily would not understand.

Out of some other self than her own self, impersonally, she said, "Charles is dead."

The room became very quiet. Nothing happened, and she repeated the sentence, like a child at school, by rote, her hands clasped in front of her. Now she had said it, it was not her problem any more. Her mother could take care of it. "Charles is dead," she said.

Lily did not immediately answer. Instead, leaning over, she rapidly flicked on and off the night light. This frightened Maggie, who had been facing the wrong way and in that instant saw that her mother's bed had been moved, so that Lily saw her sideways. The light went on and off so fast it was like being struck. And the darkness was then deeper than ever.

"What am I to do?" she asked suddenly. "What am I to do?"

Lily grunted, but in the darkness her cigarette wobbled, so her hand must be shaking. "What do you mean, dead?" she asked. "I thought he was at Bolinas."

"He was."

"What were you doing up there?"

"I drove up."

"Of course you drove up. I didn't think you walked," snapped Lily. She seemed to be thinking hard. When she spoke again her voice was weary. "What time is it?"

"I think about three."

Lily lay back in the bed. Maggie could begin to see better now in the darkness, but she could not imagine what her mother's expression was, not, at any rate, by the sound of her.

"How long ago?" asked Lily after a while.

"I don't know. I came right here."

"I was asleep," said Lily, as though taking part in some other private and necessary conversation. She turned on the light again and this time left it on. "Come over here," she said, not looking directly at her daughter, but with a sly glance that Maggie had always feared far worse. "You'd better have a cigarette and sit down." Leaning out of bed, she fumbled clumsily with her cigarette case, gave up, and threw it to her daughter. Her eyes looked not at Maggie, but at the familiar details of the room. She sighed deeply.

"Did you kill him?" she asked. Her voice was bland.

"No." Maggie was startled not by what was said, but by her mother's expression. "No. At least, I don't know. I can't remember."

"Oh yes you can."

"I can't."

Lily dragged herself up in the bed and reached for her bed jacket. "He's dead," she said. "I believe he's dead. And even if you didn't kill him, you wanted to. What I want to know is, how bad a mess did you make of it?"

"He fell against the coal scuttle." She hesitated. "I went up to Bolinas to ask him for a divorce. He just laughed at me. Then he fell down. He was drunk."

Lily shrugged and dabbed at her eyes with an edge of her bed jacket. "They'll think you killed him," she said. She thought about it. "Why should I help you?"

"No reason." Maggie tried not to flinch. "I wanted to phone Luke. I didn't dare. I thought they could trace the call or something. I couldn't think of anybody else to come to. There isn't anybody else I can trust."

"No," said Lily. "I don't suppose there is. But I won't have Luke here. It wouldn't look right."

"That isn't why you won't have him here, though."

"That may be true," admitted Lily calmly.

"If you won't wire him, I will," said Maggie. "And I don't care what happens."

"You will, though." Lily watched her avidly. It was not the sort of watching that was easy to bear. She seemed to forget about both Luke and her daughter. "I suppose you followed him there?"

"I went to see him."

"And hid the car under a tree. What were you planning to kill him with?"

"I didn't kill him. I told him I would, but I didn't."

"But you did tell him you would? And if you had, though of course you didn't, how would you have done it?" It was not exactly sarcasm; it was something else.

"I just said it. I didn't mean it."

"But you thought about it," said Lily. She threw back the covers of the bed, showing that she was wearing a nightgown of pale blue nylon that hugged her big body in uncomfortable places. Slowly she pulled herself up and gathered the bed jacket around her, as though it gave her assurance.

Maggie watched her uncertainly. "What are you going to do?" she asked.

Lily did not answer. She went into the bathroom and closed the door behind her. Maggie stood where she was looking futilely at the rumpled bed. When it seemed that her mother was not coming back the door unclicked and Lily came out again, apparently calm, but with her fingers twitching. She had changed into a robe; it must have been hanging on the bathroom door. The robe made her look larger than ever, but less clumsy. She was carrying a glass of water and two pills.

"Very well. You'll sleep here," she said. She stamped her foot. "Maggie, wake up." She took her daughter's arm, though Maggie flinched away from the grasp, and led her out into the dark and now very cold hall. "You didn't wake the maid?" she asked.

Maggie shook her head and Lily looked relieved. "Ethel's deaf as a post. I'll say you came down late last night."

Maggie could not speak. She wondered uneasily which room she would be put in. It had been so long since she had stayed in this house, and all the rooms in it had an evil meaning for her. They went past her father's door, that could never be closed too tightly, and Lily led her into a room, switching on the light.

Maggie saw that it was her own old room. She did not like that. Lily looked around the room with some satisfaction and drew down the bedspread from the maple-posted bed.

"But it's made up," said Maggie.

"It always is." Lily sat Maggie down on the edge of the bed and Maggie allowed herself to be undressed. When that was done, Lily went to the cupboard and took out a nightgown. "It's old," she said, half smiling, "but it should fit." Abruptly irritable she threw the nightgown at her daughter. Maggie pulled it over her head, tugged it down, and slipped into the bed. The sheets were stiff with cold and the room had a damp, shut-up smell. Then she remembered and sat up in the bed.

"What is it?"

"I left something in the car. A paper bag."

"It can wait." Lily gave her the glass and the two pills.

"But it can't. . . ." Maggie did not want to tell her what was in the bag.

"I'll see to it," said Lily. She went over to the window, but did not lift the blind to look out. "You're right. In the circumstances there isn't anyone else we can trust. Or that you can, which I guess amounts to the same thing. I'll phone Luke." She moved rapidly about the room, setting down the glass. Then she picked it up again and took it with her. By the light switch she paused to look back at Maggie.

"I don't want to help you," she said. "But I won't have it said Charles was murdered, either. Charles was too clever to be murdered. I won't have that." She flicked off the light and closed the door behind her.

Maggie got up and without raising the blind slipped between it and the window, so that she looked out across the lawn.

She saw Lily leave the house, holding up the skirts of her robe to protect them from the damp grass, and move swiftly to the car. A flashlight went on. Finally her mother straightened up, holding the bag, and poked into it with the beam of the flashlight. The flashlight went out, but before it did her mother glanced up and Maggie saw the expression on her face. It was not one of anger. It was one of loss.

In the new darkness, and clutching the paper bag, Lily angrily slammed the door of the car and marched back across the lawn, holding the bag stiffly out in front of her, her face averted, as though it were something dead.

Maggie stayed at the window for some time, until drowsiness made it hard for her to stand. It seemed to her that the room was growing warmer, and leaning down to the radiator she felt the hot air pouring into the room and realized what her mother was doing. Her mother was burning something in the furnace. Obscurely relieved, she stumbled over to the bed. She felt that if she could sleep until Luke came, she would be safe. And in this heavy house there was no other refuge than in sleep. There never had been.

Luke was in Los Angeles, and San Francisco is not only four hundred miles from Los Angeles. It is also in another country. South of San Jose the palm trees and the madness both begin. Those of the north consider themselves to be cool and chic and properly restrained. Those of the south think themselves alive, alert, and fashionably legendary. About each other the two parts of the state have mental reservations that never amount to war, but there is a certain amount of sniping in the foothills. For a northerner, to go south is to go into exile. For Luke it was somewhat different. He had been beaten back there. The north would have none of him and he knew why. Nor was he likely to forget it.

He worked there for a small law firm and was doing well, better than he would have done to the north, where age is important and personal connections even more so. But he seldom felt at ease. There were times when he wanted to go back and crack the north, just to show them that he could.

He had a small, hot apartment, impersonally decorated with pretentions to bad style. This meant that the drapes and sofas were upholstered in flowered cloth and that the furniture was aggressively but cheaply modern. It was a place to sleep, but beyond that only a cage. Being unmarried, he seldom entertained except in hotels and restaurants. Usually the apartment suited him well enough; but on this night it did not suit him at all. The weather was sultry, he was lonely, and he had been thinking too much to be able to sleep. When the phone rang it woke him easily.

He had tied the bedclothes into a knot and wriggled free of them while cursing the phone. He never knew whether it was worse to have a phone that did not ring, or to have no phone at all. The world did not know him well enough for him to be able to cut himself off from it.

He picked up the receiver and vaguely recognized the voice. At first, even so, he could not believe that it could be Lily. She sounded irritable but determined, and he grinned at the irritation, wondering what it could be that would force her to speak to him.

She sounded as though she were afraid of being overheard, and he wondered where she was as he looked at his watch. It was three-thirty-five.

"Look," she said, with that cavalier brusqueness that made her no friends, "you've got to get up here as soon as you can. It's urgent. Professionally urgent."

"How do you mean, professionally?" Despite himself, he thought at once of Maggie. But it would not do for him to say so. He wondered what the devil the old woman wanted and his pride asserted itself. "I can't just come like that," he said. "Can't you get Thompson, or Christie, or your own lawyers? I take it it's a lawyer you want."

There was an undercurrent in Lily's voice he had not heard often. It made him uneasy.

"Is anything wrong with Maggie?" he asked, fully awake now.

"Of course not. Why should there be? She's sound asleep in the guest-room and has been for hours." Whereby he knew that something was wrong with her, and that Lily would not say what. "It's about the estate. I wouldn't bother you if it wasn't so important. You always handle these things so well."

"I'm glad to hear you think so," said Luke, trying to angle behind her voice.

She paid no attention. "Jump on a plane. You have to be here before the banks open to-morrow."

"To-morrow's Sunday," he said.

There was a long, annoyed pause. "Get on the phone and catch the four-fifteen plane," she said quietly. "You can shave here. Throw some clothes on and come as you are."

He glanced at his watch, knowing perfectly well he had never worked for her in his life and that she would never, of her own volition, have employed him. Perhaps that was what she wanted him to know.

"Can't you speak out?" he asked.

"No. But perhaps Maggie could tell you something. She's staying down here. I'll meet you at the airport."

"Suppose I miss my plane?"

"There are other planes," she said. "But you won't miss it." She stopped to consider. "I think you would be sorry if you didn't come."

He did not answer and she spoke up sharply. "Can you hear me?"

"I'll come," he said. He heard her sigh and then she

hung up. That was good strategy, he thought. They disliked each other intensely.

He blinked at the phone, rang through to the airport, and made a scramble for the bathroom. He nicked himself shaving, and had no time to make repairs, shoved a styptic pencil in his pocket, and ran for a cab, daubing blindly at his chin. Out of defiance he had been careful to put on his most Los Angeles suit. It would do no harm to remind her why she did not like him.

Three-quarters of an hour later he was in the plane. Once the safety sign went off he went to the washroom and tried to fix his face. In the washroom mirror he looked wide-eyed and scared. That gave him pause, and he carefully re-brushed his hair, as though that would help. He went back to his seat considerably sobered and no longer angry with Lily.

For so short a journey the time seemed to pass interminably. It was not light enough to read, but it was too light for the overhead lamps. He fiddled with the cold air blast, screwing it round in his face to wake himself up. Below him the countryside lost its arid softness and began to become rich, inimical, and hard. The night air rose in steam off the land, and the mountains, from above, looked wrinkled and helpless.

Dawn came slowly as they pulled north. The airport was south of the city, built on tidal lands shut off from the townships beyond by a long mountain. The bay was a stagnant pewter mirror that reflected nothing. Mt. Diablo flushed against the eastern sky, which was edged with pale green and pale rose. They banked and circled. He was eager to get it over with, for this was the country that had rejected him.

The windsock hung limp at the tower. It was a dirty orange in colour. The control-room below it hung in space like a giant zircon, catching what rays of light there might be. He shivered. The suit he had worn was too thin for this air. If he could have done so, he would have held back the night. He did not want to get mixed up with these people again. Nor was he sure that he wanted to know why he had been called for, or to admit why he had come.

But when they had landed and taxied along the concrete strip; when the landing stage had been pushed up to the door; and when he had ducked his head to clamber to the ground again; he did not show this. He was just another young man, too slim, with black hair that was too coarse for the heavy cut it had, anxiously but proudly professional, as men too young for their professions are apt to be. And his face was a brown blank entirely, unless one noticed his eyes. Since he talked with his eyes, his eyes said too much about him.

He looked round him warily.

It was desolate at the field, cold and between sleeping and waking. He did not think his arrival was noticed. Only later, if his coming had some importance, would somebody remember having seen him. In such circumstances somebody always did. He went through the wicket and into the dirty waiting-room, and so out into the parking area.

Lily was there, all right, waiting in the big black Cadillac she used for state occasions. The car was part of her defensive equipment, so he knew she must be nervous. Reluctantly he went over to the Cadillac while she held the door open for him.

Large, but not quite shapeless, with a heavily powdered face and a beauty spot that, no matter what her hurry, she never forgot to apply, unless of course she slept with it on, she gave him the impression he had always had of her: of sickening force hidden under a smile. And under her grey bangs her face was so carefully made up that he sensed she had kept herself calm that way. With the beauty spot went the too many diamond rings whose settings were never cleaned, because she could not bear to take them off, even in bed, and the shabby furs around her neck, to hide her wrinkles. That last echo of beauty was pathetic. He had learned years ago that it was also a weapon she knew how to make full use of.

He got in and shut the door. She had had the car idling, and now careened out of the gateway on to the salt flats and the highway. Fast driving was her speciality, for she was not afraid of accidents. Accidents she could pay for.

"It's Charles," she said, staring right ahead of her and putting her foot down on the accelerator. There were no preliminaries. She wasn't pleased to see him, she despised him, and she did not pretend otherwise. Of course he had known, at the back of his mind, that it was Charles. And it was Charles he was really afraid of. Lily was rude, but predictable. Maggie was more or less predictable. But there was no telling what Charles might do. For two years now, from a discreet distance, he had watched Charles doing it, sometimes even with envy.

"He's dead," said Lily. As though sensing that that meant more to him than it should, which displeased her, she looked away from him into the flat purple salt pans and did not speak again until they had swung up the by-road to Atherton, safely green on its slightly higher ground.

The suburb was still asleep. She went through it as quickly as she could manage, as though afraid to be seen. The car was powerful and therefore almost silent.

"Killed?" asked Luke.

"It was an accident," said Lily drily. Then she added: "Maggie was there," glancing at him for the first time.

"She was there?"

"I don't know what she did," said Lily. "That's what you've got to find out."

"When?" he asked, not being quite able to absorb it, searching in his mind for something that would give him a clue to it.

"Early this morning, at Bolinas." She braked the car, turned off the ignition, and got out, walking across the lawn with heavy determination. She had an air of being lost, and it seemed to him assumed. If she was at a loss, it was certain not to be in any of the usual ways. He followed her into the shuttered house, across the dew.

The hall was not empty. Maggie was sitting half-way up the stairs, leaning against the banisters. She was pale and thinner than he had ever seen her. When she saw him she half got up and then, catching sight of her mother, settled down again uncertainly. Lily stripped off her gloves, and instead of leaving them on the hall table, put them in her purse. Though the hall was shadowy, she did not bother to turn on the lights.

"We'd better go into the library before the servants get up," she said. She always spoke of the servants that way, though she only had one.

Together they trooped into the library, which was at the back of the house, overlooking an uncouth lawn. Lily bolted the doors behind them and went over to the mantelpiece. Above it, in a badly carved oak frame, was a portrait of her husband, but by a once fashionable painter so long forgotten that it had become meaningless. All the same, when there was anything of importance to be talked of, she stood under it, not for reassurance, but clearly to blot him out. Somehow she did blot him out, though she was not a tall woman. Long habit, probably, had taught her how. Luke wondered what it was that she had always been afraid of. Through the windows, beyond the shrubbery, he could see the eucalyptus trees swaying restlessly.

Maggie sank down into a deep wing chair, as though it would help to hide her. She did not look at her mother but she sometimes glanced at Luke, when she thought that neither of them was noticing her. Luke was uncomfortable. He did not really feel at ease in this room, or in any room like it.

"Very well," said Lily. She squared off at them, so that the hardness showed under the powder, but some of the pathos, too. It sounded as though she were mouthing a prepared speech, and she had had hours of night to prepare it in. "I don't know how he died, and Maggie is in no condition to explain anything. He was at Bolinas, and she went up there. She knows he is never to be disturbed there, but that's beside the point. Apparently she left him in the living-room, lying on the floor. It was an accident, but it probably looks like something else. It doesn't matter now what it was. It does matter what it looks like. The house up there is isolated and Charles was not precisely friendly with the neighbours. It's quite likely nobody's found him yet. Maggie said to send for you. Apparently she trusts you. So there it is."

They looked at each other bleakly. "I didn't kill him," said Maggie.

"You don't know what you did." Lily was snappish. She glanced at the portrait behind her, as though it explained everything, and Maggie drew back into the shadows of her chair. "Whatever you've done, you've been foolish, and that doesn't alter the fact that Charles is dead. After all, we aren't unknown round here and neither was Charles. It isn't going to be easy." She stopped to consider. "Either way, he wouldn't be dead if you hadn't gone there, so we have to be very sure that you didn't go there."

"I don't matter, do I?" asked Maggie.

That seemed to hurt Lily. She looked exasperated.

Maggie got up. She was trembling. The sedative was wearing off.

"You don't believe me," she said.

"What does that matter? It's what the papers tell people to believe that matters, and this will be in the papers. Have you thought of that?"

"You don't care about anything else, do you?"

Luke tried to interrupt them. "It matters a good deal," he said.

"If I killed him, I'm glad I did. I wish I had."

"I know you do," said Lily, and clasped her hands at her sides with an angry gesture Luke had never seen before.

"I can't stay here," said Maggie. "I'll go back to town."

"You can't face it alone," said Lily. "You'll crack. You always do."

"I won't have to face it." Maggie made for the door.

"You're here now," said Luke, as gently as he could. He was frightened of her, as well as for her. Lily watched them sardonically and that made him mad. "It might be better to stay. It would look better."

"I'm tired of looking better," cried Maggie. She did not even seem to see him. "I don't want to look better. I want to look myself. I want to rest. There must be somewhere I can rest, even in Charles's house. It was mine once."

Lily frowned but did not move. Maggie opened the door, wrenched away from Luke, and with a white-faced look at her mother stumbled outside. Luke and Lily stared at each other. They were both alarmed at that hysteria. For the moment it was the real thing that almost made them understand each other. Lily stared across the room at a cluster of silver picture frames on a low table in front of the windows.

"You'd better go after her," she said. "Let her go to town if she wants, but get the truth out of her. Maybe you can. I can't. I'm too tired."

He went out, leaving her standing in front of the portrait of her husband, staring into the garden. It was only in the garden that anything seemed alive. Hearing a car door slam he quickened his step.

Lily stayed where she was for a long time, feeling filled up with a sadness she had got used to and which for the moment showed in her face. Then she went up to her sitting-room and went through some old letters and decided, as usual, that she could not burn them.

They were old letters of her own, and perhaps they had always been meaningless. But reading them helped to clear her mind. She was determined to hush the thing up. Hushing it up would be like paying back an old debt so long overdue that it, too, was meaningless. No one, she was determined, should ever know anything about her but herself. It did not occur to her that perhaps no one any longer wanted to.

IV

LUKE HAD SMALL FEET THAT made it difficult for him to sprint across the steel grass. But he got to the car and opened the door. Luckily Maggie had not been able to get it started.

"Move over," he ordered. She gave him a frightened look, as though she would have liked to speak, but couldn't. She moved over. He got in and fumbled for the keys. Driving the car gave him the quick feeling that the situation was under control. As he swung the wheel, narrowly avoiding Lily's Cadillac, and as the shrubbery leapt up dangerously near him, he felt something of Maggie's dread to get away from this house. In the old days he had cringed in the same way, but he wasn't going to cringe any more. It gave him some satisfaction to realize that now they could not do without him. But Lily was still frightening. Perhaps that was because her house was too big for all of them. Perhaps it was something else in her that he refused to recognize.

As they left the drive, Maggie seemed to settle more easily into her seat, as though she no longer felt compelled to hold herself erect. As usual, there was something neat, cool, and far away about her that had always moved him. He realized suddenly that this was her old car, and that he had driven in it before. Maybe she realized it, too.

They left the treed suburbs and turned north along the express highway which skirted the bay and led back to the city. Even at this early hour there was already too much traffic, most of it coming towards them. It came too fast. He could see that it made her nervous to see it coming. They faced that long green barrier mountain which separates San Francisco from the south, and up whose shores climb mean houses and dingy marble cemeteries. He remembered that in the folded valleys of that mountain there grew pale blue irises close to the ground. He had gone there with her once, to pick them. It annoyed him that it was only in such abandoned places that there had ever been any ease between them.

"I didn't think you'd come," she said, watching the mountain nervously.

"I'm glad you thought of me."

"Are you?" She did not look at him. "We used to take this drive sometimes."

"Twice," he said.

"Oh."

It was a bleak oh. He felt contrite. He did not want to hurt her. He could not blame her for his own presence, for he had come of his own free will. Therefore he had no right to hurt her, and only himself to blame.

She also did not want to show that she was hurt. "Charles loved the city," she said. "I think it was because he came from Santa Barbara. At least he said he came from there. It's hard to imagine him coming from anywhere."

"Why think about it?"

"I don't know. I think about a lot of things."

Luke slowed down as they approached the village of

South San Francisco and the factory zone. They came in full view of the bay, with the land around it treacherously low, and the Berkeley Hills still in shadow in the distance. He wondered why it was that you always had to approach American cities through their slums. Slums made him nervous.

"I don't want to cause any trouble," she said.

He wished she would not talk. It made it all the clearer when she did that she didn't know what to say to him. They had an uncomfortable ride until they reached the factory district, passed over a canal, and headed for the centre of the city. The streets were still empty. Here and there a pile of newspapers lay bundled outside a shuttered tobacco shop. A little fog lingered in the low places, making the buildings seem sad and obscure. He took another turning.

"This isn't the way," she said. She clutched at the window of the car, rolled it down, and put her head out into the air.

"We're going to Bolinas."

"I can't go there."

"You'll go wherever I think we should go," he said irritably. He caught sight of his eyes in the rear view mirror and cooled down. "You may have forgotten something. We've got to be able to prove that you didn't go there. We can't let anybody else prove that you did."

"I didn't forget anything."

"No?" He reached down to the floor, where he had seen it, and picked up a eucalyptus nut and held it out to her, dropping it into her palm. She stared at it and he threw it over the side.

"Oh," she said. "But Charles is there. . . ."

"That can't be helped."

She did not answer. She retreated into herself. It was the effort of not crying that kept her like that, and he knew that she would be better if she could cry. Besides, it would make it easier for him. They had to touch each other sometime. If he was to do anything for her at all, they had to get over that barrier.

But they didn't get over it. They never really had. He went over the bridge and plunged through the tunnel at the other end, coming out over the fishing village of Sausalito, with its rotten hulks of brigantines half buried in the mud flats. The morning was only slightly dusty. He forced the car on. In half an hour he had reached the divide of Mt. Tamalpais and saw below him, as she had seen it in the night, the long desolate sweep of sand spits and sharp cliffs jammed against the ocean. There was something evil about this country: it was too empty. It was haunted, and that made it just the sort of place Charles would choose to hide himself in.

He had never been to Bolinas before, and yet it seemed oddly familiar to him, like a town in the south. Only the fog-clogged atmosphere was different. He went slowly down the main road, towards the bluff at the end of it, facing the sea.

"Where did you park the car?" he asked.

"I don't know. Over there, under the trees, I think. You see, I didn't want to wake anybody up."

"You didn't?"

"You don't understand."

He didn't suppose that he did. He found the place where she had parked and eased the car back over the faint tyre marks.

"You'll have to come with me," he said. "Then, if anybody interrupts us, well, I drove you up to see Charles about something, it doesn't matter what, and we found him together." He took her arm and helped her out of the car. They went silently down the empty street of the town, in the smell of the sea. She turned instinctively towards the beach, so he knew where to go. He thought it was a funny abandoned kind of place, but he had heard it was a Legionnaire town. That would have suited Charles. Charles was Irish. As far as Luke was concerned Legionnaires were a good group to avoid.

The house surprised him. He had not realized that Charles had really climbed far enough to get exactly what he wanted. The house had a blind discretion that must have been expensive. It must have cost somebody plenty, for Charles was a shrewd lawyer, if nothing else.

The oddness of the place impressed him, for he was sensitive about other people's houses. It was clearly not the sexual hideaway of a businessman. Neither was it a house to be lived in. But it was very much the building of a man who did not like to be watched. Who perhaps did not dare to be watched. He pushed open the front door with his glove and went inside. Then he, too, stood, as Maggie had done earlier, in that non-committal hall, perplexed by the superfluity of doors. Maggie came in after him, not quite closing the door behind her, as though she were afraid of being shut in here.

"It's easier to go in," he said, seeing her stare at the double doors. He slid them apart, but even he was not prepared for that living-room. It was cold now. It had the disreputable smell of a room that has been used all night before anyone has come in to clean it. The fire had long since burned out. There were a few charred stubs, but the logs had burned through. Where they had been was only a heap of slightly smoking grey ash. And there was Charles.

Except for his smudged picture in the financial pages of local newspapers, Luke had not seen him for years. Charles, besides, had had that ability to hide his face even when talking to someone directly. So Luke looked down at Charles. There had always been something wrong with the man's body. It was too long, too thin, too painfully articulated, so that it seemed hollow, as though controlled by some trick from the head.

The head was even worse. The head was that of Michelangelo's most unctuous white Piétà, with the same straggly beard to hide a weak chin. Or so Luke supposed, for Charles had been too sensible a man to wear a beard for any other reason. The marble whiteness and thinness of the flesh over the bones was as it had always been. Only those large brown eyes, in life so usefully dishonest, were a little closed. The hair was awry and the skin looked damp. But what was surprising was that in death his face had a look of boyish eagerness, an almost trusting, hopeful air, that certainly nobody else had ever seen before in Charles. Luke stood there looking down for quite some time. Perhaps it had taken death to make Charles a human being.

He took Maggie's arm and she smiled at him wanly. "It's all right," she said. She sounded puzzled. "But he looks different."

"Are you sure he was dead when you left?"

"Yes, he was dead."

"But he looks different?"

"Yes."

Luke went rapidly through the house, but there was no one there. He had the feeling that someone had been there. When he came back she was as he had left her, still staring at Charles. He made her sit down. "We'd better go over it," he said.

She was not prepared for that, but she began. He thought she had never understood, and never would, that anyone could ever accuse her of guilt in anything, Lily was like that, too.

"I don't know," she said. "He liked to needle people. It gave him pleasure. He didn't like people to be here. Last night I decided I couldn't stand it any more. I decided I'd have it out with him, so I got the car. It wasn't midnight, but the street was quiet. I had to do something or go crazy. I just didn't want to be seen. I didn't have any reason. I parked under the trees and walked in here. I was scared. Charles isn't easy to face up to.

"He was sitting near the fire. He didn't say anything. He only looked scornful. Not even surprised. That was the way he always looked when anybody did anything he didn't like. I think he was stewed.

"I told him I was going to get a divorce. He said I couldn't. He was Catholic, you know, when he felt like it, and he said he wouldn't let me. He said Lily wouldn't either.

"I said I was of age and neither he nor Lily could stop me.

"He said I knew what would happen if I tried anything. I asked him why he wouldn't divorce me. He didn't care about me. He said it didn't suit him to and

47

went on drinking. He was pretty cold-blooded. All he did up here was sit and drink. It was the only thing he enjoyed doing and he liked to do it alone. It didn't make him drunk. I don't think it even amused him. He got up and spread his hands in one of those funny gestures he liked to use.

"I was pretty mad. I said I'd kill him if he didn't give me a divorce, and he laughed. Then he fell down against the coal scuttle. It has a sharp rim."

"Why did you want a divorce?"

She looked at him cautiously. "I couldn't stand it any more, that's all."

It was probably true, but he did not think that it was all the truth. There never had been much truth about the Barnes. It was something they did not like to have too much of.

"Who knew about all that?" he asked.

"Nobody. Who would know? He didn't like me to have friends. And you know Lily."

Yes, he knew Lily. It seemed to him that Charles could hear them. He hoped not. It was a distasteful idea.

"You didn't murder him," he said. It wasn't a question. It wasn't anything.

"I told you I didn't."

"I don't care," he said. "I have to know, if we're going to get you out of it. But I don't care."

She looked at him doubtfully. "I don't think so," she said. "But Lily thinks I did. Sometimes I can't remember things."

"What are you talking about?"

She drew reproachfully into herself. "I hope Lily burnt the bag," she said.

"What bag?"

She told him about the bag and he watched her while she spoke. "I don't want her to have anything else over me," she explained quietly. "And there may have been blood on those shoes and stockings. I couldn't look to see."

She was afraid of something much more than she was afraid of Charles's death and he did not think that something was Lily. "What does she have over you?"

"I don't know," she said. "Charles watched me all the time. So did Lily."

He believed in her, but he didn't believe in what she said, and that made him angry with himself. He was in no position to believe in her, and he didn't expect to get any thanks for it. He was bewildered and a little resentful.

"Charles *does* look different," she said.

"I know," he said. He led her to the door. "Go out and wait in the car. If anybody comes near you, you don't say anything except that you're waiting for me. Do you understand?"

She nodded solemnly. He watched her go down the drive. When she was safely out of sight he went back to the living-room and went through Charles's pockets. There was nothing in them, but he did not think they had been searched before. When he had done, and not much caring for the look of Charles, he faced the rest of the house.

There was nothing in the kitchen or the bedroom, but he did have the feeling that someone had been there. The house was beginning to get on his nerves. Charles seemed to watch everything with unblinking eyes, the way he always had. And the house baffled him. It had been bought out of a shop, though a smart shop. Charles, he suspected, had thought that everything could be bought out of a shop. And he had been very nearly right. It made it no easier to pin him down.

He was puzzled that in the house there were no papers, no books, no accounts, nothing personal. Charles must have kept private papers somewhere.

The bedroom was monastic. It was like that narrow, white-washed, well-hidden bedroom in which Franz Joseph hid himself. Its simplicity was ostentatious. The bed had been turned down but not slept in. There was no mirror, no table, and no chair. The far wall was a deep window, double to prevent the transmission of any sound, so that looking down at the beach was like gazing into the depths of a silent film. Beneath the window was a low tier of built-in drawers. The drawers were not quite flush, and if he knew Charles they would have been. He went through the drawers.

At first he found only the slightly too expensive but unmonogrammed shirts and underwear that Charles had affected. Then, under some pyjamas, he found a roll of ten dollar bills shoved into a handkerchief case, and under the case a picture frame. It was small, of brown leather, and when he opened it he saw that there was a fresh tear on the leather and that the celluloid protector was cracked. There was no picture in it, but if it had been hidden, then it must have been something that had some meaning for Charles. And there were so few things that had any meaning for Charles. Thoughtfully Luke slipped the frame into his pocket. It seemed safe to do so, for he did not think that many people could know that it even existed. He put everything else back as carefully as he could and let himself out of the house. He did not close the front door. He superstitiously left it open, as though closing it confirmed Maggie's guilt.

Certainly she was guilty by intent.

He hurried down the drive with the obscure sensation that they must leave as soon as possible. He found Maggie sitting blankly in the car. She asked no questions.

Neither did he. Maggie probably knew as little of Charles as he did, and nothing about this house. Maybe there was nothing to know. He turned on to the highway, relieved when they had passed the indicative crossroads unobserved, and so might have come from anywhere. It was a clear morning now. The sea was a blue-grey mirror and the world had an innocent look. The air was still enough for them to hear a bird call three pastures away, in the salt marshes by the sea.

The police car passed them on the upgrade to Tamalpais, its siren uselessly blaring. Maggie flinched, but Luke had seen it coming and his touch did not alter on the wheel.

"They've found out," she whispered.

"The house was searched."

"That means somebody knows," she said. He saw that she was beginning to realize that she was in a trap, but he could not help her there, except to try to get her out of it. And Charles's death had locked her away from him far more than her marriage to Charles had done. "But who?" she asked.

"You haven't any idea?"

"I don't know anything," she said. "That was what was so horrible. He wouldn't let me know anything at all."

He felt the picture frame in his pocket. "Did Charles have a picture of you?" he asked.

She was surprised. "No," she said. "Not that I know of. He never wanted one."

He felt, somehow, that this was true and that Charles never had wanted one. He turned the car towards San Francisco and was silent, trying to think. Far more than of the police he was afraid of the newspapers. Friendliness did not go with righteousness, and at the moment the papers were being righteous. They had exhausted the sex scare, the bomb scare, and the Russians, and that left them righteousness.

THE SHANNON HOUSE WAS NEAR Alta Plaza, but nobody called it that. They called it the Barnes house, for it had belonged to Jerome Barnes, Maggie's father. Luke did not know anything about Jerome Barnes. Of Alta Plaza he knew slightly more.

It was that residential section of the city that lay along a ridge of hills which rose from the yachted Marina, running between that once fashionable Van Ness Avenue on one side and the sombre promontory of the old Spanish Presidio on the other. It had a fine view of Alcatraz, the island prison in the bay.

In the old days, before the city expanded, Alta Plaza had been a pleasant wild place, from whose heights one could watch the four-masted ships clogging the bay. Later, until the fire of 1906, it had been on the fringes of fashion. But a city is always restless. It moves ceaselessly from one side of itself to the other; and its social life inexplicably takes off in a swarm, after its regnant bee, for no other reason than that it is the season for swarming.

So that was Alta Plaza, a quiet, steep neighbourhood with too few trees, except for its fogbound and mysterious hill-side parks. Here you could see an old wooden mansion, its windows shuttered, its rococo plaster peeling from a pediment. And here and there, in a vacant lot thick with nettles, a stone stairway rose up into nothing, blackened with soot and cracked with heat, last memorial of the earthquake and the fire of 1906. Once, as a girl, he supposed, Lily must have gone up stairs like that. Now she went to other houses, but the stairs remained, still leading nowhere. Not for nothing did the city fathers, after that holocaust, remove the Ionic portico of some gutted house and set it in a quiet corner of the public park, on the other side of a shallow, scummy lake, and call it The Portals of the Past.

Here, on a still street that never got enough light, Jerome Barnes, or his father, had built the Barnes house. Lily had given it not to Maggie, but to Charles. Which was typical of Lily. It was a two-storied house in the Normandy style, with mullioned downstairs windows of yellow sandstone, but the facing of pale pink brick. The house stood back from the street, across a small city lawn trimmed with privet. It was a solid house.

Luke drew up before it reluctantly. It was part of a San Francisco he had never been allowed to enter, and now he did not think he wanted to enter it at all.

Though some effort had been made to make the house appear classical from the front, the land at the rear of the lot sloped so steeply that the floor plan was irregular. There was a large oval hall, with at the far end windows giving on the bay towards Alcatraz and down to a disused garden fifty feet below. The staircase not only rose to the second floor, but also descended through the hall paving to the floor below, which had been fitted up as a rumpus room, never used. The panelling of the hall had been stripped down to a fake Georgian simplicity, enamelled white in the style of some advanced House and Garden magazine of the first World War. It was a spacious hall but shadowy. At night the stairs seemed endlessly to wind up and down through space.

Now the hall was piled with luggage. That stopped them both as soon as they saw it. Luke closed the front door slowly, knowing that at this wrong of all moments there was going to be a scene. It was Lily's luggage, of course. It was indigo cowhide roughly stitched with white, and she had brought far too much of it. There was a two-suiter, because men's luggage was more capacious than women's; a vanity; a large hat box; and a small rectangular box that could contain almost anything. These were ranged neatly in order of size by the console to the right of the door. Lily, of course, would have had the taxi driver so arrange them, vigilant to see that he scratched nothing, and waiting calmly to undertip him. Lily's ideas of service and expense had not changed in thirty years. It was her own way of saving money, though she never thought of it like that. She always called it "keeping up standards".

"I can't face this," said Maggie. "I can't." She leaned back against Luke. "I've *got* to be alone for a while."

"She certainly didn't waste much time."

They found her in the living-room and she had not wasted any time at all. She had even brought her own magazines to read while waiting.

Luke had been in this house only once. He had never come back. He had only been allowed to know the Barnes at Atherton, or, to be more accurate, to know Maggie at college. He found the house, which had then seemed unattainable, now merely large and slightly displeasing. The living-room was too long for its width. The chairs and sofas were agreeable, but seemed to have been moved there from some other house. There were no flowers. The light came half-way across the rug from the windows, but the centre of the room was always shadowy. Lily was sitting on one of the sofas, her legs sleekly crossed, her fur thrown down on the seat beside her, pretending to read a copy of *Vogue*. She had not bothered to take off her hat, but when she saw them come in she reached up and removed it, as though she had only just arrived, and put it on top of the furs, which were slightly ratty stone marten.

"Where have you been?" she asked amiably, but there was always something insolent in that amiability and he did not miss it. Her attitude was that they had inconvenienced her by not being there to receive her. She had changed since early morning. There was no longer anything soft or uncertain about her.

Maggie sat down in a chair slightly away from her mother. There was a sudden heavy calm about her that Luke did not like the look of. He stood by the mantelpiece, waiting to arbitrate.

"We went to Bolinas," he said. "I thought we'd better check up."

"That was foolish," said Lily mildly. "She didn't forget anything. She brought it in a bag. And as for the bag, we'll say I burnt it, if it ever existed in the first place." She glanced coldly at both of them.

Luke caught her eye and saw very well that she knew exactly what she was doing. It seldom took her long to get back the upper hand.

"I shouldn't have come until it hit the papers," she

went on. "But I thought you wouldn't want to face the reporters alone."

"You shouldn't have come at all," said Maggie. Luke was startled. He had not known that she was as afraid of her mother as she sounded now. He tried to look reassuring, but he thought probably she was scared of him, too.

"Somebody had to protect you," said Lily.

"Or you?" asked Maggie sharply.

"If you wish it that way." Lily smiled blandly, and though the rest of her face showed nothing, her eyes looked tight and observant and maybe a little hurt. She was good at getting people not to notice her eyes, unless she wanted to look angry. Luke always noticed them. That was no doubt one of many reasons why she didn't like him. "We can't afford publicity."

Luke thought, watching her, that she was apt to overdo the publicity. He wondered how she had come to think of herself as so important.

"Luke can help me." Maggie did not sound too convinced of it.

Lily snorted.

"I just want to be alone, Mother. Can't you understand that?"

Lily stopped playing with her hat and looked directly at her daughter. "It isn't safe," she said. "How am I to know what you might do?" Luke was not astute at the psychology of women, but he thought she was acting. She leaned forward, as though she did not want to have Luke see or hear her. It was a planned gesture. "I don't *like* to have to watch you," she said. "You know that."

"I know nothing of the sort."

"Yes, you do," said Lily. Luke had heard that tone of utter sincerity before and had himself been tricked by it. For the moment Lily always believed what she was saying. That was what made her trickery so efficient, for there was self-deception in it, too, and it was that that took you off your guard.

"Besides, you can be alone in your room, if you want to be alone. The house is big enough, God knows." Lily looked round the room in search of some familiar object she apparently did not find. "I could never understand why Charles didn't like flowers," she said. "They're so good for the nerves."

"Charles didn't like anything," said Maggie. It was said to annoy Lily, and Luke wondered why. It wasn't the time to annoy anybody.

Lily looked round the room again, perhaps hoping to find something of Charles in it. There wasn't anything of Charles in it. "Luke can't stay here, you know," she said.

"I'll stay at the Fairmont and come over," said Luke firmly. He wasn't going to be beaten at whatever game it was she was playing.

Lily smiled apologetically, which was her technique. "It wouldn't look right with Charles scarcely dead."

"He isn't buried yet," said Luke. "I thought you got me up here to help bury him." He was angry with himself. He had been pushed around by Lily before.

Maggie looked pale. That state of auto-intoxication that had kept her under control was beginning to wear off.

"It's bound to look odd if he comes here too much," said Lily.

"You just want things your own way. You can't always do that," said Maggie. "I want him here."

"I'm afraid that isn't the point."

The three of them stared at each other. Luke was uneasy. He had himself to think of, as well as Maggie. The thought that Lily knew that and was counting on it decided him to fall on Maggie's side.

"In that case you can pay my retainer," he told Lily. "And it's steeper than it used to be."

"I'm sure it is," said Lily coolly. Despite her weight she was still a pretty woman, not with a prettiness of feature, but with something she had deliberately invented that suited her very well. She thought it made her invincible.

"You had to phone him," said Maggie. "There was nothing else to do."

"And he came," said Lily, and chuckled. He did not want them to quarrel. It made them ugly and he did not like to see Maggie ugly. Her eyes had the rabbit anxiety of an animal that would like to be stroked but is afraid of being eaten. But they were not really quarrelling over him, but over something else. He did not care to be their symbol.

"There's something you'd better know before you go on with this," he said. "We went to the beach house. It had been searched. As we left the police car was coming down. Whoever searched the house probably called the police. And if I know Charles, whoever searched the house wasn't there casually."

Lily thought that over. "What did they find?" she asked.

He felt the picture-case in his pocket but saw no

reason to mention it. He needed something on his side. "I don't know," he said. "That's not the point. The point is, what were they looking for?"

Lily looked considerably less at ease. Maggie merely looked blank. Whatever it was either of them knew, it was Lily who knew it. He was pleased.

"I haven't the faintest idea," said Lily. "Charles never kept anything."

"Are you sure?"

"Of course I'm sure." But she did not look sure.

"You've no idea what it could have been?"

Lily hesitated. "No," she said. "Nobody ever went up there. Even I've never been up there."

Maggie got up and made for the door. Lily half rose and then sank down again, with a glance at Luke. She folded her hands, thinking, and pretended to examine the cover of *Vogue* on the sofa beside her. Luke followed Maggie outside.

He found her standing in the hall. He took her arm and led her up the stairs. She was walking compulsively, and he tried to slow her down. He had never been upstairs in this house before, but he gathered that she would make for her room.

In the upstairs hall she stopped. The arrangement of this part of the house was odd. The oval of the stairs touched the wall. Closets were set on either side of a door, and the door itself led to a dark corridor that was much too narrow, so that the light was dim, coming from either end of the house and never meeting in the middle. The upstairs corridor had a shut-up look that suggested that Charles had not precisely encouraged guests, but it was spotlessly clean.

Maggie turned to the left and stopped again.

"Which room?" he prompted gently.

"I don't know." She stared at the closed doors. "I don't want to go in alone. You'd better come in with me." She opened a door and let him step in first. It was a small bedroom furnished in a decorator's idea of what a woman's room should be, and hence offensively feminine, with a sly masculine touch that only brought out the flounces. It contained a chair, a bureau, a bed, and a dressing-table. It gave the impression that people did not live in this house, but camped out in it. She looked round the room nervously, eyeing the far door. He thought he understood.

"Would you like me to take a look round?" he asked. She nodded and he went over to the door. It led to a large dressing-room, lined with drawers and sliding panels, and lit by a skylight. Half out of curiosity, half to reassure himself as well as her, he pulled open the drawers and slid back the panels.

To his surprise he saw that Charles's clothes occupied almost as much space as her own. Charles appeared to have had a passion for buying things in sets of two and five. Everything was of the best quality, but everything was smartly nondescript. His clothes were like uniforms. The shoes, for so tall a man, were absurdly small. The jewellery, in a neat blue box, was of silver, not gold.

His clothes were much better kept than Maggie's. Maggie's seemed to be crowded in grudgingly, in any loose corner. Luke closed the drawers and closets, wondering if he should go through the pockets of the suits, but sure that he would have found nothing there. He opened the door of the bathroom. It was finished in turquoise tile with chrome plate, and it told him nothing. Charles's toiletries were in the cabinet above the wash basin. He had used almost anonymous cosmetics, neither cheap nor well known, but he had also used a straight razor. There was a worn and obviously old case of them, carefully placed on the bottom shelf of the cabinet. They were in beautiful condition. There was also a stick of lavender pomatum. He was puzzled by it until he remembered that, of course, it was for Charles's beard. He put it back and went into Charles's bedroom, which was closed up and thick with shadows.

He quickly drew the curtains, but even daylight did not make the room reassuring. It was much too narrow for its width, like the living-room, and was not in good repair. The green wallpaper was stained near the ceiling and the ceiling itself could have done with a coat of paint. Clearly Charles was indifferent to where he slept. The furniture was heavy Victorian walnut. There was a turkey carpet on the floor. The top of the bureau displayed only the cardboard stiffener from a shirt, together with two pins. In the top left-hand drawer, pushed to the back, behind white handkerchiefs edged with black lines, was a small automatic. Luke looked at it thoughtfully, but did not touch it. On the bedside table were some books: an anthology of the basic thoughts of St. Thomas Aquinas and a detective story. The bed was not turned down and had a red velvet spread.

There was something familiar about the room he could not place, until he noticed the green glass shade on the brass lamp and realized with a start that it was furnished to resemble Abraham Lincoln's bedroom at the White House. He did not quite know what to make of that. He went out of the room and locked the communicating door to the dressing-room loud enough so that Maggie would hear the click.

When he came back Maggie had taken off her shoes and was lying on the bed, staring at the dressing-room door. The soles of her feet had been perspiring and had darkened her stockings. He went over and sat on the edge of her bed, placing the key to the dressing-room on the table beside her. He forced himself to take her hand, afraid of what touching her might make him feel. He had invented a Maggie for himself that made the real Maggie difficult to face. He no longer knew how he felt about her. He had never really known how she felt about him. He was not altogether sure that he could face the risk he would have to take, and he knew that though both of them would take his help, neither one of them would help him. And it wasn't his city.

"I'm so afraid of her," said Maggie.

"There's no need to be."

"You don't know," she said. She did not say anything more about that. "Will you stay?"

"I'll be round when you need me," he said. He caught sight of himself in the mirror, and it was true, he did not look right in this room. "I can't move in here. She's right about that. But I'll do my best."

"I'm so frightened," she said. She said it as though she was just discovering it to be true.

He got up and left the room. On the way downstairs he turned into the corridor and taking the key out of Charles's door, put it in from the outside and locked the room. It was not a gesture he could explain, but it seemed to help. He left the key in the lock, in case the locked room should look odd.

When he got down to the living-room he found Lily waiting for him. He ran a hand through his hair, conscious of his own appearance, and tried to face up to her.

"She's resting," he said. He thought that this house seemed to upset her, too. She watched him.

"What are you going to do?" she asked.

"There isn't much I can do. Once the news has broken, I'll go down and see his lawyer. Who is his lawyer?"

"His own firm, I suppose." She was cautious.

"Was it usual for Charles to go away and nobody to get upset about it?"

She hesitated. "He disappeared sometimes."

"Why?"

She shrugged her shoulders. "He was like that." She sighed, staring down at her gloves. "He could be difficult at times. He never told anybody anything, really."

He was exasperated with her. "What are you afraid of?" he asked bluntly.

"What makes you think I'm afraid of anything?"

"You are. You know you are."

"I should never have let Maggie talk me into this," she said. She was not at all friendly now.

"Oh, don't worry. You'll get your money's worth. But that's all you'll get."

"There's no need to talk that way, Luke."

"Isn't there?" he asked. "I think there is. Well, you've got me into it, and we've got to find out who was there. I can at least try the lawyers. They might know something, even if you don't."

Lily stood up, smiling vacantly, as though dismissing him. "Just keep us out of the papers. That's all I ask," she said.

He thought, privately, that probably she would ask for a great deal more than that, but it was no time to say so. He told her he would be back later. She didn't bother to answer him. He let himself out of the house.

VI

HE SHOULD NOT HAVE COME BACK for any reason. He knew that. To be back with these people, or even in this city, gave him an uncomfortable feeling. He had no friends here and he knew it. The only friends he could make here were friends he did not want to have. Apart from that the glare upset him: the streets were too bright. It was hard for him to fit back into these people's lives, for he had changed too much and they had not changed at all. Nor did he any longer know how he felt about Maggie. He had been away from her for too long.

Once in the centre of town he felt better. He had the old relaxed wartime feeling of anticipation and cool-headedness, the poignancy of walking down a street which even if it was there to-morrow, might not be the same. He had no trouble at the hotel: they gave him a room at once. He went for a walk and bought half a dozen shirts and some socks, half to pass the time and half to smell the city out. He had always known the importance of a good address, and it seemed to him that if his part of this came out into the open, the better his address the safer they would all be. Besides, he enjoyed the prestige, for it was not so long since he had not been able to afford it.

But he found everything slightly changed, and in particular the hotel. The hotel should not have changed. He had seen old pictures of it, after the earthquake, an immense shored-up shell with blind windows dominating the city. And he remembered the hotel as a mysterious social aquarium full of ormolu mirrors and a lot of red plush, inhabited by observant elderly and immobile fish. Now the place was merely fashionable. It did not remind him of that slightly legendary city of the past at all.

He left it and walked down the steep hill, through that damp air that smelled always of iodine and the sea, to Union Square. Union Square was bright with clipped beds, short hedges, transplanted yews, and the old Dewey column, its tarnished Victory perpetually bearing a laurel wreath into the east. It was an exhilarating city, built on hills, rich, prosperous, and vain. It was not a male city. It had the chi-chi of a city built for women. It had the native, boyish style that belongs to cities that are cosmopolitan but not international.

He had business to do. He wanted to see Charles's partners before the news broke. He walked down into the commercial district, where the office buildings grew taller, forming cool canyons of their own.

The offices of Madge, Foster, and Shannon were on the twenty-fifth floor of the Heist Building, a steel and green terra-cotta skyscraper in the ornamented Aztec style of the early 1930's. The offices occupied the northwest side of the building, and hence faced the harbour. Prominent in the foreground was the white tower of the Federal Customs House, on whose top floor was a detention centre in which those Orientals who had entered the country illegally were temporarily jailed. It was not long since a Chinese woman had leaped from one of its windows. She had been held there for four years.

Beyond the tower he could see the harbour and the small policed area of the international zone, behind its guards and its barbed wire. Despite the sunshine, it was a melancholy view. It did nothing to reassure him.

The offices had that cramped luxury of very expensive space. The receptionist was a motherly woman of about forty-five, wearing steel spectacles and obviously loyal to the firm. Mr. Madge had died years ago. Luke said that he wanted to speak to Mr. Foster.

"You'd better say Mrs. Barnes sent me," he said. He did not quite know why, but it seemed to produce an effect. He saw no reason to mention Charles until absolutely necessary.

The receptionist looked him over, with particular attention to the cut of his suit, and he smiled back at her, watching her do it.

She flushed and went down the hall. In a moment she came back and ushered him into Foster's office.

From the size of the office, Foster was the more important surviving partner. Then Luke realized he was the only surviving partner. The room was lined with legal books set in walnut shelves to the ceiling. It had a prosperous Persian rug, two comfortable green leather chairs, and there was a portable bar and television unit in one corner. The desk, massive and ornate, was a survival from some earlier period of correct legal furnishing.

Foster was a short man with the vestiges of a tan, plump but tight, with a friendly beaten face hidden behind thick glasses. He stood up and the two shook hands.

Foster then sat down behind the desk, teetering back and forth in his chair, playing with Luke's card. He did not seem in the least surprised to see him.

"I remember who you are now," he said. "You're one of Senator Ford's young men."

Luke didn't mind. Law was one of the few professions in which age was still an advantage and youth a drawback. He was used to that attitude. He had also learned that Ford's protégés did better in the south, but since he had done well in the south he did not mind that either. They talked about Ford for a few minutes, aimlessly. Of course while they talked they watched each other. Foster was not the sort of partner Luke would have expected Charles to have. There was about him nothing that was either unctuous or glaring. He was a quiet, competent man. Luke told him that Charles was dead.

"How do you know?" asked Foster. He did not appear to be much moved one way or the other, but he did reach instinctively for his appointment pad.

"I saw him."

Foster shook his head. "It might not be wise to say so."

"I don't intend to say so." It puzzled him that Foster seemed neither surprised nor particularly upset. Instead he merely watched Luke patiently.

"And?" he asked at last.

"The point is someone searched his house and took something away. It might be a good idea to find out who and what, for a number of reasons."

This did not seem to surprise Foster either, though it affected him more than the news of Charles's death had done.

"Lily Barnes is a strange woman," he said suddenly. "I can't say that I know her well, but I've known her for a long time. I don't envy anyone who has to work for her, and I've handled her accounts for thirty years."

"I don't quite follow."

"Just advice. You shouldn't underestimate her, that's all. Nor dislike her too much, even if she does dislike you. At the back of her head she means well. At least she's loyal to something, though maybe even she couldn't say what."

Luke was baffled. "But does she know anything about Charles?"

Foster seemed embarrassed. "I don't think anybody knew anything about Charles," he said. "What was taken?"

Luke threw the empty picture frame on the desk and Foster looked at it gingerly and shook his head. "I've never seen it," he said. "It's not like Charles." He turned it over and examined the back of it. "It's pretty cheap."

"You've no idea who could have been there?"

"None. Charles wasn't an open man."

"But somebody must know him. He must have friends. There could have been a woman."

"No, that was the trouble. There wasn't anybody. That was what made him . . . a little eerie."

"How was he to work with?"

"Brilliant. Ambitious. In a way I'm not sorry he's gone." Foster stood up and going to the window, stood with his back to the room. "Lily did a lot for him, of course. She brought him to me. Oh, not openly. But I began to be invited down to the Atherton place more than usual, oh, three or four times rather than once a month, maybe. I knew what was up and I knew what was expected of me. He had an odd effect on women. Hell, we were in low water and she bought him in. That is, she threatened to remove her affairs, just mentioning the possibility, you understand, casually, over dinner. And he got money from somewhere: he put up fifty thousand. That was long before he married the girl. I've often wondered how he got it."

"Where did he come from?"

Foster shrugged. "I gathered from Santa Barbara and Stanford. Lily did the talking, and he never said anything about himself. I had the feeling sometimes he didn't have any past. You didn't get to know him. Even after his marriage he didn't open up at all."

"It isn't much to go on."

"No, it's not much." Foster sighed. "I asked him out to our place at Belvedere once. He came and he was a good guest and it was as though he'd never been there at all. He was all the time watching things, too. I took off my shirt, while we went sailing, and saw him looking at the label in it. He wouldn't ask me where I got it, you understand, but he found out. Charles always found out. And he didn't buy one like it, either. He went to the same shirtmaker and bought something else."

"He must have relatives or a family," said Luke.

"You'd think so." Foster picked up the picture frame again. "Why is it so important?"

"Maggie was there when he died."

Foster looked startled. "I see," he said.

"So now you know why I'm here," said Luke bitterly.

"I was wondering." Foster shifted his position. He seemed acutely embarrassed, though Luke could not make out why. He got up and wandered round the office, not really looking at anything, and then went over to the window again and looked out across the port to where the thick Doric column of the Coit Memorial reared out of its trees towards the sky.

"You didn't know Jerome, of course," he said.

"Who's Jerome?"

"Maggie's father." Foster was silent, gazing out across the city, his short, over-plump body slightly ridiculous when seen from behind. Finally, he sighed deeply and turned to face Luke.

"What I'm trying to say," he said, "is that if you do have to find out about Charles, I suppose you will find out things about other people, too. The little bit I know I can't tell you, and it isn't anything that will help you, anyhow. I know you don't get along with Lily. Most people don't. But if you do find it out, try to understand it. And try to understand her, too." He waved a hand helplessly. "I know a lot about them, one way and another. Lily's a fool, but she isn't a simple woman, and what's done is done. She's vain and she pretends to be a rattle, and she plots, and I suppose she can be ruthless when she's really frightened. But she's lonely and she has her reasons. We all have our reasons, and most of us get stuck with them. Come over here and look out of the window." He waited until Luke did so. "It's just a jumbled heap of stone and concrete, with a bay around it. Some people think it's beautiful; some people don't. Lily was born over there in the Palace Hotel. You can just see it if you squint out of the window. She was a Smith. There aren't any streets or parks named after them, and there are a lot of them, but in her own mind she was a Smith. She just feels that way. God knows what Smiths. Until she married she lived up on the hills behind us and out towards the sea. She married Jerome and there aren't any streets named after the Barnes, either. There used to be, but they were changed. We all lived here, in a way we don't now. That's why Lily lives down in Atherton. She can get away with living in the past as long as she stays there.

"You've got to figure out what Charles made out of it all. That's harder. You see, he didn't belong here. He didn't have any past. And in the old days small town people always wanted to come here. It was glamour, I guess. I came from a small town myself. Petaluma, in case you care.

"Well, Charles made a big mistake. He thought just being here was what was important. It's not. It's what being here means. He never belonged. He never belonged anywhere. But Lily and Maggie and me, and even maybe people like you, whatever you think otherwise, or people make you think otherwise, belong somewhere until we die. Do you see what I'm getting at?"

"I think so," said Luke.

"Then go easy," said Foster. With a last look out of the window he came back to his desk. "Lily phoned me before you came. I don't think she knows what she's doing. This has hit her hard and it's given her a lot to think about. And she overestimates herself, which doesn't make it any easier. Anyway, she wants the thing hushed up. Well, it can't be hushed up, but maybe we can tone it down a little." He looked thoughtful. "How is Maggie holding up?"

"I don't quite know. She seems semi-hysterical."

"Ummmmm," said Foster. He stood up, evasively fiddling with his glasses.

"One other thing," said Luke. "What about the will?"

"What about it?"

"It might tell us something."

"It might," said Foster, "but I haven't got it." He didn't, clearly, want to talk about it. "He didn't die intestate, you can be sure of that. Charles was tidy." He picked up the picture frame and handed it back to Luke. There was something distasteful about that torn, imitation leather frame.

"They'll have to bring it before a coroner's jury and all, because of the jurisdiction," said Foster. "If the papers whip it up, and they will, they'll need a good jury. That gives you about a week to find out what you can. And if I find out anything, I'll let you know."

"It isn't much time."

"It's all the time you've got. There's one other thing. If Charles knew anybody, it was somebody he couldn't get rid of. Somebody who had known him too long, I think. And probably a woman. He wasn't so good with men." He played with the blotter edges. "And don't get hurt."

"Why should I?"

"Nothing. I just think maybe you might. And it isn't worth it. It might have been once, but it isn't now."

Luke blushed.

"Oh, I don't care," said Foster. "I'm just an old woman. But watch out, anyhow."

Luke left. He nodded to the receptionist on the way out, and went into the corridor. It impressed him, looking at the lettering on the door, that of the partners only Foster was left. He called a cab and went back to the house.

HE THOUGHT THE STREET SEEMED deceptively quiet. Or else it was only beginning to get on his nerves. There was something anonymous about those large houses. There was something too clean and self-conscious about them. The Barnes-Shannon house may not exactly have been pleasant, but at least it had a little character of its own.

The door was on the latch, and not wanting to attract the attention of the maid, he stepped into the hall without ringing the bell. Lily's bags had been removed, no doubt to whatever room she had chosen. He did not want to see her, and neither did he want to disturb Maggie. He was therefore relieved to find no one about.

Experimenting with the doors, he found the library, slipped inside, closed the doors behind him, and went over to the windows to draw the venetian blinds. If Charles had left any trace of himself anywhere, surely it must be here. He glanced curiously round the room.

Like Charles's bedroom, it was monastic and barren. No doubt it had been cleared out to create that clinical atmosphere of which Charles had so obviously been fond, but it could never have been a cheerful room. As it was, it had a deliberate, contrived gloominess.

Luke sat down at the desk and tried the drawers. They

gave easily. He took out all the papers, heaped them on the desk, and began to go through them. He had not expected to find much, but that he could find nothing upset him. In all that assemblage of household accounts and old letters there was nothing that bore so much as a personal name, unless you included the notebook in which he kept a check on the servants.

Luke looked at these for some time, surprised and faintly disgusted. There was a row of names, a series of zeros and checks, and under some names an emphatic line. It took him a moment to realize that Charles must have allowed them so many demerits and then sacked them. At the rear of the book, in a neat, square hand, was a list of minor things to be done about the house. It included the precise alignment of linen on various shelves of the linen cabinet. It was his check list for efficiency.

It occurred to him, with some repugnance, that if one of these notebooks had been kept, then the habit indicated that there should be others. He rummaged down in the drawers again and found wedged at the back another notebook. It contained lists of people with the same notation of checks and noughts. There were more checks than noughts. His first impulse was to burn the book, for he knew some of the names. Then, at the end of it, he found Maggie listed, and even his own name, with a question mark after it. There was a chart of her wardrobe, of the people she knew, of restaurants and clubs she had once gone to, of what trips she had taken and why. The word "Napa" recurred several times. The ink here was angrier and he wondered why Napa should bother Charles. It was a pleasant enough place in the middle of the wine country. These entries were recent. Apart from them, he found only a map of names in rotation, with dates, some for dinner, some for lunch. It was arranged to run to the end of the year.

Thoughtfully he stacked the books in front of him. They were uniform, bound in black leather, with small binder rings holding the sheets. The ink was blue and the handwriting done with a broad-nibbed pen. He did not know what to do with the booklets, but they upset him. He pulled them to him again, searching for Lily's name, but it was not in them. Perhaps she had merited a separate notebook of her own. Carefully he detached the pages dealing with Maggie and slipped them into his pocket. He saw no reason why she should ever see the proof of how closely she had been watched; and there were a good many reasons why nobody else should see it.

There had been nothing in any of the books that had anything to do with Charles. They had all dealt with other people. Faintly nauseated, Luke turned over the other papers on the desk. They were mostly receipts for bills paid. No doubt Charles had had the habit of tearing up letters as soon as they were answered. He could see from the bills that he had lived frugally, but had spent a lot on alcohol and on clothes. The alcohol was divided into two accounts, one for Bolinas, the other for town. The Bolinas account was limited to Scotch. That for town ran to gin, vermouth, and bourbon. The combined liquor bills came to slightly more than did the household accounts. The Bolinas bill was marked to Charles's personal account.

It was clear that Charles had run the house. Maggie's personal bills were included, which surprised him. He had always believed that Maggie had money of her own. He rammed the papers back into the drawers of the desk, but he still did not know what to do with the black leather booklets. For the time being he left them on the edge of the desk.

The door clicked and Lily came into the room. He took off his glasses and looked up, which was one of his standard defensive manœuvres. She had changed into a light dress with vertical stripes that made her seem younger. She did not look surprised to see him there, but she did look displeased. She glanced at the top of the desk.

"I didn't know you were back," she said quietly. "Did you go to the lawyer's?"

"Yes."

"And found out nothing, I suppose." She was still leisurely examining the top of the desk.

"I was looking for the will," he said. "I thought it might prove something. Surely he made one."

"Oh, yes. He made one."

He swivelled round in the chair, watching her. "Do you know where it is?"

She sat down in a chair facing him and lit a cigarette before she spoke again. She looked oddly self-satisfied and amused. "Yes," she said after a while. "I have it."

He was astonished and he showed it. She smiled at him, and caught sight of the booklets which were now at her eye level. She picked one up, saw what it was, and sniffed. "I'd forgotten about these," she said. "It was very like him, that habit. You went through them, I suppose."

"I did."

"No doubt you felt you had to." She shrugged her shoulders and placed the booklet carefully back on top of the stack. "It wasn't a form of spying, really. He just had to know everything. It wasn't one of his better traits, but as long as you understood it, it didn't do any real harm. But some people might not understand. Perhaps we should burn them."

"We can't burn everything," said Luke. He wondered why she was so confident, unless she had got to the booklets first. Her manner towards him was guardedly indulgent. Also, she was trying to give the impression that she was comfortable in this room, which he did not think she really was. He lolled backwards, not liking particularly to sit in Charles's chair, but damned if he was going to look any less relaxed than she did. "Tell me about the will," he said.

"I'm not altogether sure I should."

"It will have to be probated, you know."

She folded her hands in her lap. "Very well." She leaned forward, like a croupier who has a full table and a magnet under it, with a look of slightly foxy pleasure. "It's two years old. I had him make it the day after his marriage. It's correctly drawn and virtually unbreakable."

"He could have made one since, you know."

"No, I don't think he would have done that. Besides, until two years ago he didn't have much to leave." She sounded vaguely contemptuous. He wondered why she could never bring herself to accept sympathy from anyone. He rather thought that at the moment she might be going to need a lot of it.

"Well?" he asked.

"Charles had about one hundred thousand in the bank and he owned the beach house at Bolinas outright, as well as this house under certain conditions that aren't important. Oh, well, he had a life holding, but could not dispose of it. The will allows for hundred-dollar bequests to each servant who had been with him for more than eight months at the time of his death. There's a small bequest to the College of St. Ignatius, and another to augment any legal scholarship at Stanford University, at the discretion of the trustees, provided that his name shall not be mentioned. He went to Stanford, you see. The possession of this house reverts to me. The beach house at Bolinas goes to Maggie."

"That's crazy."

"He had his ironies. She has it on the condition that she either sell it to strangers in two years or else tear it down. Everything else I've got IOU's against." She leaned forward. "That was an agreement between us. Charles could be grateful. I suppose Foster told you I bought him into the firm."

"Not exactly."

"Well, I did. And I believe in protecting my investments."

He did not quite know what to make of it, except that it seemed to please her very much. "What about Maggie?" he asked. "There's such a thing as community property, you know."

"Maggie's money is in trust until she is thirty. Under the circumstances I don't think she'll quarrel with the will. It's harmless enough, anyhow."

"I'd call it damn odd."

"I don't think it matters what you call it." He wished

she would stop acting. It was that that made it so difficult to talk to her. He had never learned how to act.

"People sometimes make personal bequests," he prompted.

"Charles didn't. There was this, though: he'll be buried in the Barnes vault. I think he'd have liked that, so I had him put it in. But that isn't exactly a personal bequest, is it?" Her mouth slipped suddenly sideways and she got up and went to the window, gazing out over the city much as Foster had done. But unlike Foster she did not speak to him. Around the silhouette of her body he could glimpse the blue bay, dotted now with the white triangular sails of little boats that the warm weather had brought out of their harbour. She did not seem to be looking at the view, but beyond it.

He wished there was not that old barrier between them, to make this new barrier the higher. If she did not turn around, it was clearly because she could not speak to him. This period between death and discovery was not doing any of them any good. He reached over and took the black booklets and slipped them back into their hiding-place. They would have to stay where they were, for there was a limit to how much of a man you could destroy before he was even legally dead. Whatever damage had been their intention, they could not do that damage now.

He sat there restively, wondering what was wrong with her. The room was not a nice room, and sitting in that chair was like sitting inside a dead man. Yet Charles still seemed very much alive. He did not like to think of that body lying unidentified in some hot county morgue.

He could not think of anything to say to Lily. He wondered what he was waiting for.

Somewhere behind them both the front door slammed loudly. He jumped up from the chair, catching sight of Lily's startled face, from which some private, previous thought had not yet been erased. He dashed through the living-room and up the stairs to Maggie's bedroom. The bed was a rumpled mess and she had placed a chair with its back cocked under the closed door to the dressing-room. He did not care for the look of that chair. The bureau was open in disorder, but he did not think she had taken any clothes. He raced down the stairs again and ran into Lily standing at the foot of them.

"Where would she go?" he asked.

"I don't know. But she mustn't be seen. She mustn't."

"I'll go after her."

Lily looked genuinely scared. "Be careful, Luke," she said. He had never heard her use his name with less condescension. "She may say anything. We've got to get her back."

He went out of the house, forcing himself to walk sedately until he was down the block, in case anybody was watching. At the corner he saw her high above him, at the top of the hill, going towards the park. He started after her.

HE HAD A STITCH IN HIS SIDE when he reached the top of the hill. It was so steep that steps were cut in its paving, and up these he had jumped as fast as he could. At the top of the hill was Alta Plaza itself, a big undulating park. Underfoot he could hear the cable of the trolley running in its purple metal groove. Looking east, he saw Maggie boarding one of the cars. Impatiently he waited for the next one, but fortunately there was a double up and he did not have to wait long. He swung aboard, sitting at the front to see if she left hers. He jammed irritably into his pocket for small change.

The second cable hit the stop signs all the way down into the hollow of Van Ness, and then up the other side as well. Sometimes, when the first cable breasted a rise, he all but lost sight of it. The trolley bell clanged incessantly. He could not figure out where she was going.

From Alta Plaza they dropped down into the commercial district, and then rose through tight squalid houses towards Nob Hill, and the open air. There the buildings were cleaner, fresher, and more impersonal. They passed the cathedral and the large hotels and began to descend the hill again. Maggie got off the cable at the corner of Grant Avenue and he began to understand. He followed suit.

On the right was the old red brick Catholic church, swallowed up by the Japanese-Chinese community. He followed some way behind her. She did not seem to be moving aimlessly: it was as though she were making for a burrow, and he began to suspect which one. The street was busy with tourists, so that it was difficult to keep her in sight.

It was the time of the New Year festival and tall wet branches of peach blossom stood in pots along the streets. Maggie turned down to the small square where the steel statue of Sun Yat Sen was, standing with its immaculately folded stone hands, gazing indifferently towards a German Art School. She did not go down the hill, but doubled back, crossing Grant Avenue at the far end, where dried ducks lay crinkled and luminous brown in the stores; and where live rabbits and coloured eating fowl stood shaking in their small boxes. She went down a small street that at first seemed to puzzle her. It was a tall street of cheap rooming houses and restaurants with many balconies. She stopped to buy some sweetmeats in a shop. He could see her earnest face in profile, staring down at a counter. There was music from the balconies, Chinese music. From one of these balconies he had seen a sailor jump out holding a white cat and land on the paving uninjured. It was a rowdy street.

He knew now where she was going and it made him sadder than if she had just aimlessly been wandering around. He slackened his pace, and bought some crisp, somewhat unsatisfactory candies, the water lily root that tasted of rancid sherry, the coconut with sugar, and the frosted melon.

She reached the end of the street and passed through

the crowd of vendors, where almond blossoms already shed their petals on the asphalt. Hesitating, she went doubtfully down a dark alley, as though she had forgotten her way. He did not follow her at once. Instead he stood on the corner, looking across the narrow street at some bad blue vases in a laundry window and at a dingy tortoise-shell laundry cat. When he thought he had waited long enough, he went slowly down the alley. It was dark and dirty. At the end was a pink neon sign. He approached it and went through a doorway.

The outer lobby was gaudy. It was like the inside of a temple. In the middle stood the lacquer rickshaw that gave the place its name. The folded-back roof of the rickshaw was brittle as lizard skin. Dubiously he went round behind it and into the bar, a long, dark room with shoulder-high cabinets let into the walls. It was from the cabinets that the only light came. A curio dealer, half to advertise himself, but partly because he had an interest in the bar, had filled the cabinets with mildly erotic curiosities in marble, crystal, ivory, and wood. Some of these were in themselves beautiful. Some of them were not. Glowing in the obscurity of that quiet place they had a mysterious effect. He had discovered this bar for himself, long after it had first ceased to be popular, and once Maggie and he had come here often to drink and talk together. For him it was an intimate, personal place, but he had carefully forgotten it, because it had meant something to him. He had always thought that she had forgotten it, too.

She was at the far end of the bar, squeezed down in the darkness, in front of a Tibetan passion Buddha covered with coral and turquoise. Luke stood in the doorway and then went over to her. He sat down one stool away from her and held out a brittle paper bag, already stained by the candy inside it.

"You didn't buy any melon," he said. "So I got some." He picked out a piece of the yellow stuff and handed it to her. "It's better than the coconut."

She took the melon and began to nibble it, looking at him seriously out of the darkness.

"The place hasn't changed," he said. "It's just the same as it ever was."

"I've never been back. It always seemed so lonely."

He put his hands on the counter and crooked his head at the bar-tender. He felt more at his ease here. "We'd better have frozen dacquiris," he said. "That's what we always did have." He spun round on the stool, feeling almost exultant. It was as though everything was going to be all right now. "We can take them off into the corner and play some music."

"What kind of music?"

"Oh, just music," he said. "Any old music will do." He got up and went into the back room, where the juke box was. He put in a quarter and pressed three buttons at random. It was not his fault that one of the records turned out to be an old song called "Don't Blame Me". He sat down beside her, munching his melon and not saying anything. When the song came on she began to cry.

"Oh, hell, Maggie," he said. There wasn't anything else he could say. He took the two dacquiris and led her over to a dark table in a corner. She sat down and fumbled for something in her bag. The song played on remorselessly. He gave her a handkerchief and felt both completely helpless and happier than he had been for years. In here that song still meant something to them. Outside it wouldn't mean a thing.

When she had stopped crying she wadded up his handkerchief and put it in her bag.

"You must think I'm pretty terrible," she said.

"You're keyed up."

"I mean," she said, speaking with difficulty, "about the marriage. I guess it hurt you."

"Tell me about it some other time. You'd better finish your drink and have another." It seemed better to shut her off.

"I had to go somewhere. I couldn't stand the house. This was the only place that meant anything."

"It's a nice place," he agreed, and pretended to look around, as though to see just how nice a place it was. And it was a nice place. It was hidden away from the world, which he guessed was the reason he had always brought her here. It hadn't been so easy then. It wasn't, when he came right down to it, any easier now.

"I didn't know what to do," she said.

"It doesn't matter." He did not know whether she was still talking about the marriage or about Charles. He was surprised to find that her hand was completely dry, like the hand of an observant child.

"I'm frightened," she said. "I guess I always have been. And I wonder if he knows I didn't kill him." She watched the waiter bringing the second round.

"He's dead, Maggie."

"Is he?" She did not sound as though she believed it. "I don't think Lily thinks so."

"Lily's nuts."

It was the wrong thing to say. She looked at him out of some wide-eyed pit that he couldn't see to the bottom of. She looked as though she had been slapped.

"Drink your dacquiri", he said, "and have another."

In the end they had four apiece. It was nice to sit there for a little while. When he thought she had had enough to drink he told her they would have to go back.

"I know." She was watchfully still and her smile faded.

"It won't be for long. I can at least promise you that."

She put her glass down, touched his hand, and then stood up, slim and troubled. She was no more troubled than he, for they could not seem to establish any contact at all. "Very well," she said, "take me back." Her passivity was alarming.

He took her back in a cab. He could not tell whether she was really calmer or not, but he hoped for all their sakes, and especially for hers, that she was.

They found Lily's car drawn up in front of the house and when they got inside the hall there was a chaos of baggage. It was not only Lily's. As soon as they entered Lily appeared on the landing at the top of the stairs. She was wearing a black seal-skin coat and had her hat on, a trim hat with a veil, which she pulled down and tucked under her chin. She gazed directly down at Luke.

"Is it all right?" she asked.

"Yes, it's all right." He wondered uneasily why she was being so dramatic. "We went to Chinatown and had a drink."

Lily was taken aback. She put her hands on the balustrade, as though being above them gave her an advantage she badly needed. He had the sneaking feeling that whatever her other emotions were, she was also enjoying herself enormously.

"Foster phoned," she said. "They phoned him first. So now officially we know. I told the maid to go out and buy every newspaper she could lay her hands on. She'll be back soon." She avoided catching Maggie's eye. "They want someone to identify the body. You can't do it and Maggie can't do it. I said she was prostrate. So I'll go. They've got him at Sausolito." She made an odd gesture and started down the stairs. Then, pausing, as though not wanting to come too close, she once more leaned on the balustrade. For some reason he felt profoundly sorry for her.

"What are you planning to do?" he asked.

She began to come down the stairs again, very slowly, fiddling with her gloves. She spoke to him and not to Maggie.

"I'll be about an hour and a half," she said crisply. "When I get back I'm taking Maggie down to Atherton."

"No," said Maggie. She had been watching her mother closely and now she stood away from Luke, in the centre of the black and white marble floor, and looked up.

Lily shrugged. "We can't have any more irresponsible outbursts like this. The papers will be out soon and that means the reporters will be here. The whole city will be watching us and somebody has to take care of you. You can't be trusted."

"I won't go."

Lily was annoyed. "Of course you'll go. There will be reporters, the police, and phone calls day and night.

People you haven't heard of in years will be offering their sympathy and hoping for a little inside gossip. Who's to know what you might say?"

Luke thought that she was right. "It might be better," he said. He took Maggie's arm to stop her from shaking.

"You don't understand," said Maggie, as though her mother were not even there. "I can't be alone with her."

"Why not?"

"I can't," she repeated, and watched her mother come on down the stairs. Lily was in no hurry. She paused on the fourth step, looking at both of them with what was supposed to be composure. She gave a short grunt.

"Who would help you but me?" she asked softly. "And I don't have to help you, you know."

"Oh, yes, you do."

Lily's manner was that of a trainer with a dog. "Do I? Suppose I washed my hands of it? Suppose I did?"

"You wouldn't dare."

Lily waved her hand irritably and came down the rest of the stairs. "Luke, you'd better stay with her until I get back." She didn't bother to wait for an answer, but marched firmly out of the door. For once decision seemed to be an effort for her, and her eyes were sad. They heard her drive off with an irritated authoritarian clash of gears.

Maggie stood irresolute and then walked briskly into the living-room. He shut the front door and when he joined her found her sitting by the fireplace, smoking and looking thoughtfully into space. The clock seemed both very loud and very slow.

"It's probably the best thing to do," he said uncomfortably. "She's right about that."

She glanced at him but did not speak.

"What is it, really?" he asked.

"What is what?"

"This is no time to play games," he said. "You might lose one. Have you thought of that?"

"Yes, I've thought of that."

"Then what is it?"

"It's a lot of things," she said. "It always has been a lot of things. I guess it's always going to be."

"That isn't very helpful. I only came to help you, Maggie. You know that, don't you?"

"I don't know what I know," she said.

"It's not Charles. I know it's not Charles."

She looked up at him. "I can't be alone with her. You don't know what she's like."

"You don't know what a scandal can be like, either," he told her.

"What scandal?" she asked sharply.

The obliviousness of it made him blink. "Charles."

"I don't want her to do anything else to me, Luke. I daren't be alone with her. She isn't the way she looks at all." She seemed somehow relieved.

"I can't stay in the house, Maggie."

"No, I suppose not."

He did not like the way she said it. He had no intention of abandoning her. He did not want her to feel that she had been abandoned. He stared at her, baffled. It occurred to him that he did not know her very well, after all.

There was a tap on the door and the maid came in with the papers. She was bright-eyed and avid, and she tried to peer over his shoulder at Maggie. He soon got rid of her, but it made him realize how right Lily was.

Maggie was in no condition to face up to that kind of scrutiny.

He spread the papers out on the coffee table. They were extras and the ink was still wet on them. At first she sat hunched up away from them, not saying anything. But then she edged closer to him on the sofa and took his hand. He squeezed hers, but it was impersonal and tense.

There were three papers, two tabloids and the conservative *Chronicle*. There was a big smeared photograph of the house at Bolinas, taken from the beach, with a diagram of what one of the scandal sheets called "the death room". There were dotted lines from the chair to a Maltese cross marking the place where the body had been found. There was an old photograph of Maggie, probably taken after her coming-out party, or at college, and one of Charles, looking alive and self-confident. One of the papers called him a prominent socialite, one a society lawyer, and the third a business man. The conservative *Chronicle* had a photograph of the "death room" taken by flash-bulb. They did not call it murder, but they clearly hoped that it was one. Maggie looked down at the papers for a long time, but without touching them.

"What on earth do they mean by 'socialite'?" she asked.

"They mean you have money."

"It's horrible," she said. "It wasn't like that at all."

There was no point in telling her that as far as the papers were concerned the truth was anything that would sell and remain unsueable.

"How they must hate us," she said.

"It's just policy." He realized that public opinion was something she had never thought about. He leafed through the papers. It took him a long time to find what he was looking for, and when he did find it it didn't tell him much. The obits were skimpy. Apparently only the *Chronicle* had an adequate morgue.

That depressed him. If the newspapers knew no more about Charles than he did, perhaps there wasn't anything else to know. And yet there must be, for someone had been at Bolinas. And if Maggie had been seen, he did not like to think what might come of it. As he re-read the best of the obits one phase caught his eye: "Before attending Stanford, Mr. Shannon was educated at the Sacred Heart Academy in San Francisco." He stared at that thoughtfully, wondering if it was true, and if it was true, if it meant anything. It was not much, but it was the only thing he had seen about Charles that he had not known before. He went hastily through the other two papers, but there was no mention of it in them.

Charles, of course, was Irish. So were the Barnes. He always forgot that, because they all made such a fetish of being respectable. It was not a thing that people usually forgot to boast about, and if Charles had made nothing of it, therefore perhaps it meant something. He stared down at the paper.

Maggie lay back against the sofa and shut her eyes. It was clearly the only way she could hide, so he said nothing to disturb her. Perhaps sitting there quietly with him might do her some good.

They were still sitting like that when they heard the car drive up and its door slam. Maggie opened her eyes and stood up. "I'll go get my coat and bag," she said. She gave him a sudden, crooked smile. "I'm all right now. Really." She looked round the room. "It's better to go. I used to love this house, and he made me hate it." She went out of the room.

He heard Lily come in and the two women speak briefly in the hall. He could not hear what they were saying. Lily came in quietly. Under her veil and under her makeup her face looked unexpectedly severe and old. For a moment it seemed that her eyes no longer dominated her face. He saw that she had at last realized that Charles was really dead. She glanced at the papers, but made no attempt to look at them. She looked genuinely frightened.

"Luke," she said, "the cat's gone."

"What cat?"

"Charles's. He kept one up there. A Siamese or something. Some people took care of it during the week. It's gone."

"Cats come and go."

"You don't understand. Charles liked it. It had a bassinet and a coat, and I don't know what all. It's all gone."

"Oh."

"You'd better follow us down," she said, not sitting down. "I'll get you a room at the hotel in Palo Alto." He saw that she was badly shaken.

They heard Maggie come down the stairs. They moved towards her in unison and Luke let them out of the door. Just as he held the door open the telephone began to ring. It rang insistently and for a long time, and they stood staring at one another, wondering. Through the open doorway he could see the maid settling one of the bags into the rear of the car. With a glance at Luke, Lily went down the path and Maggie followed her.

The preliminaries were over. It wasn't a private matter any more. Reluctantly Luke shut the door and went to answer the phone. Before he could reach it it had stopped, but he knew it would ring again. Faintly perplexed, he got his hat and left the house. The reporters could wait.

He had decided to try the seminary. They might know something there. On the way, in the taxi, he found that he did not know how to begin. He knew nothing of Irish Catholic life and did not feel at ease in it. It had not occurred to him before that Charles, despite the name, might have that background. It made a great deal of difference. For one thing he was uncomfortably aware of where he stood with the Irish: they were not particularly kind to anybody but themselves.

They ran local government, the way they ran it everywhere. Once in a while they threw a bone to the Italians, but that was all. They were not much noticed in the public, or the social, or the cultural life. There were not interested in public or cultural life and they had their own society. They were interested in politics, which had made them rich. With the money they sprinkled the city with convents, seminaries, and churches. Their ideas of taste came out of a shanty, and what they built had a shanty look, but they built anyway.

The taxi deposited him in front of the school. It was an ugly building of yellow cement Byzantine with a lobby that smelled of Fels-naptha and rubber. Once inside and he felt more at his ease.

He finally got himself conducted into the presence of a Father O'Leary, the registrar. Father O'Leary had, if anything, a Lutheran appearance. He had black hair and a prognathous jaw and his eyes were sympathetic. Luke did not think he could have stumbled on a better man.

"Oh, yes. I read about it. It upset me." O'Leary's voice was matter of fact. He picked up a penwiper and began to twiddle with it, glancing at the office door, which was half glass. "The point is, why are you here?"

It wasn't an easy question to answer. There was a green and brown map of the state behind O'Leary's back and Luke looked at that, wondering how much he should say. "Mrs. Barnes is a client," he said.

"Yes," said O'Leary, "I've met her." He smiled at Luke. "It bothered me."

"It may bother a lot of people."

"I don't think so," said O'Leary. He breathed deeply and pulled out a handkerchief.

"It's funny. I never realized he was Irish."

"Or Catholic? Well, he was born Catholic, if that makes him one. And as for being Irish, I'm afraid he was ashamed of that. A lot of people are, and Charles had his eye on things where being Irish isn't always a help." O'Leary looked at Luke with amusement. "It doesn't always help, you know." He coughed gently. "I remember him well. I looked up his record after I saw the papers. He came to us when he was twelve and left when he was sixteen. He was a good learner, a little too bright, if anything. I taught him logic." He considered. "That was a mistake, I think. Logic is an excellent science, but not a way of life. I suppose what bothered me when I read the papers was that I didn't like him. Nobody liked him; and I don't think he wanted anybody to."

"And then?"

O'Leary shrugged. "Then he left."

"A boy of sixteen can't just leave."

"That's what he did, though."

"What about his family? He must have had some family."

O'Leary looked uncomfortable. "He didn't. At least, not so far as we knew. He had a guardian, a woman who brought him here. I never met her."

"But there must be some record of all that."

"Oh, yes, there was a record. To-day I looked for it, but it wasn't there. They're kept in open files."

"Somebody took it?"

O'Leary seemed put out. "I imagine he took it himself. And recently. You see, I forgot all about him until a few years ago. Then I bumped into him at some political rally. It upset him, I think. Later he came here. He came once or twice and said he wanted to do something for us. He said he wanted to make a donation. He even made several. They were anonymous."

"Why should he want to destroy his record?"

"That's what I wondered. I think it was because he didn't want to have any past. And well—the donations were rather large. It seemed better not to say anything."

Luke understood. He wondered just when O'Leary had discovered that missing file.

"He had a knack of meeting people who were useful," added O'Leary.

"Is that all?"

"Yes and no." O'Leary looked at Luke more sharply, as though he had just then become interested in him. "Charles was frightened," he said slowly. "He was badly frightened and he was frightened all the time. He wasn't frightened of being murdered, if he was murdered. He was afraid of dying. I think he always felt that he was dying and that he had to hurry to catch up. He wasn't ever really young, and once he was over thirty he resented what he'd missed. So everything he wanted he either bought or stole. I don't mean outright. But he managed to get what he wanted and he always felt cheated once he had it. And yet he didn't want anything that couldn't be bought. It couldn't have been very pleasant for his wife."

"It wasn't."

O'Leary drew his eyebrows together and then sighed. "What is it you have to find out?"

Luke decided to trust him and told him about the beach house.

"That won't be so easy," said O'Leary.

"But a boy of sixteen doesn't bury his own past," said Luke. "At that age he doesn't have any past."

"Charles just wanted to be somebody else," said O'Leary, and stopped. "It probably was a woman, but I don't think you'll find her. She'd be very old by now."

"He probably forgot her."

"No, I don't think so. There must have been some people he couldn't forget, because they'd have known all about him. He couldn't get rid of them; so he must have conciliated them in some way. The question is: what way?"

Luke got up to go, but O'Leary waved him back. "I'm not through yet, and you may as well listen to me. That's what you came to do. The point is, which one of them do you want to save?"

"I don't understand."

"Yes, you do. You see, you don't have many people to draw on, really, and I gather you don't have much time, either. And it must have struck you that of the people you do know, Lily Barnes is the only one who could have known anything about Charles at all."

"She'll scarcely speak to me."

"You might think it over, all the same."

Luke was put out. He didn't like to have the tables turned on him, particularly when he didn't know what the tables were. He rose again, and O'Leary examined him candidly, placidly aware of his irritation.

"I wish you luck," he said.

Luke said good-bye and left. Outside there was no cab in sight and he did not want to wait while somebody phoned for one, so he decided to walk. It was not a section of town he knew very well. For one reason it was recent. Formerly it had been the burial district of the city. Now it was jammed with cheap houses which bore an unpleasant likeness to the anonymous white marble jumble of a derelict *campo santo*. Nothing lived there. He came to a corner and saw that he was on the edge of an old cemetery, so he decided to take a short cut across it. It had been demolished to make way for new housing. Headstones had been flung down on their faces; and here and there a corroded coffin had been cast aside under a bush. The roof of the columbarium had fallen in and the empty chamber was crowded with nettles. He hurried on. O'Leary had upset him very much indeed. O'Leary had reminded him of Lily, and Lily reminded him of his own past, and he did not find that agreeable.

He found it even less agreeable by the time he had taken the one and a half hour trip to Palo Alto on a slow and smelly commutors' train. The only person he could look up in Palo Alto was Senator Ford, and he did not want to see Senator Ford right now. He read the evening paper, had a tasteless dinner, could settle nowhere, and went for a walk in the campus grounds.

The Stanford campus was large, pretentious, and at night rather eerie. The blue moonlight lent it a hostile glamour, and there was almost no other light. In front of him stretched the Mall, bordered by dishevelled palm trees that rattled in the night air, and by a wood with an underbrush of needles and aromatic leaves. It was a lonely road. Far ahead of him he could see the mosaic façade of the college chapel, glittering in the moonlight. He struck off into the trees and came to the family tombs of the Stanford family, the one a miniature pyramid, the other a small temple guarded by lipsticked lions. He walked out across the fields and past the stables towards the golf course. Even from a distance he heard that long forgotten but familiar whirring sound. Because the climate was so mercilessly arid there, the golf links were watered only at night. The sprinklers turned in the moonlight, perhaps ten of them, casting sprays of silent water twenty feet into the air, where the moon mirrored the individual drops. Slowly the sprinklers circled on their pivots, their double wings of water like enormous moths, stately, slightly unreal, and silent except for that incessant metallic grinding of bearings that imitated, but did not reproduce, the song of absent cicadas.

Luke sat down on a ragged stump, watching the sprinklers, and lit a cigarette. He had been here, but it wasn't really his Alma Mater, and he did not want to cry. At the same time it was wrong to come full circle, and that was what he had now done. Lily and Maggie had got him back into the same old trap again by a woman's trick that had nothing to recommend it.

X

HE HAD BEEN ONE OF SENATOR
Ford's boys and Senator Ford had pull. That was what
had got Luke in, for Stanford, like most small private universities, ran on the quota system. The college
was co-educational, but by maintaining a ratio of three
men to each woman they had managed to keep the
money in the family. They also encouraged intellect.
That is, they would admit almost anybody of sufficient
intelligence, so long as the intelligent did not take up
more than 10 per cent of the student body. This system
may not have made the intelligent particularly happy
while they were there, but as long as they became distinguished afterwards and developed a fine alumnal
glow the university really didn't care about that. What
it did care about was that the intelligent had an unfortunate tendency, purely apart from lacking gymnastic skill,
to be of mixed descent. Hence the quota. South Americans, if well-to-do and of a neutral tint, were always
welcome, particularly if they had Scots or Irish blood
and were not Catholics.

Luke was not South American nor, for that matter,
was he strictly Catholic. He was a Spanish-Mexican
from Los Angeles and looked it.

He was not unhappy, but he was not happy there

either, for he had self-knowledge, and those who have that can never be happy. He was impelled by impersonal ambition and he knew it. Of all the forms of ambition that is the worst, for it is inexorable. For himself he had no ambitions at all. He would have been happier playing pool. He liked the swagger and the jazz of the marginal life he came from. But he knew it lived under a shadow. He knew the importance of a social role and of comfort and a reputation. He knew this and it made him sad. He did not want to better himself. He did not need bettering. But if you belong to a minority you have to put yourself beyond the range of insult. Minorities should be both transient and rich.

His one real ally was, of course, Senator Ford, but Ford was not much actual help. He could be sympathetic when he chose, but he seldom chose. He was old; he was fickle; he was sexless; and he was primarily concerned about himself and his own reputation. He was indulgent, but he was neither understanding nor kind. He saw his protégés once a week and was agreeable to them. The rest of the time he was busy with his autobiography. It would never be finished. It would never be published. And Senator Ford knew that.

One evening, not having anything else to do, Luke was in one of the libraries, slightly sullen with boredom, when Maggie came up to him. He remembered now that she had been wearing a white sweater and a tweed skirt. He could also remember how he had felt about her at that moment, a curious mixture of wariness and curiosity, wondering who she was, what she wanted, and how much sting there might be in either; together with the acute, angry discomfort of not knowing quite what to do which was always the by-product of his having wandered into a world that did not quite belong to him.

But they saw a lot of each other. She was neither so simple nor so naïve as she appeared. She already had that hard naïveté that American women do have, with the difference that in her it was not grasping.

Because they were young he had said that he was in love with her. Sometimes he was. Now, when he thought it over, it was a scrambled memory. What he had liked best about it was the sense of belonging. It had been some time before he had realized that, in a different way than he, she too was in between the frontiers of society. In her case they were other frontiers. Unlike an army, a society sees no bad strategy, and often exists only because it fights itself simultaneously on a hundred varying fronts.

He remembered many things about her. Once, in a sudden rainstorm, they had hidden under the canvas of a haystack. There was an adolescent perfume then well advertised called New Mown Hay and he had thought that the stack would smell like that and be somehow pink. It didn't and wasn't. It smelled damp. The hay was corded with bailing wire. They rearranged the bails to make a sort of house and laughed in the rain until the campus patrol car stopped to investigate. That was funny too.

And once, after a party, late at night, they had driven home on a steam-roller. She had the assurance to do something whimsical like that. It was not until he had been to bed with her that he learned that that lopsided decorum which was her usual mask, and which he thought she had been bred to, was actually the personal disguise of some puzzled terror underneath. She was always acting. And she persisted, blandly, in being so much more adult than he was that she often hurt him.

Nor was the sexual side of their relationship satisfactory. She kept the two sides of herself always disparate, and each was more vehement, the one violently, the other with decorum, than it should have been. He could never make her two selves match up, and both were evasive. That such nocturnal episodes took place, as was customary with the college students, at the ring of auto courts and motels in the outlying districts did not help matters much. The one they usually went to was a featureless blank in his mind, except that its garden contained painted lead statues of dwarfs in yellow caps and that the fountain was topped with a boy in a smock, carrying an umbrella whose iron shaft had been bent almost double, so that the water, spraying out over the umbrella top, fell chiefly into a bed of dirty asters. And in bed he lost identity for her. She did not seem to care who he was, and that disquieted him.

One night, and for him the night existed in his memory as something inexplicably hideous, they had walked back to the campus, a distance of perhaps two miles, through the suburbs. There was a moon and the air was clogged with haze. They passed a vacant lot thick with candytuft and wild mustard. "Do you love me?" she had asked.

"Of course I do."

"No, you don't. Nobody does," she cried. She clenched her hands and ran into the vacant lot. He stood for a moment, startled, and then went after her. She was sitting crumpled up on the grass. "Oh, I shouldn't have said that," she said. "I shouldn't. Now you know."

"Now I know what?"

"You do," she said, and began to cry. The only thing to do was to sit down beside her, which he did. Through the tall weeds he could see the empty sidewalk and hoped nobody, particularly a policeman, would come by. She didn't want to be touched. She went right on crying. He finally had to push her down on the grass and shut her up, and he was shaking himself. Her skirt was smeared with the wet yellow mustard. She stared at him. She had lost her composure and never again with him did she regain it.

"Don't tell anybody," she said.

"Why should I tell anybody? Tell them what?"

"Oh, nothing," she said. He could not decide whether she was acting or not. She got up and the rest of the walk was uncomfortable. He did not see her for several days. He did not, somehow, want to. He had his own reasons for wanting the whole relationship to float in limbo, for he knew how circumscribed it was. He preferred to keep it that way. He did not put much faith in it, but not seeing her did make him realize how important seeing her had become, as a sort of daily anchor to keep him from drifting. It manufactured memories: long sun-drenched afternoons on that lake above the post office where every year someone always drowned. Now it was winter and the lake had run away into the ground, as it always did, leaving only a shapeless puddle in a bowl of cracked mud.

He began to miss her. Then, quite suddenly, he bumped into her outside the university post office. He did not think it was entirely by chance. He had learned that Maggie's nature was such that one seldom saw her unless she felt like being seen. He was upset to find what pleasure it gave him to see her. She had become something familiar in an unfamiliar world. She smiled at him confidently, but it was not an open smile.

"Come on, I want you to meet Mother," she said. He could not tell if she was being deliberately provocative. She must know perfectly well that he didn't want to meet Mother and she must know why. He did not want to be tested and found wanting.

"Oh, do," she urged, while he thought it over. "She doesn't bite."

So he went. The car was parked several blocks away. It was the big black Cadillac Lily still had. The car glittered with a special insolence. Lily leaned out of the window. She was, of course, driving. He was taken aback by that big, confident, heavily powdered face and the eyes that looked out of it, cold, cursory, polite and evasive. He tried to regard her as an older, bigger Maggie, but that was not quite true. Lily insisted upon taking the two of them to lunch.

He got uncomfortably into the back of the car, sure he was not dressed properly for wherever it was that Lily would choose to take them. The car was big and he was slight, and he sat alone in the back seat. Maggie talked incessantly. Lily, he noticed, was watching him in the rear view mirror, and he wanted desperately to comb his hair. He did not know how he knew that the two women were having a quarrel. Perhaps it was because Maggie was talking much more intimately to him, emphatically so, than she ever did when they were alone. She was parading him in front of her mother, to make her mother mad. It made him feel important and inferior. He knew perfectly well that to a woman like Lily he was not the right kind of young man at all.

All the strip of highway south of the university was lined with over-decorated restaurants to which the local matrons went for lunch. They had the same kind of massive simplicity as had Lily's car. They were geared to transient power. It was difficult to keep talking and his voice had not the right sophomoric drawl.

The restaurant was *chic*, a series of interconnecting ranch-house rooms, painted white and turkey red, with awnings, fowling pieces, napoleon ivy, a good deal of white-painted wire, and bird-cages with flower arrangements in them. The bar was mannish, for the fraternity trade. The place smelled faintly of patchouli. It was a recent habit of the management to put all small change in an acid bath, so that it came out sparkling and new. Anyone who pulled out a handful of change showed instantly where he had been. It was a canny piece of advertising. The two women left him to go to the powder-room and he stood watching the half-deserted bar. It was one of many recent lessons in the applied techniques of glamour.

He watched them returning and had a minute to look at Lily before she saw him. There was certainly something going on between the two of them, and Maggie looked both defiant and squashed. Lily, he saw, was younger than she looked and more attractive. Seen from his distance, unobserved, she was a different kind of woman, with a personal swagger and pathos to her that he had been too embarrassed at first to notice. There was something hopeful in the way she looked at people round her.

But once she saw she was being watched the mask slid down again. He wondered what it was that she felt she had to be careful about. She had that habit of swimming through a room which he envied in people, and of course she made a point of knowing the waiters, whether she knew them or not. Lily reduced Luke and Maggie to the kindergarten level. She moved her judicious way through lunch.

"We'd better begin with grapefruit," she said. "It's hot today. And then curried shrimps, I think." She leaned forward. "Is that all right, Luke?" She made a conscious effort to make the "Luke" sound friendly.

"Yes," he said uncomfortably. "That would be fine."

Lily continued with the menu. She seemed then to ignore both of them. When she was finished, and not before, she went on talking.

"Maggie says you're from Los Angeles," she said. "Do you know the Petersons?"

He did not know the Petersons and he knew that she knew it. "Los Angeles is a big place."

Lily ran her thumb down the side of the menu. "I suppose so," she said doubtfully. "But no city is big once you get to know who's in it. Then it always suddenly gets so small. What part of Los Angeles?"

"Central," he said. "Figuaroa."

She blinked and looked at the grapefruit. The crushed ice was too coarse and the grapefruit slid around in its cradle. He jabbed at it miserably, wanting very much to leave. Maggie said nothing. The whole meal was like that.

"This place has fallen off," said Lily, when they got up to go.

Catching her eye by accident he was startled by her expression. It wasn't what he had expected at all. It was erotic, speculative and personal. Or was it only that they all had had too much too drink? After all, she was Maggie's mother.

But Lily looked several different ages at once, and none of them suited her. Seeing she had been caught out she made a point of ignoring him, even as they walked out of the restaurant, through the flunkeyism of the owners, bowing her out. Did she come there, he wondered, just for the pleasure of being bowed out? Besides, though there are many kinds of sexual attractiveness, it did not seem to him that he possessed any of them. Lily had embarrassed him.

She also seemed to have embarrassed herself. She talked too volubly to Maggie all the way back to the campus, and seemed pleased when they both got out of the car. She drove away immediately.

Maggie looked after the car and frowned. She seemed discouraged. He felt discouraged himself. It was all very well to pretend with her that they were equals, but he had been slapped up against the world she came from. He looked down the *allée* of the campus. Though not more than fifty years old, it seemed ancient, not in the sense of venerable, but in a primitive sense that was even more depressing. It was inimical to him.

Maggie pretended ease. "Did you like her?" she asked.

He said yes.

She looked at the now empty road from which the car had passed. "Oh, you were horrible," she said. "How could you be so horrible? Why couldn't you talk to her?"

He was angry with himself. "Nobody could talk to her."

"But you don't understand," she said. She turned and walked up the row, in the impatient sunlight, under the well-bred trees and he did not follow her. He did not try to follow her, for he quite suddenly realized that as a couple they were noticeable.

On that social campus everybody watched everybody else: it was part of their training for suburban life. The buildings, with their monotonous arcades, seemed suddenly too complicated for him, and he struck away from them and went to the outdoor pool. There only, with his compact little body cleaving the green water, he felt more at ease, for in childhood to swim was something he had learned how to do and it had shaped him.

For several weeks she avoided him. He had known that she would. And apart from missing the company he was not sure whether he cared or not. There is a difficulty with mothers: they show other people what their daughters are apt to become. Perhaps she was nervous about that.

Once, when he was down in the village buying oranges, he saw Lily in a caterer's shop. She was bending over an excelsior filled bin, plump and judicious, with a sly grin on her face, while the clerk watched her with exasperation. Luke watched her himself. She was wondering if the peaches were ripe. She took first one and then another, splitting them expertly in half to see. She laid the halves down, carefully, and he could see their yellow flesh and the scarlet capillary filaments gripping their stones. She smiled vaguely and chose six more. She rejected the broken peaches. The clerk looked at those with anguish: he would have to pay for them himself. Lily was like that. About her daughter he was not so sure.

He took to remembering Maggie at night. It made him sleepy for his morning classes. At eleven he went to the co-operative cafeteria to bring himself to. It smelled of too many people, rancid toasted cheese, young pine wood, and a sort of self-satisfied masturbation. It was always filled with the deliberately stylized awkwardness of the very well brought up young. He was thinking about that when she sat down beside him. She seemed a little uncertain.

"I haven't seen you in ages," she said.

"No, you haven't."

"Things got complicated," she explained. "Don't be a damn fool."

"Maybe I am a damn fool."

She sighed and twiddled with the straw of the iced coca-cola she had brought with her. "Don't be mean," she said. "Sometimes it isn't so easy for me. I want to go somewhere."

"Sure. Any old back street will do."

She looked at him swiftly. "I want to."

'O.K. You want to."

She looked at him again, curiously, piece by piece, and as she did so he could feel his image shaping in her mind, starting with the hair, a little too long and greasy perhaps (it was a year of crew cuts), the mouth, which was too full and too red, a pretty good neck, the sweater, the dirty trousers, a little vague and hasty this, and then down to his shoes. He was wearing blue and white argyles.

She took out her keys. "Sam's away," she said. "He's out on a drunk."

He knew Sam slightly. He was a St. Louis Jew, mournfully handsome, with lupanar proclivities. His family, prosperous psychiatrists in St. Louis, paid him to stay away from Missouri, and he was putting himself through college that way. He had an apartment in town. Luke felt a slight pressure in his groin that told him he would go. They got up to leave. Some people noticed them and some did not. They got into her car, which she drove, with the same worried fury that her mother drove with. He did not like her always to drive. It made him feel like a clay pigeon coasting down the treads of a water shoot. But the car meant something to her, and she would only let him drive in the open country where there was no one to watch them. They didn't say a word all the way down to the village.

The university was a tribute to Henry Richardson, but since it had red tiles it passed for Spanish. For the building boom the village had mocked the Spanish, too. The apartment was in the midst of an aborted *paseo*. There was a courtyard with a fake well. The effect owed more to Humperdinck than to Lazarillo de Tormes. The ground floor cloisters were devoted to gift shops. They got out and climbed steep, dank, smelly, monastic stairs to the front door. She got out Sam's keys and opened the door. They stepped into the upper part of a studio about twenty feet high, but very small. It smelled musty. The gallery led to the kitchen, cluttered with dead soldiers and plates of half-eaten toast. Steep stairs, more like a plastered ladder than anything else, led down to the tiny studio itself, which had big windows closed with cracked, yellow bamboo blinds. They went downstairs, found half a bottle of Noilly Prat, and drank it. There wasn't any radio. They were thrown back upon themselves and on the Noilly Prat.

"I love you," she said. The vermouth was stickily cloudy. It left rings on the table. The room was too small. It never got a proper airing.

"No, you don't. You're only here for spite." As soon as he had said it he knew it was true.

She knew it was true, too. She did not answer him. She got up uncertainly and tried to pull out the bed, which slid on casters into the wall below the gallery. They had done that before and had giggled about always expecting to find a corpse in it. Once they had found Sam in it. He always hid there when his hangovers got too bad.

He went to help her. The bed was not made and that made him sentimental, or perhaps the vermouth did. He knew he wasn't really a tough guy. He looked like hell in jeans and besides he wasn't tall enough to master the proper stride. He was sentimental as mush.

When she was doing something like this her movements were too practised and deft and automatic. She was virginal up to a point and then experience broke through.

The real trouble, though, was that there wasn't any radio. It made them both awkward and self-conscious. He would have liked to be romantic and undress her, but she would not let him do that. She did not like to be looked at. He began to shuck his clothes. He might be small, but he had nothing to be ashamed of. She watched him with that frightening divided attention that always made him want to slap her awake. He never knew whether it was insolence or hysteria. Besides he could not love her in bed for in bed her personality disappeared. He only loved her afterwards when he was sleepy.

It did not work out very well. She was nervous. He felt as though he were being watched, and as the daylight grew less, for they stayed there a long time, they became introspective and gloomy.

"I can't stand it here," she said.

"It's the only place we've got." He was angry both with himself and her, for the nothing that had happened. With her, very often, nothing did.

"No," she said. "Let's go home."

She had never suggested that before. He did not like the idea.

"Yes," she said. She got up and went into the bathroom, carrying her clothes. "It's okay. Mother's out with Charles."

"Who's Charles?"

"I don't know," she said, by which he knew she did not want to say. He sat on the edge of the bed, looking towards the bathroom door. She came out of the bathroom, not looking at him, and went up to the kitchen. He heard her opening the icebox door and stared at his shoes, half-keeled over before him on the floor. Then he began to dress.

"Why do you want to go home?" he asked.

She banged the icebox door. And then she banged it again. It occurred to him that the best thing would be to get her out of there, and as she banged it a third time he struggled into his trousers and shoved his shirt down into them. He knew he had to go with her, for he suspected it was another social test of the sort he had become accustomed to and often flunked. If for no other reason than rage he was determined not to flunk this one. When she was upset or disgusted she liked to scramble above people, for the safety of being able to look down on them. Out of carelessness he had let her do that before this. She would not do it now.

"Okay," he called up the stairs. "Okay," and wedged himself into his shoes. If it was not okay, he was not going to let her know it.

So that was how he met Charles. And remembering now how he had felt that night, going to that house for the first time, he thought that in a way he could begin to understand Charles much better.

Outside it was much later than he had thought: they had spent a long time at the apartment. The street lights were on and glowed misty through a heavy somnolent haze off the bay. Palo Alto was not attractive at the best of times. As does any university town that is younger than its college, it had the air of being a squatters' settlement, necessary but impermanent. Then, he was nervous. Like so many of the insecure he both overestimated and underestimated the rich. He either thought they had more money and more pomp than they had, or else could not conceive of expensive simplicity. For the rich do not only have more money than we do. It is more that they are fresh water fish, in a world four-fifths salt, limited in their ambience, but living in their own element with their own diseases and squalor. Glamour is not an interior thing. Once within any charmed circle, and it disappears.

He knew that Lily Barnes, and therefore Maggie, lived in Atherton. It seemed to him sacrosanct, not because there was any exclusive mystery about it, but because he had no reason for going there. It was not precisely hostile territory; but it was a country of which he did not know the language. Besides, he came of one of the shorter races. Life for him was always out of scale and always would be. It gave the Anglo-Saxons an advantage.

It was not far to Atherton. They had only to cross that concrete bridge on the highway and pass through Menlo Park, a squalid town wedged between two better places. In the half darkness the roses along the campus fence glowed the colour of dried blood and their sun-baked leaves rattled in a helpless evening breeze. When they reached Atherton the air felt different. It was not only his imagination. The rich are surrounded by their own silence and their own smell, the smell of those high-piled beige-coloured rugs that spread from wall to wall in fashionable stores, like a universal element.

Atherton pretended to be the country. About its nocturnal insect noises there was something as deliberate as an Esterhazy quartet, and as arrogant. It was orchestrated to soothe. In those days the development was not built up. There were many vacant spaces underneath the eucalyptus trees, so that each house was a dim bulk in a wood. He braced himself as they turned up the drive, between hedges of ivy made to simulate old yew at least by its density. There was no moon and the haze cut out the stars, bathing the world in a diffused, expensive light.

They came out of the drive and the house stood across a tousled lawn. He could remember even now the sharp, snake-like slithering of the gravel as the car swirled over it. Maggie had not slowed down. He had only an uneasy impression of the house as it then was, crocketed and draped with wooden lace, with high dormers, a mansard roof, immaculate white, and seemingly hollow.

The car stopped with a jerk under the *porte-cochère*, and looking out of the window he found himself on a level with a cracked wooden statue of a jockey, once brightly coloured, but weather-beaten now, holding out a brass ring. The paint had peeled from its eyeballs and from its face, so that it looked both scrofulous and blind. Maggie sat fishing through her bag. The house was in darkness.

"We'd better be quiet," she said. "Ethel's probably asleep."

"Who's Ethel?"

"The maid," she said, and bit her nails. He knew that was not why they must be quiet. She got out of the car and banged the door. She went on up the steps without waiting for him. Hesitating, he got out and followed her. For some reason he felt like a lackey. He did not know why he was here. He was anxious about the servant. He felt furtive because she was being furtive. She clicked the latch and disappeared into darkness. She did not turn on a light. She turned it on only after he had come inside and closed the door after him.

He had never been in so large a house before. He was not awed. But he was impressed by the weight of solid wealth. When she turned on the light he saw the polished floor and the staircase rising to the landing, where he dimly caught sight of the outline of closed bedroom, if they were bedroom, doors. It was like straying on to a movie set after the technicians had gone home for the night.

She watched him staring up at the closed doors and she clearly did not like it. He was sure they would not go upstairs. He would be allowed to intrude so far, but no farther. People like him had to spend their lives on the ground floors of other people's lives.

"We'd better have a drink," she said. She wanted to get him away from the hall. He half-expected an avenging angel to appear on the landing.

She pushed open the sliding doors on the left and flicking on the lights, went into the living-room. It was furnished in blue, gold, and white; and it was very long. She was restless. She did not want to sit down. She moved ahead of him through the house flicking on lights as she went, through the living-room, a glass gallery giving onto the garden, the dining-room, the breakfast-room, and the pantry. He struck the piano in passing and found it was out of tune.

They came up short in the kitchen.

"Get some ice," she said, so he got the ice, swinging open the heavy refrigerator door. The refrigerator was jammed with lettuces, tomatoes, half a honeydew melon, a pot of salmon caviar, fruit, vegetables, and meat whose surface was crystallized with the cold. He got out the ice-trays and took them to the sink. They had a long handle, a novelty in those days, by which they could be extracted from the forms, and when he pulled the handle the ice made a ripping sound. She handed him a kitchen bowl to put the ice in and again he followed her through the house. She did not put out the lights behind her. He had the feeling that none of these rooms was ever used.

She took him into a room he had not seen yet and which was different from the rest of the house. It had less the air of empty waiting. It was the library, pine-panelled, but the panelling in an English style, with an elaborate mantel whose shelf was supported by a Greek metope. The lights here were less clinical. He could feel at once that this was a room Lily used, and yet it was a man's room. Deep windows gave out on the lawn. The sofa and chairs were comfortable, the desk empty, and unlike the rest of the house, there were shallow dishes of flowers on the tables. He put the bowl of ice down on a coffee table and looked around him. The most noticeable object was the large oil painting over the mantelpiece, an old-fashioned society portrait of a man with rather prominent eyes. The sofa and coffee table being opposite it, it seemed to dominate the room.

"That's Father," said Maggie, seeing him stare at it. It was the first time she had ever mentioned her father. Not looking at the painting, or at him, she pulled open the bar, fitted into an empire commode, and took out two whisky ponies and a bottle of Black and White. She handed him the bottle and he sat down on the sofa to split the seal with his finger-nail. She sat down beside him, but not close to him, and poured herself a stronger drink than she usually took. And then she drank it. They were both waiting for something.

The house was full of waiting. He was sure she knew for what. It did not help to put him at his ease. The room was out of scale for him. He sat on his coat and it bunched under him. Irritably he pulled it out.

She finished her drink and poured another. He settled

uncomfortably against the back of the sofa, afraid of staining the table with his drink, the glass colder than comfort. She suddenly moved around and put her head in his lap, so brusquely that he upset his drink. It soaked into the floor as alarmingly as a bloodstain.

"Leave it," she said. She began to cry. "What am I to do?"

It was so abrupt, so puzzling, and somehow her grief, whatever it was, made her older than he was, so that he soothed her awkwardly, like a child that doesn't know what to do when it sees its mother or its father cry. He stroked her hair and let her sob into his lap until his trousers were damp. But while she did that he found himself listening for every noise in the house. And also watching. Because of the way her body was his line of vision was limited, and he saw on the edge of the coffee table a thick smoky jade ashtray, carved in the shape of a leaf, and the pearwood inlay on the table edge and on the leg, and a bit of the pattern of the rug. Usually he never noticed little things in a house. They were only things to use. But now he realized that the ashtray had cost more than he could spend to live on for a month, and that everything in every room of any house cost so much money, and the things in this room probably more money than he had owned in his life; and that other people were more aware of these things than he and would judge his own possessions accordingly. No doubt to Lily he was consciously worth less than that ashtray in which, when he was not here, they stubbed out their cigarettes without thinking about the matter at all. These people were barricaded behind their possessions. He had no business among them. He tried not to look at the ashtray. He tried to concentrate on Maggie. Somehow the ashtray got in the way and made him feel cheated. So he just sat there while she cried.

The front door slammed. They didn't have any time to hide, not with all the lights on. His heart jumped. He could feel Maggie grow tense. She straightened up and looked at him with almost terror, as though she was about to be caught out in something she had not even done. She reached for her purse but she had left it in the hall. He gave her his handkerchief. She wiped her face with it. The two whisky ponies stood in front of them, on the table, like pawns.

He wondered, looking at them, if she had wanted him in this house to defy her mother, or to defeat her. The library doors slid open and Lily stood there. Part of the party flush, if she had been to a party, was still on her face. He had the feeling that neither of them, for she was with a man, had expected to find anybody there, but were only puzzled about the lights.

Seen by night Lily was a younger and more determined person. Only her eyes were old. She was not fat, but she had a generous body, still well taken care of, and her hands were shoved down into the pockets of a heavy mink coat whose hairs glistened in the light with the colours and texture of an oilskin. She was wearing a round hat of brown pheasant feathers that made her look chubby and infantile. He did not want to look at her. He looked at the man, whom later he knew as Charles. He was tall, slim, and in evening clothes. He had so little flesh over his bones that his skin had the sweaty texture of cold marble; and his eyes were brown but cold. His hair was slightly awry, high on his temples, and he had a short brown beard. Though he was young there was nothing boyish about him. He looked cool, detached, deliberate, and faintly amused. He glanced swiftly at Maggie. Luke could tell that Maggie did not like him. Then he looked at Luke and from Luke down to the ashtray, whose colour was so much the colour of his own face, and he did not have to say anything. It was that look, now that Luke thought about it, that helped to explain Charles. Charles always knew the cost of everything and sometimes the value as well.

Luke had flushed.

Neither of them entered the library. Lily stared at them both, and he thought that when she looked at him there was a special, intimate anger in her eyes.

Then Maggie did what he knew Maggie would do in any crisis, even of her own causing. She did not even try to help him. She got up and rushed uncertainly across the room. Charles made way for her with a special kind of irony as she squeezed out of the door. They heard her hurrying across the parquet to the hall, her footsteps interrupted by the rugs.

Lily slipped off her coat. She was wearing a long dress of grey and white stripes. She did not seem in the least annoyed. "You'd better go now," she said. He looked at her and stood up. She went over to the liquor cabinet. "Go on," she said, and there was a quick personal fury in her voice. "Get out."

He had nothing to fight back with. As he went to the door he had to pass Charles, who smelled faintly of some smooth Cologne that hovered round him. And it seemed to him that Charles gave him a glance that, though it was amused, had in it, too, something of the special pleasure of someone who has vanquished an opponent before the fight, an opponent equal, but with less efficient training.

It also seemed to him that Charles and Lily had reached some agreement about him, even before Charles had met him; they had that marital quality of making up their minds about events before they let the events occur.

He walked down the drive and all the way back to the university, that being the only place he had to go, over the golf links, where the sprinklers had been turning over the lawns, as they did now. He had not stopped to watch them then. He had only wanted to hide.

But now he thought he knew very well how Charles had felt and how his mind had worked. It was that inward glance at him and at the ashtray. That glance, even now, lingered in his mind.

That had been ten years ago and the stump now was littered with stubbed-out cigarettes. It must be three in the morning and he had sat there a long time. His joints were stiff and no matter how long he sat there the sprinklers would continue to revolve and to chirp incessantly.

Ten years ago was the year of the war. He had turned on the radio one lonely afternoon to get some music and had got Pearl Harbour instead. As far as the university was concerned the war was social. They had turned the track field into a compulsory ground for commando tactics invented on the spot; and all the undergraduates, shivering with cold, in that bad winter, had had to practise commando tactics during their gym periods. It was like going out for track and he was not good at track. Neither was the university very good at commando tactics.

After graduation he joined the navy and for some reason had the good fortune, he supposed because he was Spanish-Mexican, to have a good war. He spent most of it in Puerto Rico, working in a prophylaxis station. Once or twice he saw faces he had seen round campus on the stairs of the naval brothels. He enjoyed the anonymity and the uniform, which suited him, and Puerto Rico, and the time to think. He had a lot of time to think. In between the boredom and the alcohol he learned a lot and sometimes, because he was shoved off into a corner again, he thought of Maggie.

She still fascinated him, because nothing had ever been finished or settled between them. He still wondered whether he loved her or not. It did not matter. For when he got drunk enough to cry out, while his head went round and he stank on his pillow, it was her name he repeated like magic, to exorcize the alcohol. Next day if, for instance, he went swimming through the gelatinous Caribbean water with that special muscular joy that was the only pride childhood ever gave him, he didn't think of her at all. It was only that she had some kind of permanent hold over him that some day he would have to loosen or resolve. Puerto Rico, as did everything else, left him between two worlds.

After the war he wasn't an officer and in his position, even with Senator Ford to back him, a Senator Ford grown less powerful and more senile now, he got nowhere. He gave up and went south to Los Angeles, where he belonged; and in a small way he had done well.

He gave it up, stubbed out his last cigarette, and walked down through the campus to his hotel, wanting another cigarette long before he got there. In the morning he would go and see Ford. Maybe Ford would buck him up.

XI

UNDER THE LAWS OF THE UNIversity, which was in those days land poor, those professorially employed by its colleges were allowed to build houses upon the property, usually on the upland hills, upon a lease to last their tenure of office, or if they should retire from the university rather than remove from it, for their lifetime. In this way the university profitably became landlord. Senator Ford, who had wielded some power in the past, though joining the faculty in an honorary capacity and late, had been granted the same privileges and had his house there.

Such clustered houses, usually in a Spanish style, though built of wood, were both patriarchal and pleasant. Senator Ford's was neither. Perched on the edge of the golf course was an old and shapeless house. It had once sheltered the local bootlegger and had even been a store. It was the only house on its road, unless one counted some squatters' cabins in a gully beyond it. Built on several levels and shaded by acacia trees, it had behind it unfinished and abandoned rooms, a refuge for old bottles and forgotten newspapers. The part of the house occupied by Ford was much the same. The long glassed-in gallery at the side, many of its windows broken, which had once been the store and had served as an office during the bootleg period, was now a ruined clutter of papers, books, broken furniture, and old newspapers. Ford collected pictures and they lay deserted out there, the rain and damp destroying them, the mice eating them. Upstairs there were four bedrooms, of which three were abandoned and locked. Luke had stayed in one of them once, a dirty room with the acacia trees ceaselessly brushing over the tin roof of the porch. Ford lived like a well-dressed ferret. He was a neglected dandy in a long-forgotten style, with an egg-stained waistcoat. In addition to this he kept cats. The cats were predacious and brought down sparrows, small birds, and lizards, which they brought into the house and left there. These small game were left undisposed of. You might find them anywhere, for Ford was afraid of death, and unless someone came by who could be induced to remove them, would not touch even the corpse of a sparrow. For some reason they did not putrefact, but mummified; therefore you could always find a few of their dried-out bodies, either in the gallery, or swept furtively under chairs and tables. It had once been Luke's duty to remove them, but as Ford withdrew more and more from life, and saw fewer and fewer people, they remained there longer and longer. This, combined with the sulphurous powders which he burned to dissipate his asthma, gave the house a musty smell like that of the patchouli jars that on old mantelpieces held the rotten, verdigrised petals of roses.

Luke called him up the next morning. His voice was as contemptuous, mannered and rasping as ever, but slightly more senile; and with an undercurrent of warmth in it that was no more than bored loneliness. Luke took a cab out to the place directly after breakfast.

He found Ford in the garden. It was not a garden at all, but only the property around the house, a wilderness of yellow mustard, nettles, unturned earth which gave unexpectedly underfoot, and of forgotten plants which came up year after year, steadily growing into a sterile mat, like the uncombed hair of crazy women. In this wilderness, with no particular skill and puffing with asthma, Ford yearly set out hundreds of bulbs, most of which he begged from friends and neighbours, very few of which he ever had to buy, and a good many of which actually came up, with twisted stems and the phthisic blooms of neglect. He did not care. He did not even look out the window at them, or pick them to put in vases. He had been victimized by a mother who would not die, for whom for forty years he had set out the bulbs of iris and tulip, and the act had become automatic with him. As long as there was a show of colour somewhere he was content. Filial piety with him went that far. But he did not look at them and he would not have them in the house.

When the taxi dropped him Luke noticed that some speeding car had staved in the square posts which, California style, supported the porch and that the break was so weather-beaten, no effort had been made to replace them, though the accident must have happened years ago. Ford was like that. Now he was out of politics he did not care much about anything.

Beside the porch was a steep flight of waterlogged wooden stairs leading down to the garden. Luke found him there, bent over a spade which he used languidly, turning up the clods of adobe earth mixed with loam.

He had already done a patch about six feet square. The broken, already wilting stems of wild mustard stuck out of the clods every way, determined not to die, brandishing their roots. Luke stood on the stairs, dismayed to see that the old man shuffled now, though he was still handsome. He had an enormous lower jaw that in old age had saved his neck from resembling that of a turkey.

Ford looked up, as though taken by surprise, and grunted. "Go into the house," he said. "I'll be up." And that was all the greeting Luke got. It was all the greeting anybody ever got, but Luke could see that the old man was resentful of the cut of his suit, full of Los Angeles prosperity, and of a cockiness that had made him what he was. He went into the house, for the front door was never locked. In six years nothing had changed. It was a double living-room, the outer half-tinted green, the inner maroon, and flooded with light that only made it look the shabbier. It was lined with books and plaster sculpture and pictures, and in the fireplace, for some reason, stood a moth-eaten stuffed ibis swathed in toilet paper, somebody's idea of a joke on the old man that Ford had been too lazy to remove.

Luke knew this house well. He had even once been impressed by it, briefly, chiefly by the culture strewn round it. In the old days it had given him a false sense of having a surrogate home, though there was nothing home-like about it. He knew he would not be offered anything to put him at his ease. Nobody ever was. The kitchen cupboards were lined with gift goodies from S. S. Pierce, that were only opened at random for the cats; and with half cases of Noilly Prat that were never broached for anyone, laid up against a party never given.

It was not a comfortable house, and yet Luke felt oddly comfortable, perhaps because this was the one place in the region that he knew well.

He heard Ford coming up the stairs and sat down to smoke a cigarette. The chipped ashtray was filled with the cinders of Asthmador. Opposite him, propped against the bookcase, was a Paul Cadmus he could not admire. He tried to think of something to say about it. It was an old man's room and a sick, wistful room. He had outgrown it.

But Ford was well-connected. Ford had the drop on everyone. Ford, if he wished, could tell him what to do.

It turned out that he did wish. If his kindness was skittish and undependable, there remained the malice of the man. The malice was always helpful if you knew how to evoke it.

Ford came in. He was more stooped than before but otherwise little different. He was too tall to be old and knew it. He folded himself down on to the couch.

"I read the papers," he said. "I thought you'd probably be here." Then, to play for time, he lit his Asthmador. The Asthmador operated on the principle of those children's toys called snakes and the fumes rose quickly, until Ford's old eyes peered out among them like those of a sibyl of the wrong sex. He was wheezing badly. "It's the old bitch," he said. "I always told her that."

Hissing more slowly in the ashtray the fumes began to die down, leaving a smell in the room like the theatric presence of the devil in *Don Giovanni*. Luke knew all about the Asthmador. It was a stage trick to play for time.

"Still in love with the girl?" Ford asked.

"That's not the point."

"I don't know," said Ford, looking at the ashtray. "It *might* be, you know." He was being sarcastic. "What the hell are you here for otherwise?"

Since he didn't know the answer to that, Luke didn't say a thing. In the circumstances possum was the only thing to play.

"Oh, hell, the Barnes," said Ford. "You've got a lot to learn about the Barnes, my boy. I was thinking about them this morning. A come-uppance is about the only thing they haven't got. Why not let nature give it to them?" He chuckled and took out a cigarette. Luke flicked up his lighter and saw the old man look to see what kind it was. Apparently it was the right kind. "They've got it coming. They really have."

"It depends on how you look at it," said Luke, wondering just how he did look at it.

Ford stretched his legs out in front of him and puffed at his cigarette. He did not drink, but he smoked as other people drank.

"You've come a long way, I guess," he said. "Or have you? And probably you think it's no thanks to me. Well, I got you here. And I got a lot of people here. It taught them where they didn't belong, if nothing else. I don't belong here myself. But I do know the Barnes. That's why they don't see me any more. I know them too goddam well."

Luke saw that familiar blend of childish malice and pleasure on his face that had always been so unreliable. It might be a good deal more reliable now.

"Autobiography," said Ford. "You want to get the

kid off. It doesn't matter whether you're stuck with her or not, but you want to get her off. Okay?"

"Not exactly."

"Nothing's ever exact. That's the beauty of it." He seemed to contemplate the beauty of it with some dissatisfaction. "Getting even," he said, in a shorthand all his own. "It's inexact." He knew he was being provoking.

"Now take you," he said. He enjoyed being hostile about sex. It gave his own sexless life a meaning. "They both knew you'd come back, and you did, and you knew it, too. My advice to you is, save your own neck. You won't take it, but that's my advice." He ran a withered finger under his collar, automatically, rather than to illustrate. "And now you want me to tell you something, but you're damned if you know what, and I'm damned if I know what either. But being scared of Lily is no help."

"What makes you think I'm scared of her?"

"I brought you up. I damned near brought her up for that matter."

There wasn't any answer to that.

"You've done pretty well so far," said Ford. "But this isn't your sort of thing, boy. Let 'em stew."

"Why?" asked Luke. It was the right thing to ask. He sort of thought it might be.

Ford looked interested. He clearly wanted to talk. But looking at him, Luke wondered how he could ever have admired him at all and also, uncomfortably, if he would ever turn out the same way. He doubted it. The stock was different. Ford came from Sandusky, Ohio, straight Scots descent, and proud as Lucifer in a way that suggested matches burning out and not the devil. Little Mexico didn't turn out that way. Little Mexico knew the devil when it saw one.

"Look, son," said Ford, and was only half lying. "Maggie doesn't matter. Maggie never did matter. She's only her mother's daughter. Nobody ever loved her and nobody ever will. If you want to be romantic, don't bother me. Be a fool. That isn't my line. But you know that's true as well as I do. What matters is something else. Something we could use Maggie for, you and me both. Suppose she murdered the bastard? Nobody cares about that. He was better dead. He never lived anyway. He was just one of those things. I saw plenty of him and I can tell you that. You know why you're here? It's because you want your own back. So do I. Son, you're on the wrong side. Not that there's any right one, mind you, but you always have been and you always will be. You belong back where you came from. You went back, I'll give you credit for that. Go back again."

Luke looked at his own tie, his suit, and his shoes and his finger-nails and tried to think of something to say, but Ford did not give him time.

"Take Jerome," he said. "Jerome Barnes. He's almost my age now, and God knows where he is. Funny duck, but clever. Always wore a dirty panama hat he'd picked up somewhere. He picked Lily up somewhere, too, and she ran him into the ground. That's the answer to it all. She ran everything into the ground and she still wants to. She's happier keeping things buried. She'll bury you, too, and she tried burying me, but I was too smart for her. I knew the score.

"Oh, she doesn't count for much now. She made her

mistake and she paid for it. But she used to run things, and she kept on thinking she still could. Charles slapped her down on that one. I slapped her down myself. That's where she made her mistake about Jerome, for a woman can't run things in this state. It takes a man. She can do a lot with a man, if she wants to, but still, it doesn't matter what kind, a man has to be in front.

"Why the hell should I help you," he said abruptly. "You can't even help yourself." He looked around the room. It did not seem to comfort him, but then perhaps it was not comfort he was looking for. "You used to be pretty bright," he went on. "At least I thought so. But you're not being bright about this. Maybe the old woman scared you. She can do that. She even tried it on me. And maybe the girl is worth saving. I don't know. If she murdered that fool, she wasn't the first who wanted to. Did she?"

"No."

Ford chuckled. "You wouldn't tell me anyhow. I never liked her. Sort of mousy. But that doesn't mean she has to hang. And you know what that means. That means Lily."

"Lily hates my guts."

"She probably wanted you once," said Ford. "She isn't what she looks, not by a long shot. She used to have parties, you know. She'd ask the football team up when Jerome was sick in bed. She did all right. And then suddenly she didn't like the team any more. I guess she got tired, or maybe somebody told her something she didn't want to hear, or maybe she just wore it out. And then there was Charles."

"Charles?"

"Sure, Charles. Why the hell not? I guess she got bored. He was slimy, but he had something, you've got to grant him that. And by then she'd learned she couldn't run the county, let alone the state. Jerome could, but she couldn't. Jerome was a pretty good guy. But Maggie, hell, she can't even run herself."

"Meaning?" asked Luke.

"Not meaning a damn thing. Except sometimes it's better to keep your nose out of things. But if you have to stick it in, concentrate on Lily and keep the girl aside. Lily's had her run. It's about time someone caught up with her. It's a thing I'd like to see. Oh, Lily's the answer. She's the answer to a lot of things. And all you have to do to beat her is outgrow her."

"You'd like to see her beaten, wouldn't you?"

"Wouldn't you?" Ford glanced away from him. "Jerome was a friend of mine. I loved the guy. Pull her down. She pulled everyone else down, and now it's her turn. Pull her down and let her rot." He reached under the sofa for the Asthmador tin and couldn't find it. "Oh, hell," he said. "When you get to be my age it's time to quit. I used to know the people who ran everything, and that was living. It's all gone now. She kicked me out of here, you know. She was a trustee."

"And Charles?"

"Charles?" Ford seemed to hesitate. "Oh, him. He was just an ambition that blew the wrong way."

Somehow Luke didn't think that it was quite that easy. Nothing ever was. But there was no point in telling Ford that. Ford was a shabby old man with a grudge. He always had been. The grudge was wrung out and there was nothing left of him at all. Ford was somebody he had outgrown. He was beginning to wonder now if he hadn't outgrown the whole lousy crew. Life was better in the south. He didn't have any part in the hatreds up here. He had wanted a part in the loves, but that was another matter: the hatreds shut him out.

Even now, when he rose to go, though Ford didn't have anything to say to him, he didn't want him to go. Nobody wanted him to go. They all hung on, not out of affection, but because they needed something. He left the house in disgust.

Somehow, because it had, he admitted, seemed glamorous and important once, it seemed shabbier than ever now. The trouble with him was that he suffered from a spaniel loyalty that was not even properly fed.

Just to work it off he called a cab and took a drive through the hills. They at least were primitive and green. He didn't want to succeed in the world really. It was just that he had to do it, because everybody else did.

XII

By the time he swung down towards Atherton he felt better. For one thing the orchards were in bloom. He remembered once that one spring afternoon, as the rain was blowing south, he and Maggie had sat in the mustard and the grass under one of these trees, on an abandoned farm above the campus, and had been happy. The petals, wet and clinging, as they fell down sometimes fell on her face, like beauty spots, and on his own, like kisses. He put the remembrance away.

He did not enjoy the taxi. It was ridiculous through that country-side. He would have preferred his own car. He had the driver drop him outside the gates and stood there until the taxi had driven away. Atherton did not seem so fearsome now. Only the silence was disturbing, for it was a brooding silence. For the rest it seemed smaller than it had ten years ago, dustier and more forgotten, despite the new and smaller houses with their bright curtains and raw wood.

He walked up the drive between the walls of ivy. They were less well taken care of than formerly. Some of them were yellow with some kind of rot, and there were spider webs among the vines. The gravel was hard on his shoes. He turned the curve and came in sight of the house, stripped down to an uncomfortably fake Georgian elegance that did not fit its shape. He stood there for a moment, at the distance of the lawn, looking at the house, but except that one of the french windows was open, it looked deserted and non-committal. The sunlight was not kind to it. He did not want to go inside, so stepping across the lawn, which was sopping wet, he made his way round the living-room wing, through heavy hydrangea shrubs with bruised exhibition blooms. He did not know why he did this. Perhaps he was subconsciously reconnoitring.

Buried in the shrubs was a small formal garden with a moss floor and a pool with a plaster statue of a plaster boy holding a discoloured plaster trout. The fountain was not running. Maggie was sitting on a bench, staring down at the turf below her. He stood where he was, watching her for a moment, his head lost in the hydrangeas. He was very close to her and could see what she was watching so intently. It was a double thread of ants moving efficiently towards the other side of the bench. She was completely absorbed, and he thought that in that mood of frighteningly inconsequential absorption, which came over her from time to time for no discernible reason whatsoever, she would be capable of anything. The ability was random, catatonic and amoral. What bothered him was that she seemed so utterly content and pleased by those ants. And it was certainly true: she had never learned to tell the value of one thing from another.

Ford had said save her and it was what he wanted to do, but he couldn't tell why. It was not quite love. Perhaps it was only the idea of love, which is more durable than the emotion itself. He felt that if he watched her any more he might change his mind, for there was nothing positive in her for him to grasp.

He parted the hydrangeas, dodging his face, where they splattered him with water and stepped out on to the lawn.

"Where are they going?" he asked quietly.

She wasn't startled. She seemed to take his appearance for granted. She had been very thoughtful and the sun sparkled in her hair and cast unexpected shadows on her face. She looked up and smiled at him happily. "Hello," she said. "Isn't it lovely?"

She seemed so unaffectedly pleased, that he was shocked. But after all, what the hell do you say the morning after an unregretted death? She made room for him on the bench and he sat down. Unexpectedly she turned round and kissed him. She broke whatever there was between them just like that. At first surprised, he drew away, and then did not draw away, and slowly felt his arms going round her and his fingers splaying out below her shoulder-blades, slightly astonished to find that there was a real self inside her that he had forgotten, somewhat older than the self he had remembered, and nicer. He remembered, too, that she was not exciting ever until you touched her, and then she became excited herself. It was like knowing two people you liked equally well, but in different ways.

"Things will be better now," she said, with a simple, childish faith that they would be.

"Yes, I guess they will." He was sobered by the dangers of that disparate outside and inside of her. He did not know which one he was attempting to defend. "There's still Charles."

"I don't want to talk about Charles."

"You may have to."

"I have had to. The police were here. But that isn't what you mean, is it?"

"What do you mean, they were here?"

"Oh, why talk about it?" she said. "I was only his wife. What would I know?"

"At least you know he's dead."

"Oh, yes, I know that." She looked at him earnestly, drawing her index finger along his thigh. "It's funny," she said, "you've changed, too. And yet you haven't. I hoped you'd come out here. That's why I was waiting, watching the ants."

He looked down at the ants involuntarily, and as he looked up he saw the windows of the house and Lily standing at one of them. He flushed, seeing that she had been there for some time. She didn't do anything. She leaned with one arm against the door, watching them. Maggie looked up and saw her, too.

Lily bit her lips. "When you're through you'd better come in, Luke," she said. She sounded angry. He glanced at Maggie and went into the house, following the trail of ants which still moved from the house towards the bench. He wondered vaguely why, and then saw that Maggie had laid down a trail of chopped-up apple. It was the sort of useless, concentrated thing she would do. As he turned to shut the french window behind him he saw her bent over the ants again, thoughtfully.

Lily was standing in front of the fireplace. As far as he could tell standing in front of fireplaces was what she did best. In the bright light he looked at her and wondered how she managed to keep a firm hold on her looks. She had slimmed down a lot in the past years.

"Sorry about that," he said.

"It doesn't matter. Did she tell you the police were down here?"

"Yes." He hesitated. "Did she get through it all right?"

"Yes. After all grief wasn't exactly called for. Not from her, anyhow."

He didn't ask her what she meant by that. He thought now that he knew what she meant by that. It surprised him how conscious she made him feel of himself, not anxiously as at San Francisco, but here, on her own ground, absurdly sturdy and irrefragable. Perhaps she felt it, too. If there is ever an involuntary attraction between two people that is not satisfied, perhaps it then persists until it is satisfied. And this one never would be. He sometimes wished he had not been so naïve years ago. Now that he knew so much more about Lily he felt a curiosity to know more. For maybe, like her daughter, she also had two selves. He was happy that by her standards his suit, which was a rich blue with a wide white stripe, was too assertive for this room.

Such things were the wrong things to think about. He thought about them all the same. And as though feeling that some tension had eased between them, he sat down. She joined him and opening a green leather box, offered him a cigarette with fingers that still wore too many dirty diamond rings. He glanced away. Her fingers showed her age.

She lit his cigarette. "I never liked you," she said.

"I know that."

"But now it doesn't matter." She eyed him through the

sudden smoke from the cigarettes. "Well, I'm not afraid of the police. We have friends and we have power. I guess they can be managed."

"Then what are you afraid of?"

"I?" she asked, as though the idea were new to her. But he saw that it was not new to her. He realized she was trying to establish some kind of tentative contact with somebody, anybody, now that Charles was dead. He wondered what he should say about that. It might be worth a try to say something. On the other hand he didn't want to antagonize her either.

"Why did she do that?" she asked. "The ants and the apple, I mean. She always does something like that, and you can't hold on to her. Perhaps you could, but I can't. Maybe she *is* mad. She might be. If the worst came to the worst, we can get her off that way. Maybe it should have been arranged before, just like . . ."

"Just like what?" he asked quickly. But she wouldn't look at him or answer. He saw she was abruptly scared, but of something he could not put his finger on. "No," he said. "Maggie's not mad. She's lonely and she's scared, but she's not mad. She hides whenever she can, but that doesn't make a person insane."

"Doesn't it?" she asked. "I've seen her afraid of madness." Her voice was both worried and at the same time self-satisfied.

"So that's the way you've always worked it."

"It's the way her father went. I thought you knew that."

"No, I didn't know that."

She flushed. "She wasn't an easy child," she said. "She never has been easy."

"Why should she be?"

"I worried about her."

"Yes," he said, "but what way?"

She did not like that. He saw not only that she had over-extended herself and wanted to draw back, but also a good deal else that he had not seen before. With something like pity and disgust he saw it now. You clever bitch, he thought, you goddam clever bitch. So that's how you got a hold on her.

He looked round the room and saw suddenly how the house could have madness in it, if you worked it right. And he was sure Lily had worked it right, with that horrible, sweet, understanding, social kindness that was the real weapon women always use on each other. There was the portrait in the library, and the room upstairs, and suddenly he felt sorry for Lily. He thought that for once he saw her, not the way we usually see people, as something observed from the outside, complementary to ourselves, but from the inside of herself, restless and bitter and locked up in a body too old for her; afraid that some day somebody might find out just how little there was inside, and how easily it could be hurt; and sticking pins in Maggie to see how much she could stand herself. He decided to try sticking in a few pins of his own, the other way round, to take them out of Maggie.

Unexpectedly Lily reached out and took his hand and patted it. Her skin was shockingly, prematurely old, and the frigid temperature of a dead turkey. In a few years the brown spots would begin to appear on it. It made him sit up with a jerk.

"I went to see Senator Ford," he said.

"You were one of his boys, weren't you," she said innocently. "They say he's got doddery. And spiteful. He always was spiteful."

"Honest, though," he said.

"Do you think so?" She sounded contemptuous. "I could tell you things about him that would make your hair curl." She looked at his hair. He needed a haircut and the long ends were curling slightly out of place. It didn't disconcert him one bit. He was enjoying himself now and wondered if Maggie was still watching the ants.

"Don't you know who that woman is?" he said.

She stopped inspecting his hair. "What woman?"

"At the beach house."

"*Was* it a woman?" she asked blandly.

"Yes, it was a woman." He was sure of it now, but how did he know? Perhaps because with Charles it always was a woman. He tried to suggest that anyhow, and was rewarded with an angry shrug. He looked at Lily curiously, wondering if she was keyed up enough to crack. He rather thought she might be.

"We don't want trouble," he said. "We'd better find out. And if you don't know, who does?"

"I told you I didn't know."

"But you do know what I mean, don't you?"

"No," she said. "I don't." If she hadn't said that he would have let the matter drop, but she was so patently lying that now he wanted to hurt her. Somebody had to hurt her some day.

"Why not? Charles was your lover, wasn't he? He certainly wasn't his wife's."

It didn't have the effect he thought it would have. "Yes," she said drily. "He was my lover." She sat back on the sofa and lit another cigarette. "For five years. Why not? Her father went insane and there wasn't much in Maggie. A woman can get lonely. And then he married Maggie."

"Yes, he married Maggie. Why?"

"I suppose he wanted to," she said coolly. She relaxed a little. "It kept it in the family."

"That was the idea, wasn't it?"

"It was his idea," she corrected.

"Was it?"

"It certainly wasn't mine."

"Why not?" he asked, and wondered why they were having what only seemed a matter-of-fact conversation about something he had hoped would make her flare up and give herself away.

She looked down at her dress, retreating inside with the same intensity Maggie had, but more contemptuously. He didn't mind. If retreating contemptuously was the sole defence she had, she was welcome to it.

"Does Maggie know about you and Charles?" he asked.

"Of course she knows."

"Did she know when he married her?"

"I presume so. Why on earth shouldn't she? Maggie does as she's told."

"She didn't this time," he reminded her. It was the only thing he had said that made her angry.

"You're cocky," she said. "But you're a fool. If you want to play adolescent games in the shrubs, you can, but you won't do it in my garden. Or in my house. Nor in Charles's house."

"You don't want her to have anything, do you?"

"She doesn't deserve anything. That isn't the point. But I won't allow it, and the papers won't like it. And the papers might find out."

"That would be foolish of you," he said, but he was frightened.

"Do you think I care?" she demanded. "Do you think I care about *anything*?"

"Yes, I think you do," he said, and he did not say it angrily. She glanced at him, surprised at his tone, and he looked back at her, trying to see what there was behind those eyes. But she would not let him see.

"Leave her alone," she said. "If you've got any decency, leave her alone. At least for a while." She glanced round the room irritably. "This house is so empty," she said. "It always was." She stood up and walked towards the door in her high heels that made such a hopefully young sound. She left him where he sat. He did not move. He could hear her moving through the house, making rapidly for the hall, and it seemed to him that from the sound she was going up the front stairs more quickly than she might have done.

He heard a door bang and he thought he heard it lock. And it occurred to him that that was what was wrong: that the house was empty and that it always had been. It did not make him like her any the more, or like Maggie any the less. It solved nothing. He remembered, unpleasantly, how close and warm and different Maggie had felt when she had kissed him, and he thought of Charles, with his cold, hard flesh. He became so aware of Lily that he got up and left the house.

"You're not old," he told himself. "Nobody is ever old. But you aren't young any more either."

Outside the ants were still trooping towards the apple, but Maggie was not there. If she was still waiting for him she was waiting somewhere else, and he took a walk to investigate. The garden was no longer kept up. It had gone to seed. And perhaps for that reason the farther he got from the house the happier he felt. He stopped and frowned, and found himself staring at a scarlet pepper bush, its long leafy antennae withered by the heat, even here, in the shade. He would have to tell Maggie he loved her some time. It might as well be now, if that would help to keep her calm. He would compel himself to love her, for that was the only way to save her. Therefore love her he would.

XIII

Lily stayed locked in her room. There was no one in the house, but that didn't prevent her from locking her door, chiefly against that corridor with its bedrooms that were no longer used. There were five bedrooms apart from her own. She went in them sometimes, when the house was empty, just to be sure that there was no one there.

Maggie's was at the far end of the corridor, beyond the well of the hall, and looked over the front of the house. It had not been re-done for ten years and it was still a girl's room. She remembered when she had had it done that way. It was before she met Charles and she had had the room done up as a surprise for Maggie. The three guest rooms were never used. They were redecorated when the house had been made Georgian, the first year she had known Charles. Ford had slept in one of them once. So had the Governor Ford and Jerome had selected for that term. But they usually stood empty. She had them cleaned once a week and always kept them made up. Then there was Jerome's room, which faced the back of the house and which had never been remodelled. Sometimes when she was alone in the house and Ethel had gone to bed she would get up and lock the door to Jerome's room. It was always kept shut. But she would not have the blinds or curtains drawn. She liked the sterilizing light. It was furnished in heavy mahogany, simple yet massive, that had come round the Horn. It was a room whose contents she could see only too clearly. Beyond it was the room Charles had always used when he had stayed the night. The decoration of that he had supervised himself, but the effect was cold. It had a bathroom attached. Once, a year ago, Ethel had been cleaning up in there and left the hot-water tap running. Lily had heard it soon enough and turned it off, but Ethel could be careless at times. The doors of these rooms were always shut, except that belonging to Maggie, which was left open to let light into the hall. It was a cheerful room. It was a pity it was never used.

Lily lay on her bed listening to the clock. It was one of those brass clocks under a glass dome which have four balls that ceaselessly revolve, and though it made little noise, that little was oddly perceptible.

It was almost dark, but she did not bother to turn on the light. She knew these rooms well. She had had the wall knocked out and an arch put in, so that the sitting-room, with its efficient desk and sprigged chintz furniture flowed naturally into the bedroom, which contained nothing but a night table and the bed. No one ever came into her rooms but Ethel, to clean, and Charles, once. And a few people before Charles, though nobody since.

She had undressed and put on a négligée, but she had not really gone to bed. She kept jumping up to fuss with things, or trying to read a detective story, though she had given that up hours ago; and it seemed to her, in the empty silence of the house, that the downstairs rooms were full of people who did not like her. She went into the bathroom and flicked on the overhead light.

"You were young once", she said to her reflection, "and now you won't be young ever again." But she did not say so aloud. She did not want to hear it. Ageing was something she had never been able to understand, and she did not understand it any the better now. She stared at herself in the harsh, unflattering light and then went back to the bedroom and lay down and wondered if Charles had ever really liked her. It would have been nice to believe that he had.

Even when Maggie was away at a private school and not old enough for college, and chiefly because Jerome was too ill to bother with, she had given parties for people from the campus. And not only because she was lonely. Originally, she supposed, it had been Senator Ford's idea. He liked other people to give his parties for him. When she first married him Jerome had helped to run the local political machine, and Ford had had great hopes for him. And later, when Jerome went odd, Ford had had the idea that they should cultivate young law students or anyone else who was likely, not so much to bring them over to their side, as because it didn't do any harm to know people. Ford believed in catching them young.

She wasn't much more than forty-five in those days and she had looked younger. She had forgotten, with Jerome, what it was like to be young and drink too much and have fun. Of course Jerome had always been a stuffed shirt and she knew why she had married him, yet sometimes she wished the stuffing would come out once in a while. But as Jerome began to fail and she had to take over the reins herself, which meant fighting Ford all the way, and even giving in to him more than she wanted to, until the whole setup began to dwindle away from them both, leaving them with not much more than the county, she saw less and less of Ford. She also saw less of the law students and political science majors whom he had encouraged.

Stanford meant a lot to her, perhaps because she had never gone there, or because after all it was the one local college that mattered, and she began to make a thing of throwing parties for the football team after a big game. The team and the lawyers didn't mix too well, but it was easier to laugh and forget things with the team. Some of them were nice; besides which, of course, Ford had become impossible, and as he began to draw the younger politicians away from her, though she knew what he was up to, it made it all the easier for her to keep what new acquaintances she made of her own.

She kept the house full in those days and it was amazing how cheerful it could be when it was full. She never got over that, for it had never been cheerful before, and she and Ethel, whom she had brought with her from the hotel as her personal maid, got a lot of fun out of planning the parties themselves, down to the last *canapé*, and for really big occasions a small band. Jerome had put his foot down about the band, but now the big Capehart did just as well. Once in a while it went crazy and threw records all over the room. If it did one of the boys always knew how to fix it.

On the 5th January 1940, when Maggie was fifteen, and away with friends anyhow, she gave a real party to celebrate the Rose Bowl game, or anyway, to celebrate. Ethel and she had really knocked themselves out. She was late getting ready, and of course before she went to her room she had to go in and take a look at Jerome, to say good night.

There wasn't anything wrong with Jerome actually. Not if she admitted the truth, anyway. But he liked to save himself, he didn't like to talk, and he could be difficult. He was difficult that night. It took her a long time to get away from him. Outside in the hall she had looked at her watch and scampered into her room. She had a new faille dress, the colour of a young Siamese cat, or colours; and she dressed with great care, cheering up as she watched the evening taking shape in her mirror.

It was true she was getting somewhat plump, but not too plump, and she was not beautiful: she had a spaniel face. But it was a quizzical, engaging face; and she knew that everybody thought she was a good scout, except perhaps Jerome and Ford, neither of whom could be expected to know what a good scout was. Being a good scout was her speciality.

"All right?" she asked Ethel, and Ethel said yes, it was all right. Gathering up her skirts, she went down the main stairs, and that was how she met Charles. He was in an ill-assorted clump of people—she couldn't remember who they were now, or ever afterwards—but he had come alone and he sort of stood out. Besides, she had not seen him before, and almost everybody else there she either knew only too well or did not want to know at all. She stopped half-way down the stairs for a moment, looking at him, and she knew that he had noticed her as well. He had to be nice, she thought, for she was his hostess; yet all the same she felt suddenly timid and wondered if perhaps her dress was not a little too full around the hips.

For that matter Charles had been pretty full around the hips himself.

Hesitating for that minute on the stairs she hoped that she really did look her best, and that—she supposed—was the beginning of it. It was not falling in love or anything like that. Nobody falls in love. It was that, catching his eye, she saw instantly that, whoever he was, they understood one another. And since understanding herself was the last thing in the world she would ever admit to doing, not with these fresh-faced boys, anyway, that gave her a sudden, illicit thrill. For nobody ever caught her out. The only people who could do that were people just the same as she was.

She went on down the stairs with her special party smile, a neat mixture of the maternal and the acquiescent that she hoped looked well and that she knew worked well, at least when it was sufficiently backed up by the liquor cellar and the buffet. "Hello," she said. "Hello." And wished these whey-faced boys would not look at her with awed contempt, as though she were the house matron. The girls usually did not look at her at all.

There must have been a hundred people there and that was the sort of party she liked. It cut down on the effort she had to make if she had fewer people, and tonight there was an excitement in the air that usually she missed. At about midnight she found herself pushed into the library, which was half empty, by the crowd in the gallery and the living-room. She took a deep breath. Looking up she saw him. He was standing in front of the sofa, examining the picture over the mantelpiece speculatively. She saw automatically that though his evening clothes were well made, they had not been made for him. And it surprised her that she made a note to do something about that even before she spoke to him. She had erupted into the room and she hoped she didn't look too tired or too flushed. He looked at her with that sideways smile and twinkle that he could turn off or on. There was something pleasantly memorized about everything he did.

"You shouldn't be here alone," she said, pushing back her hair.

"Well, I'm not," he said, "now am I?"

She liked his voice, too. It had a double emotional *vibrato* that she seemed to recognize. It was a little like her own when she was being sincere. She shrugged and went over to the liquor cabinet, the private one, and poured two highballs without even asking if he wanted one. She was a little nervous.

"I haven't seen you before," she said. "You're not one of Senator Ford's boys. . . ."

"No, not really," he said. "I don't think he thinks much of me." He hesitated. "It could be a point in my favour."

She glanced at him over the top of her glass. He wasn't trying to make an impression. They were talking as though they had already known each other for years. He was clever, she could see that. He knew he had already made his impression and she wondered if he had come to make it. She felt suddenly happy.

"You bet it could," she said, and she felt excited, and watched him with bright brown eyes, like a chipmunk, holding on half-way up a tree, who looks quickly to see where to jump next. And she let her eyes crinkle into a smile.

Maybe he hadn't expected it to be so easy. He twirled his glass and looked towards the other room, the people jammed with their backs to the still open door. "Don't you get tired of it?" he asked. "I should think you would." He looked disdainful and she saw that for some reason she had lost a point.

"They all go home eventually," she said. "Most of them. Or go somewhere." She looked down at the bottom of her glass, knowing damned well what she was going to say. "If you don't", she said, "it might be better to wait upstairs." She handed him her empty glass, went out of the room and had the feeling that when the others had gone he would be there.

She didn't see him for the rest of the evening and enjoyed herself thoroughly, certain, for once, that somebody would be upstairs after the others had left. She had never found her guests so amusing, as now when she no longer needed them. She knew she must look her best.

When, at three-fifteen, she did get upstairs, he was there all right, sitting quietly in a chair, smoking cigarettes and looking satisfied with a bottle of bourbon from the library, she noticed with amusement, thumbing through a big blue and gold album of Jerome's that was full of bad photographs of the Barnes that once were.

It was so very easy. She didn't care whether it was prearranged or not. She thought she could manage him. She took him down to Del Monte when the spring term was out. He had not wanted to go and she had thought it was because of clothes, so she sent him the money for a decent suit, knowing he'd go to the best local tailor; and then she went down to the tailor, scooped up his measurements, and had him sent a wardrobe. She got power of attorney from Jerome in May and that made things easier for them. It was her first adventure on a big scale and she loved all of it. It gave her something to do.

She put herself on a thirty-day protein diet and went up to town for a week to buy new clothes. And though she gave him things openly, on her own initiative, she was careful not to give him too much. As a Stanford trustee she had him granted a decent scholarship and watched him spend the money with considerable satisfaction. It was a fiction, but it was a fiction that made things easier all round; and she was proud that she had had the sense to work it out that way. The only person she worried about was Ford. He had sharp eyes. She wondered sometimes if he had arranged Charles to get her out of politics, and that gave her an idea about Charles, so she really settled down to train him. Del Monte was the test case.

It seemed silly to take the Cadillac. The Cadillac belonged to her matron side. She bought a convertible and spent a week banging it up, so it wouldn't look new; had him move into town; put him up at the town house—the first time it had been used, except for her shopping expedition, in months—and then picked him up there the next morning, with the luggage already piled in the car. He had his own luggage by now, saddle-stitched cowhide, and she looked at it with approval. He caught her doing that and smiled at her. His teeth were small and regular. It was the smile of a little boy who knows he has done the right thing, but wonders faintly why anyone should think him capable of doing anything else. In those days she didn't in the least mind his making use of her: after all, she was making use of him. And it was good to have company again, not just some lout, but somebody she could really get to know.

She never made the mistake of teaching him anything. She let him learn by example. But she did want to overawe him, for the kick of it, and it annoyed her that he was not overawed.

They made Monterey in three and a half hours, driving fast, with the radio going full blast, and she did the driving, singing to herself when she felt like it. Once they were out of the San Jose valley she forgot about Jerome and the house and the whole mess of her life. To forget made her feel younger. She hoped it made her look younger as well.

However, bright sunlight did not suit him. His flesh was too pale and his body too cerebral, and his beard looked ridiculous. Probably he had an adolescent, eggshell chin. They were out of the north and getting into the stage-set country of Carmel, Monterey, and the Big Sur. She was beginning to be a little puzzled about him. His reactions were not quite what she expected them to be. She didn't really like anyone round her who was astute. They had lunch at the wharf at Monterey, watching the white sand curve into infinity and the filthy, shipshape fishing vessels bobbing at anchor. The mountains were behind them. The sea was a flat but not transparent blue. She felt better. She did not like crowds; she was not afraid to be alone with people, but unless she could be alone with them in her own house she felt safer behind a barricade of waiters and busboys.

After lunch they drove into the Del Monte properties. They didn't stay at the hotel but at the lodge, for the lodge was the more exclusive. The properties were designed to give an impression of undisturbed immemorial time, with the pine trees and the monterey cypress, the soft indistinct shadows on the pine needles on the ground, and the long ectoplasmic streamers of Spanish moss hanging in searchlight colours from the trees.

He was not a sexual animal, she found, and was both relieved and disappointed. He preferred people with their clothes on; and in a curious way he only existed when he did have his clothes on. There was something unpleasant and empty about his nakedness. It was like the nakedness of nineteenth-century statues. He was competent in bed, but with a sort of disdainful, mutual contempt that at first she had found amusing, thinking it was a defence mechanism to cover up what he would never admit he did not know—which was his attitude about most things. Later she got to dread and avoid him. She was not in love with him. He fascinated her. And she got a special pleasure from watching him walk into a room, from seeing how he was dressed, how he held a highball in his hand, exactly how he would say something, knowing that he would say it properly. It was a pleasure she had looked for from Maggie and never found. She always knew that Charles would do the right thing, the acceptable, understandable thing in the right way; and Maggie was totally undependable. She could not read Maggie's mind. But she could follow his.

If there was anything wrong, it was that he was not an animal. An animal helps pass the time. You can watch an animal for hours. An animal crawls into your lap when you don't want it to and licks your face, until when you thought it was only five-thirty it was really a quarter to eight. He was not satisfactory that way. It was idle to be alone with him.

So she introduced him to everybody she knew and that was what he wanted. At night they stayed up late and drank, or went visiting, after a while as much on his invitations as on hers, and visiting bored her. She was always at a disadvantage in other people's houses, for she never knew where everything was. In other people's houses she knew she was there because of Jerome.

She did not want to think about Jerome.

It all happened so effortlessly that at first she did not even notice what was going on. She did notice it when she realized how nervous she was while she waited for him. At first he had been her lover. Now she was his. He had outmanœuvred her. That made her thoughtful. Usually she had got round any attempts men made to control her by going to bed. Ultimately, lazily, very deliberately, as she had long ago learnt, she could have a good quarrel and then stretch out a firm arm and say, oh, darling, drawling it slightly, give that special smile of hers that always worked, turn out the light, and down there in the animal darkness, when everything else failed, she always managed to get back the upper hand, if she really wanted it. But Charles didn't have any animal darkness. She was only beginning to learn what kind of darkness he did have. Whatever it was she did not understand it.

She felt angry. She banged her glass down on the coffee table and split it. The waiter mopped it up. Her only anxiety was that he should get the pieces out of the way before Charles came downstairs (he took longer to dress than she did), because Charles was astute at deciphering accidents like that.

She did not want him to realize how she knew that their relationship had changed, for she did not want him to go away. She looked at the mirror hanging on the opposite wall and saw herself sitting neatly and tidily inside a trap. It wasn't even her own trap. It was the one she had so carefully built for him. She practised smiling. If it came to a showdown she thought she could be just as sincere as he.

But not quite. She was a woman and she was restless. They had a corner room overlooking the golf links to the sea, and she would wake early, because the light from the windows hit her from two directions, hear the golfers down below, see him sleeping in the other bed, and wonder what in God's name there was left this morning that she could possibly go out and buy. On the last morning she saw suddenly that he was awake and was watching her with that vaguely evasive smile of his that though it was sensual had no comfort in it.

"I was thinking", she said, "that we haven't been to Marsh's. I'd like to go."

"Okay." He was suspiciously affable. He got out of bed. He was so tall and thin that his pyjamas hung around him like a flag on a motionless day, and when he tied on his robe his hips were so wide, his waist so thin, that the skirts of the robe hung round him like a farthingale. There was something sexlessly Elizabethan about him, an exotic Italianate taste for intrigue and deliberately dirty clothes. If he must use cologne she heartily wished that it would not be musk.

Outside the golfers made their ritual noises above the sound of the surf.

The reason why she wanted to go to Marsh's was it was part of her childhood to go there, not part of his, if he had ever had a childhood. He never talked of that part of his life and she could not imagine him as a child, but only as an homunculus that had gradually outgrown itself. She wanted to get her own back.

Marsh's was an oriental store. More than that it was an institution. It was the only Orient she had ever known, a rich, expensive Orient of dark corners filled with things to buy. Their establishment in Monterey was a conceit of plaster and lath, in emulation of a Chinese house, though more baroque. It had that special, hushed, reverent, attendant silence luxury stores have everywhere, in so far as they emulate luxurious houses and, of course, luxuriant houses, them. There was a miniature garden in a courtyard more Japanese than Chinese, and defaced statues stood everywhere. It was the kind of store where you can sit on a sofa and out of the canny half darkness be brought things to see. And more important, they knew her there and remembered her more as Miss Smith than as Mrs. Barnes. It was the type of store that gave you a surrogate past; and in her case, having been brought up in hotels and right now not knowing what the present or the future would be like, a surrogate past, she felt, was what she needed. They brought her boxes of feeling stones. She took off her gloves to look at them.

"What are they for?" asked Charles. She knew that he wouldn't know what they were for. Fascinated, his long fingers stole out over the twenty-four plush compartments and fondled the smooth stones, lapis, carnelian, jade, carved in abstract or vegetable shapes.

"That's what they're for," she said, looking up at the clerk, who seemed fascinated by Charles's fleshless fingers that dabbled down among the stones like chopsticks.

She took one of the stones, a carnelian fig, in her own plump hand and felt how cold it was against her flesh. But Charles would not be conscious of the cold. He would like it. And she let the stone warm in the palm of her hand and grow ripe, reluctant to put it back. He himself had strayed towards the white, abstract jade, delicately veined or cloudy as smoke. Disgusted with him she decided to keep the fig and slipped it into her pocket.

"Do you want them?" she asked. She wanted to disconcert him.

"Yes." He was not at all disconcerted. "I want them."

She sat very still feeling that she had been trumped, and again she fingered the fig. "Very well," she said, "you can have them. Except for this." She rolled the fig in her fingers, not showing it to him. He did not try to see it. Instead he stared at the empty purple plush pocket of the carrying case. "I can find another," he said. He looked up at the clerk with that smile that could be winning if he wished it to be. "I don't suppose you've got a stray," he said.

After half an hour of choosing he had the box filled up and she knew by then that she hated him. They put the box in the car with the rest of the luggage and she realized that he had checkmated her again. They drove back to town. In town she put the fig in a drawer and pretended to forget about it. She remembered it all the same and so did he. These days he always smiled blandly at her. She was afraid that he was tired of her and wanted to get out from under. She did not want him to do that.

So she let him do what he wished about Jerome, which was the worst mistake she ever made, and she did not know even now how she had made it, except that, once back in town from Monterey he seemed nicer and kinder' and somehow more understanding of her. All the same she began to be afraid of him. She felt now that even on that first night on the stairs, when she had met him, she had known that she would be afraid of him. And he had known it, too.

It was very quick about Jerome. Charles had pushed his advantage. He had not left her alone for a moment. He even insisted upon following her when she drove behind the ambulance all the way up to Napa. Of that trip she did not remember a thing. She did remember the drive back. They made the trip in the Cadillac. He watched her. She did the driving, as usual, but it did not seem to her that she was really doing it. It seemed to her that he was doing it. Napa was in the wine country. The green vines were fresh over the parched yellow hills that rose so slowly they were scarcely hills at all, but an oceanic swell. The day was bright, clear and warm. They passed not only the vineyards, but also the abandoned ruins of Italian stone presses, now roofless and inhabited by gypsies. She did not want to return to San Francisco. When she saw its dingy but sun-sparkled towers assembled at the water's edge she felt she would stifle when she reached it. It was stronger and more recent than she was. Charles lit her a cigarette which she did not accept because she did not want him to know that her hand was shaking. She thought she now knew what a guilty criminal must feel, who knows what the verdict will be but hopes against hope for a different sentence.

Charles was her verdict. She still could not quite understand how he had been a crime.

The day they finally got rid of Jerome he did not offer to come back to Atherton with her and she did not want him to do so. She wanted the illusion of being able to get away from him for a while. The drive alone, once she had dropped him in town, was harrowing. When she got into the house she knew at once, without Ethel telling her, that someone was there. She even thought she knew who. She marched through the rooms without taking off either her hat or her coat and found Ford sitting in the library with his gloves in his lap, looking at the portrait over the mantel. He did not get up when she came in.

"Are you going to take that down, too?" he asked.

She pulled off her gloves, eager to get a drink, and feeling somehow that he was not being fair. His heavy face was angry, and when he was angry he could be pretty bad. That was the way he had always won out over her in the old days.

"No," she said. "Why should I?"

He did not stir. Anger made him motionless; but his eyes grew hard and his shoulders shook the way a cat's do, tracking a sparrow. He seemed to crouch down in his chair.

"Jerome was my friend," he said. "And there's Maggie. You won't get away with it."

Her nerves were far from steady. She knew she had done wrong, but what really bothered her was the knowledge that now Charles had a real hold over her. "You silly old fool," she said. "What could you do? You haven't anything left yourself." She wondered, even then, why she had said "yourself".

"Maybe not," he said. He was visibly wounded. "But maybe I don't have to do anything. You bought yourself a barracuda this time."

"What are you talking about?"

"Charles," he said softly.

Her hands shook on the lid of the liquor cabinet and when she threw it up it hit the wall. She looked down at the necks of the bottles, like capped guns.

"Anytime I feel like it I can," she began.

"No, you can't. It's too late now. He's got you right where he wants you. You poor fool woman. I don't have to do a thing but watch."

"You'll enjoy watching, won't you?" She picked up a bottle, slipping her hand round it.

"Yes, I'll enjoy that."

She heaved the bottle at him. She saw his face clearly. He frowned and drew his head to one side. The bottle sailed over the sofa and shattered the window, but fell inside in a tinkle of mingled glass. "Get out," she shouted at him. "Get the hell out."

He glanced at her and then at the cabinet, calmly. She knew she was going to have hysterics. She was afraid to be alone.

"It's a pleasure," he said. With a look towards the

broken window he got up and shuffled out of the room, a little bent but still determined. She hoped Ethel had not heard her, but she was sure to see the glass. Fortunately Ethel knew better than to ask questions. When she was sure Ford was gone she went upstairs and locked Jerome's door, and for several years it stayed locked. Charles was the only one who ever unlocked it. He unlocked it from time to time to annoy her. It did not annoy her very much, for locking the door did not help. Now that Charles had ultimately tricked her she began to realize just how alone she was.

She tried to make the best of it, but failed. She had to have Charles, if only because there was no one else she could have. So she had to put up with whatever he felt like doing, and he took advantage of that.

In the beginning she had seen him almost every day. Now she always had to go to bed alone. There are worse things than going to bed alone, but on the other hand nothing in the world is worse. She began to drink.

If she phoned him up on Tuesday and he said he was busy, but to phone him Wednesday at eleven—and she was damned if she would phone him Wednesday at eleven—at eleven-thirty she phoned him all the same; and sometimes in her bath she would get the idea that maybe she was mistaken and that at that moment he was thinking of her and expecting her to phone, so she phoned him. He never was thinking of her, clearly, when she phoned him. And if she had luncheon or dinner with him, it only lasted for an hour and a half, she knew it would only last for an hour and a half, which spoiled even that little time. And if he came back to the house for a drink, it was only for a drink, while he sat there looking at her with that look of maddening amusement and self-satisfaction of his. At least, that little helped somehow to fill up the time. Barracuda wasn't the word. She found herself doing more and more for him.

It was easy to buy him into the partnership at the law firm. If she could not have him at the house she would rather have him at a distance in the city. She knew the partnership was his idea of right payment for his silence about Jerome, but she tried to pretend that it was a gracious woman's beneficence to a rising young man. But he was not rising and he was not a man, and she did not feel particularly gracious. He was moving horizontally through a vertical world, towards a goal she couldn't see and did not want to see.

It was quite by accident that he met Maggie. At least, she thought it was by accident: with Charles it was impossible to be sure.

Maggie took after her father. She had the Barnes jaw and the watchful, slightly sad Barnes eyes. Lily could not talk to Maggie any more. She never had been able to, if it came to that. She never knew what to say to her.

Charles could be helpful when he chose. For some reason she did not grasp, and which made her wary, he was helpful now. He was almost attentive. This surprised her, for he had made it clear that she was not to hang around him, or make him the laughing-stock of younger people who knew him. He had to have his own career, he said, and he didn't want anybody to know how he had got it. She had flared up at that. She had told him to get out. She had said that she wouldn't speak to him again.

"Oh, yes, you will," he had said. He grinned at her.

For a while she did not phone him. She went to the city less and less. It was so much easier to do everything in Atherton. She felt better there and was not humiliated. Then, after a month, when she thought she could get over him, he had phoned her up. She had been evasive but, sensing that he was about to hang up, she had said she would see him. She was surprised at his affability. He had almost apologized for not seeing her.

"But you know how it is," he had said, and turned on his warmer verbal smile.

She thought things over and decided that they could be friends. She was older now. So was he, and trying to be older than he was. Older people needed friends. She tried to make herself older yet. But if she saw him now on Thursday, or when he drove down from town and stopped off along the way to some meeting, it only made it the harder for her that she did not see him on Friday as well.

She had to see someone on Friday. She began to play bridge, if only for the pleasure of telling him she was busy on Friday afternoons. He didn't seem to care. He didn't care for bridge. He played it correctly when he had to, but that was all. There really wasn't anything he did like to do. He was moved only by an inner sense of duty. And you cannot be the successful mistress of someone else's sense of duty.

Maggie did not like him. Lily thought she saw the way out of that. She wanted him back and she wanted the house filled up again. What she really needed was a good hold over him; and she forced herself to remember, now that he was being kinder to her again, that some hold she must have.

It had all been so easy and she had been such a dupe.

She could remember the night they had caught Maggie and Luke in the library. She had felt it coming. It came earlier than either she or Charles intended, but if anything that played on her side, not Charles's. She had made up her mind what to do. She had swallowed her pride long ago. She had none left any longer to swallow. Not pride of the private sort, at any rate; and he was content to leave her her public pride. He didn't need it and he knew that she did. That was the frail last self-respect between them. In his case she suspected it was only pity.

Whatever the reason for his return he was back for a while. The night they came on Maggie and Luke he phoned and said he'd be by to take her to dinner. She went immediately to the tub and soaked in rose geranium bath salts for an hour. Then she had a shower and a rub down and looked at herself in her mirror. The trouble was that every time she let herself go she had a harder time pulling herself back into shape. She could not play both the understanding matron and attractive forty at one and the same time. Not that he gave a damn one way or the other, but she did. When first she met him she hadn't had to worry much about her dress line and now she worried about very little else. It had been seven years.

She did the best she could with a black dress embroidered with gold thread circles, slightly, but not too much, off the shoulder. She gave a final shake to her hair and started down the stairs. He was waiting in the hall. Half-way down, almost where she had hesitated when first she saw him in her house, she hesitated now, wondering what he was up to. For a moment the thought made her sad. She had seen him, once or twice, look at Maggie as he had looked at her five years ago. She did not much mind. She had known him for so long, and she knew so few other people that she just had to go on knowing him, no matter what.

She was fully aware that he did not like to be seen with her in town. They had been through all that many times. But now the town was moving out to the southern suburbs he was back. At least, she hoped he was back.

The highway south of the university was dotted with neon signs and more or less smart restaurants. They spent the evening at one of these and then went dancing. She ate mustard steak. He ate fish braised in sauterne. After they had had enough to drink she began to enjoy herself. It gave her pleasure to be seen out again with someone other than a woman with whom she played bridge. Whereas she didn't mind being seen with other women at lunch, at night it bothered her.

She had too much to drink and she knew he was plotting something. He was very agreeable. He always was agreeable if he felt like it. She looked at that tight, white, artificial head with its deceptively honest eyes and wondered what he was up to. He drove her back to the house at about one-thirty. Every light in the place was on. She looked at him, startled.

"Come in for a drink," she said. This time she knew he would. She felt exhilarated and slightly puzzled. She was aware that such an expression made her attractive. She pulled open the doors of the library, and even though she was startled, she was aware that for some reason Charles thought the scene funny. Yet he could not know that she found Luke attractive. He could not even know who Luke was. So she lost her temper since she felt she had to show off. Charles did not find that in the least funny.

After they heard Luke slam the front door he got up and pulled the library doors closed, got the two glasses from the table, put them back dirty in the liquor cabinet, poured himself a drink and sat down on the sofa. Maggie, she noticed, had not even lit the fire. She stooped down, her coat pulling against the cinders on the hearth, and lit it. She waited until the flames had caught and then rose and took off her coat.

"I want to marry Maggie," he said, and crossed his legs demurely.

It did not faze her at all, though it made her feel cold. She gave him her monkey grin. "I know you do."

"I thought you might help."

"With my own daughter?"

"It would keep it in the family. You want it kept in the family, don't you?" He drawled away at her, patently pleased with himself. She noticed how thin his legs were. He hoisted one of them over the other, at right angles, so he could hold his left ankle with his right hand: that was the gesture college boys of his generation always used when they wanted to be real sincere and grown-up. He was wearing black loafers and through his black silk sock there was a faint, distasteful glimmer of white flesh. They were the legs of a very old man, or of a juvenile playing a very old man in college theatricals. She wondered if he had ever acted in amateur theatricals. he had something of that sexless face.

"You don't care," he said. "You know that. And you certainly don't care about the girl."

That was not quite true but it was true enough.

"I thought it might appeal to your sense of humour," he explained. "If you've still got one."

"I'm not that old," she said bitterly.

"No one's ever that old. That's not the point." He was very comfortable on her sofa, in her library, looking at the portrait of her husband.

"Maggie's got a will of her own," she said. But the matter was decided already. He never said anything until matters were settled. He had that trick, she knew it, and there was no way round it.

He looked straight over her head at Jerome's portrait. "We both know how you control her," he said. "Do it again. You might see me more often."

"Perhaps I don't want to."

"Oh, you want to, all right. God knows why, but you do. I often have wondered why."

"I used to be fond of you, Charles."

"It's not so long ago." He waggled his foot up and down, looking at his loafer, and removed a speck of dirt with his forefinger from the heel of it.

"I can see the two of you on your honeymoon," she said.

"I thought maybe you could. I thought we'd go to Del Monte. Same room. Same place. But a little different in other ways, this time." He got up and left the house quietly. After he had gone she crouched down by the fire, taking jabs at it with the prong of the poker and staring into the hot burnt coals along the log. For some reason she thought of Luke.

Charles did not seem to be in any hurry. It was three or four days before he put the pressure on. One night, because he knew she didn't want him to do so, he stayed at the house. He had been out with Maggie, it was too late for him to drive back to town and he wanted to annoy her.

The marriage went through. She was ruthless about it. And Maggie agreed to marry him, she said, just in order to get away from Lily.

There was no point in telling her that she could not get away; that probably now neither of them could. And Maggie made such a show out of it: she thought she was tricking her mother. It made Lily impatient and hard.

Just for a moment, on the day of the reception, she felt sorry. One generation sucked into Charles was enough. Then, when she saw the car drive away towards Monterey, and when she drove home herself, all the way down to Atherton, she went through the house, flicking on all the lights, and wasn't sorry at all. All she wanted now was revenge.

But now he was dead she did not want it any more. She wanted him back. He was the only thing she had ever had and now she was an old woman, and it was too late, and Luke was downstairs, somewhere, with the girl. The past and the present were not the same. It didn't do any good to sift ashes. You could sift ashes all day and there was nothing to find but ashes, for whatever had got burnt up by mistake had burnt totally away. The knowledge of that did not prevent her from sifting them.

"Oh, my God," she said in the darkness. "There isn't anyone. There isn't anyone anywhere. I'm alone."

She got up and paced round the room hopelessly, bumping against the furniture in the dark. "Oh, my God," she said, "I'll be one of those well-dressed women who are sitting in the theatre when the lights go up with empty seats on every side of them, and who cry when Bette Davis or Barbara Stanwyck gets it in the neck. Oh, Charles; Oh, Charles."

A slim, woman-hating, bloodless, sexless bastard, with his head bashed in. He might just as well have been lying sprawled out in the dark here, in her sitting-room.

"Oh, my God," she said, "I'm fifty-three. Why?" And quite deliberately, because she had never done so in her life, she began to scream, knowing perfectly well it would not help.

XIV

LUKE FOUND MAGGIE STANDING in the middle of the hall, with the lights out, looking up the stairs. There was no need to ask her what she was doing there: they could both hear Lily.

"Come on," he said gently, taking her arm. "You can't help her."

"I don't want to help her," she whispered. He could sense for the first time since he had seen her again that she was agonizingly awake. "I never will."

"Yes," he said. "I know. Come away."

"No. I want to listen."

"Maggie, come away." He led her to the front door, pushed her through it and closed it after them. When he turned around she was already purposively striding across the lawn. He hurried to catch up with her.

"It's all right," she said. "I know where I want to go." She shoved her hands in her pockets and turned to look back at the house. There was no light in Lily's room or anywhere upstairs. "We always were a mixed up bunch," she said. "I thought you knew that. Everybody else does."

She stopped looking at the house, or the dark windows of the house, he could not tell which, and walked more rapidly. He did not take her arm again. He figured

177

she did not want to be touched. They reached the end of the lawn and went into the shrubs, the eucalyptus leaves crisp and brittle underfoot. "Where are we going?" he asked.

"You'll see. It's some place I always wanted to take you and never did. It's time now."

He had not realized that this part of Atherton was built over what was left of the old Flood estate, a grandiose wilderness scattered with pavilions and follies, where even now you could find a big cast-iron urn standing on a pedestal among the weeds or in the backyard of some raw new wooden house. They walked through the eucalyptus wood, fragrant in the cool evening, and it was like walking into an older place. They came to a fence. She hesitated for a moment and then followed it to the left towards a gate. He opened the gate and they plunged across an uneven field of wet grasses and lupin and circling round, went through another copse of trees. It was a small one and she slowed down as though puzzled.

"Yes," she said, "it's still there. They were going to tear it down, but they didn't." She came out of the trees and stopped.

This time he came up and took her arm, blinking with surprise. "I'll be damned," he said.

Across an open space littered with builders' rubble and torn-up foundation trenches rose a pavilion. It was mostly the Villa Rotunda, but with improvements, and a little larger, made of wood. It was about twenty-five feet high, but the eucalyptus trees were higher. It was a building from which the plaster had fallen away. Originally it must have been painted white, but the starlight turned it blue and, he thought, from the way it reflected light, that the dome had once been either gilded or coppered, it was difficult to determine which. Once he supposed there had been an avenue approaching it, but now the weeds not only went right up to the door but grew between the two small templed wings that framed the main flight of stairs. The foundation was of rose brick.

She looked at him and saw that his eyes sparkled with pleasure, so she herself was pleased. "When I was small and Daddy was around we used to come here," she said. "It's where I always come when I want to." She seemed suddenly young and charming. She took his hand and squeezed it. "Come on," she said. "It's growing late."

Late for what, he wondered. For midnight? For the Big Game Dance? For the secret of secrets? He was delighted. For the first time in many years romance settled tightly down over his head, like a helmet filled with pressurized air. It made it much easier for him to breathe.

"Let's run," she said. "Let's run."

"Okay," he agreed. "Let's." And he broke into an awkward run that became less awkward, until she stumbled. Stumbling amused her and she laughed. The field swallowed up the laughter in a friendly silence. He looked at her and saw that for her this was a good place. Dodging the trenches, which in the stubbled moonlight were difficult to see, so that they had to jump over one or two of them, they reached the entrance, where the carriageway was white with scraps of fallen plaster, like moulted feathers. There she stopped.

"Oh, Luke," she said, and timidly reached out and

put her hand in his coat pocket. That she should know about putting hands in pockets surprised him, but it didn't in the least annoy him.

She stood between the two temple wings, looking at the stairs, and he thought he understood. She was a high priestess taking the neophyte up the steps of the shrine and wondering if the conversion was sincere or not, and just what he would make of the mysteries. At the top of the steps was a gaping black hole that did not seem to lead anywhere.

"Have you ever been here at night?" he asked, thinking about tramps and not altogether liking the darkness. More solemnly now she again took his hand and began to walk towards the stairs. At the foot of the steps were other yawning black holes in the two side buildings. He supposed they had been cloakrooms or some such thing. The stairs sagged and were splintered, and weeds grew through them. At the top they looked back at the field of rubble and then plunged into the gloom. He put his arm around her in the darkness, protectively and awkwardly, because she was a little taller than he was, and felt her hair brush against his neck.

She knew the way and the darkness was only a sort of baffle or devil door. They came out around it into a big circular hall with, in the centre of it, a broken fountain on a dais. There was a hole in the ceiling, as in the Pantheon, through which he could see the stars. The stars bathed the room in a uniform, shifting blue light.

"It's all right now," she said, drawing away. "This is one place Charles never even knew about."

He did not listen. Once, no doubt, the room had been banked with palms and ferns and azaleas from the mountains. It seemed to him they were still there, and at the far end of the room was a raised platform for an orchestra, and beyond that, another gaping hole, this one bigger. He left her and went exploring, crossing the arena and jumping up on the dais. The hole was a big passage of double height. There were rooms off it and at the end of it double doors. Someone had chopped a passage through the doors and he peeked outside. Outside was a big landing platform, like a wharf, and he was puzzled by it, it so resembled the loading stage of a meat packers. He decided it must have been built to accommodate caterers. No doubt the side rooms were for the same purpose. The effect was uncomfortably eerie and he hurried back to the rotunda, stepping over fallen plaster and a timber or two. In the side rooms, as he could dimly make out, the damage was even more severe.

The light had changed. There was more of it and it was more the colour of silver. It showed up the desuetude of the place and yet made it friendlier. He looked up and saw part of the moon shining down through the circular aperture at the apex of the roof. No doubt at the right times it fell straight on the fountain, and he supposed they had played a trick with that in the old days. He sang wordlessly, to test the resonance, but because of the hole in the roof the effect was not good. Maggie was sitting on the steps of the dais under the moon. Beside her one tall thistle, dead for ages, reared up from the top step and cast a long shadow. She was watching him. Behind her the statue of the fountain was complete to the waist, above which rose a rusted armature, with nothing clinging to it but a plaster hand.

Whistling, he jumped down from the orchestra platform and went over to her. Standing at the bottom of the fountain steps, looking up at her, he felt curiously excited. Her eyes were shining and misty.

"You like it," she said.

"I've never seen anything like it."

She struck the thistle with her curled index finger, shooting it out from her thumb; and the dead flower sent out a shower of pale white seeds that bobbed for a minute in the air before they fell. She was fascinated by them. She repeated the motion. He watched not her, but the seeds leap up from the dead flower while she struck it with her small, slim fingers. Then, instead of going up the steps, he sprawled out along them, hoisting himself forward with his hands, until his head was about level with her waist, and turned over on his back. He felt for her hand and played with it. "Tell me all about it," he said.

"It used to be a ballroom." She let him warm her hand and made a surreptitious gesture back, as though they were in public. "When I was small I had some of my grandmother's dolls. They weren't like modern dolls. They were little wax-headed women with wooden bodies and wax hands and feet, and pantaloons, and big sweeping dresses. There was a man, too. He had a frock-coat and a little hat that always got lost. I suppose they looked like that here and played waltzes and, well, did things."

"That's not what I mean," he said, looking up at her, but she did not catch his eye. She was looking inside herself. "Tell me about the other part of it."

"Oh," she said. "I don't know. Father was much

older than Lily, really much older, and he was immensely tall. He was over six feet, but I don't think he was very strong. He brought me here once, that's all. It was when I read fairy-tales and I had on a white dress and pigtails with blue ribbons, and I'd just learned about tucking your handkerchief into your sleeve. And then afterwards I came by myself."

"What happened to him?"

"Nothing happened to him," she said, and started to draw her hand away. He did not let her. "He went insane," she added, and bit her lip.

"When?"

"A long time ago. I was just a child."

He stared at her for a moment and pulled himself upright. He started to take off his coat.

"What are you doing?"

"You know what I'm doing," he said. "You know very well."

"No," she said. She closed her eyes and clenched her fists. He looked at her thoughtfully.

"Take off your coat, Maggie," he said gently. "Please." He stared at her. After a while she opened her eyes and looked at him. She really looked at him as he didn't think she ever had before. She began to take off her coat. He helped her with it and spread it beside his own. Then suddenly she leaned down and cuddled up to him, half turning her face away, looking up at the moon, and he felt her blind hands playing with his shirt.

"That's better, isn't it?" he asked softly.

"Yes. Oh, Luke, yes." He held her tighter, trying to cover her with his hands which were too small; and they lay together there, slightly uncomfortably, looking up at the moon which was full now and yellow, because of the heat haze. It almost completely fitted the opening in the roof.

Its geography was very clear. They could see the rabbit pounding the paste of immortality in his pestle, under the cassia tree; and he was a nice, serious, clean-minded rabbit, concentrating on what he was doing and quite serene. After all, he did it almost every night: by this time he should know how.

You could see a lot of things in the moon if you wanted to and knew how. You could even see Coatlicue, the Mexican goddess, but he did not want to; or the big nice friendly man there, grinning; or even, if things weren't going too well, the Cheshire Cat. But on the whole things were going very well indeed. As far as he was concerned it was a fine big moon made out of blue cheese. He wondered if Maggie knew about the rabbit in the moon and the cassia tree and the paste of immortality. He didn't really want to ask her. Instead he thought of the mooncakes they had once bought together in Chinatown, years ago, and what fun that had been, and how they had tasted.

And how, really, she tasted, so he bent his head to find out.

She was not at all as he had expected. She was a different person than the person he remembered. He suspected she *was* a different person, for she had never seemed fully awake in the old days, and he had only been half conscious with adolescent embarrassment himself. The reasons he had thought he loved Maggie then were social reasons. He had always been uneasily aware of that. Even when he had come up to San Francisco this time, it had not occurred to him that she was a woman now and not a girl. He wondered vaguely but not very much where she had got experience. Certainly not with Charles, if he knew Charles. It was like being pleasantly surprised by a new person and he wondered why she hid behind the girl. He went right on kissing her, only more avidly. Then she stopped him.

"I've never been to Los Angeles," she said.

"What has that got to do with it?"

"Nothing," she said, and played with his hair that was too greasy, pulling it out from the sides until it stood out like two wings, which embarrassed him.

"Don't do that," he said. She looked at her hands that glittered with his brilliantine.

"It's just that you've changed," she said. "I think maybe it must be nice down there. You know, you never belonged here, and I don't think that I do, either."

He shrugged and tried to weasel his way in to her again, but she was thinking and serious now. "We're so dead up here," she said. "It's nice to be alive, but if you are you have to pretend to be dead, otherwise they kill you."

He hadn't thought about it that way, but it was probably true. He did not want to think about it right then. "You're so small," she said.

"That's a hell of a thing to say."

"No, it's not. Small and compact. How did you get to be so compact?"

"Swimming mostly."

"Yes," she said. "You can swim down there." She

stopped talking and put her arms around him, locking them, and drawing him closer down to her, slowly, as though she were moving the tube into place over a horizontal X-ray table; as though to say, here, this is where the infection is, you'd better start here.

It was a warm night and he thought he knew why she had wanted to do this here. It was because she wanted him in the continuity that life had broken up for her, the old continuity of life as it should have been. Then he got so excited, because she was excited, that he stopped thinking. It was like shooting white water in an open boat and not caring what you hit, just so as you got out alive. And just as he thought he would go under and the water bubbled up all around him, he shot suddenly out into the pool at the bottom, even though the boat still spun round crazily from the dwindling currents that had forced it there. He half raised his head and saw that their clothes were scattered all over the dais. Tugging at her dress he pulled it over both of them and glanced up. The moon was beginning to pass, so that the hole in the roof was divided, half blue sky, the colour of fashionable ink, and half yellow moon.

When he had been a brown-skinned kid, in the hot August days at a summer camp in the mountains, the great sport was to strip naked and shoot the rocky rapids of the Stanislaus River. He had been best at it, though it scared him skinny, because of the slimy razor-edged rocks, but being Mexican, being best at it had not helped. But now he remembered how he had felt, leaping up on a rock with his bare feet, while the water pearled on his skin, slicking back his hair, and looking at the others in the rapids with an animal pride that was the best kind of pride, for it was warm and did no harm to anyone.

His skin was still brown. Hers was pale. But it was warm now, and only because it was over for a little while would it grow for a little while colder.

"It's different now," she said.

"I guess it is."

She settled down, like a patient who has finally decided to trust her psychiatrist, after a long probation.

"Why did you marry that bastard?" he asked.

"Lily said she'd have me put away."

"She couldn't do that."

"She did it before," she said sharply, and then hurried on. "I wanted to get away. I thought I'd get away from her and I didn't think I cared what he was like. I wanted to hurt her, too. And, well. . . . Oh, Luke, I need you so."

"I'm here."

"I didn't before," she said flatly.

"No," he said. "I guess you didn't." He drew the dress more firmly around them, not because it was cold, but because the arena was getting shadowy and dark.

"We didn't get married here. We got married from the house in town," she said. "I guess it was easier for Lily that way."

XV

She was not sure how much she wanted to tell him. She was not sure how much she wanted to tell anybody. But she could remember it all.

It had been so fatally easy. It was the beginning of the war, so Luke was away, but even if he had not been he could not have rescued her. Dumbly she believed, or hoped against hope, that someone would rescue her, and the conditions of her imprisonment were so familiar to her that she could not even say rescue from what.

She knew all about Charles. She could not remember now when she had not known. But she shrank from admitting it, for the less she knew about her mother the safer she felt. She tried to ignore Charles. Then, when he had first begun to pay attention to her, or even before that, when once she had caught him watching her closely, she had thought only that it was something Lily had told him to do, for reasons of her own.

And then, as he slowly moved up and manœuvred into position she realized what he was up to. And in that big house she couldn't help but eavesdrop. She had gone into the living-room one day to fetch a book and heard him say, through the library door, which was open, the phrase, "When I marry Maggie." She was wearing a heavy silver bracelet with a Maria Teresa Thaler hung from it, and instantly she put her other hand to the bracelet, to quieten it, but she heard no more for just then the door closed.

Most of the time they did not seem to care whether she overheard them or not. She went down to the temple to think it over. She had not been there for some time. It was a foggy day and in the damp fragments of plaster from the ceiling detached themselves and dropped off, like satiated leeches. She brushed one from her hair, staring round the temple that was usually warm and glamorous but to-day was cold and shabby and cluttered with dry weeds. There was even a hole in the floor. If I can't have this, she thought, not quite knowing what this was, I can at least have that, not quite knowing what that was. She had only one line of defence left against her life and that was to give in completely.

She got a certain amount of pleasure out of watching Charles. Once you got a lever under the edge of that facile charm, it lifted off like a scab and you could see the smooth pink vulnerable flesh underneath. She also made a private joke about his beard. But she could not imagine how he would propose to her. When she was alone to think it over, it made her giggle a little too much. She had forgotten that efficiency is always quiet, and Charles was an efficient man.

Though he never took Lily up to town, he took her up frequently. One time they wound up at the "Top of the Mark" at about midnight, which was the sort of place he *would* take her. It had once been the private penthouse of a copper king, but for years now it had been one big bar slung out into space, with slightly tinted windows overlooking the night-lit city. Most of it, unfortunately, faced towards the slums or the hills, but the view from one side had been reproduced in cigar advertisements from coast to coast. She liked it because it reminded her of H. Rider Haggard's *She*, because of the lobby downstairs, and of Helen Gahagan Douglas flinging herself around vengefully in white veils. Maggie could not see herself, however, as the eternal female principle, and she did not think that Charles did, either. The eternal female principle was essentially a story-book thing.

But the "Top of the Mark" was nice, perched up in the air like a counterfeit zircon. It gave her a twenty-fifth-century feeling that came from being up high, in the lounge of some luxury space ship of the future, not going anywhere in particular, but being awfully rich and enviable.

"I suppose he feels he has to pump a little romance in," she thought. It made her feel suddenly tired. She looked around the room for the sort of blond boy she would have liked to have been there with, but could not find one. She never did find one. The room was drowsy and half deserted. They sat in the right windows and she looked out at the magic lights of the city, the harbour, the hills, and the shipping. If I had my own money, she thought, the money I should have had, the money Father would have given me if he hadn't gone away, I could get on that boat right down there and go to Valparaiso or somewhere, but then what? And she watched the lighted Chilean steamer slowly being nudged out into the open water, half hidden by the dirty white smoke of its tug.

"Well," she thought, "this is it." The ice-cubes fell

in her glass with a soft chink and she felt scared. Charles heard the ice fall, too. He reached his dead hand across the table and patted hers, with a neat mixture of avuncular understanding and a touch of the cardinalate. She might have been his niece.

"I guess you know I want you to marry me," he said. He was using the vibrato in his voice that he kept for special occasions.

"Would it help you that much?" she asked.

He did not draw his hand back, but if anything it was colder than before. It was also slightly sweaty. She did not like sweaty hands.

"Every man should get married," he said.

"Yes," she agreed. "I guess every man should."

He withdrew his hand. She guessed he thought she wanted to bargain and his eyes grew sharp, though they tried to look warm, with the knowledge that she had nothing to bargain with. You might at least pretend, she thought, that I'm a person. After all, I move and talk like one the best way I can.

"What does that mean?" he asked.

"I don't know. I'd have to think about it."

"Well, think about it," he said, but he sounded impatient.

She made him sit through two more drinks and then had him drop her at the town house. He did not kiss her, but he pumped sincerity into his eyes for all he was worth. She went into the house alone. It was not until she was upstairs in her own room that she realized that when they were married they would share this house. She supposed Charles would want to change round the furniture and have the decorators in. He usually did. He was that kind of man. It was a pity, for she liked things the way they were. It would have helped a lot if there had been anyone, anywhere, to love her.

He always rushed things a little towards their conclusion. He got impatient, she thought, because he spent too much time planning a thing and then the fun went out of it for him.

Her scene with Lily was equally quiet. It was as though they had all suddenly decided to pretend they were in a sickroom. The scene did not occur in town, but at Atherton.

It was the last week of her senior year, but after finals. She knew the pressure would be put on her that week, for nobody wanted her on their hands after she graduated. Lily was wearing her best smile. Charles used his eyes for expressing sincerity, Lily her mouth. The result was the same. Maggie looked at her mother warily, clutching her bag.

"Let's go to lunch, dear," said Lily. "You must be tired." No one would have guessed that they were mother and daughter. In a way they weren't. Lily was full of an older woman's playful bridge club gallantry towards a junior matron.

They went to the Studio Club, about five miles below the university. In shape like a progressive chicken coop it had, at the lunch hour, the atmosphere of a church social at a fashionable Episcopal church. In deference to the age of most of its clientele the management had the window glass tinted pale blue, to avoid the coarse intrusion of actinic rays. The calories were admirably balanced. It was impossible to eat too much.

The bar was large and dim. It was scattered with deep

sofas, low coffee tables, and arrangements of flowers. The drinks were too elaborately served and usually contained coloured garbage. The place, in short, was *fun*. In a corner of the bar dimmer than the others, at a large Hammond organ, a thin, elderly, bald-headed man was letting his hands wander idly over the keys. Whether it was Ethel Smythe or "In a Monastery Garden", he played it all in the proper Sir Arthur Sullivan manner, and at least the sound produced, like that of houseflies angry in a bottle, helped to keep the gossip in separate compartments. With a sigh of contentment, for because of the lighting this was one place where she did not have to worry about her complexion, Lily sat down on one of the sofas, laid her gloves on the coffee table with surgical precision, and settled back. Like a surgeon, she never tugged her gloves on, but carefully rolled them on and off, as though they were powdered and sterile. She preferred thin kid, which had somewhat the texture of surgeon's plastic rubber.

"I thought we'd have sandwiches in here, or something," she said. "The restaurant is so noisy."

So they had sandwiches in there. Maggie sat beside Lily, perversely on her deaf side. They might have been two women placidly cutting up the reputation of a third, rather than deciding her future. Maggie was beginning to realize that that was the way futures were decided, at least the only sort of futures Charles and Lily were interested in. She thought it was a pity.

"It's time you settled down," said Lily.

"I won't get my diploma for another week," said Maggie, for no particular reason, except that she could never help saying things like that to her mother because her mother never really understood the point of them. Lily could only follow one trace at a time.

"Well, we don't want you going haywire," continued Lily. It was the time-honoured beginning of all their serious talks. The rest of it bade her remember the example of her father. "You're too high strung. You need a steadying hand."

But not, thought Maggie, manacles, and wondered why her mother was going at it so easily. It isn't me she's worried about, it never has been. It's Charles, she thought. She was too tired to bargain, but she made the pretence.

"I'd need things," she said.

"That can be taken care of."

"I mean money."

"Your father's money is tied up. You know why. We can manage."

"Suppose I don't want to get married?"

"Nonsense. Everybody gets married," said Lily. She eyed the waiter bringing the sandwiches. They hadn't got round to Charles yet, but they didn't have to. Perhaps that was what disconcerted Lily. It was all so easy.

Maggie decided to make it even easier. "I'm going to marry Charles," she said.

Lily flinched, but also sighed with relief. Suddenly Maggie understood that Lily was afraid of Charles now, and wondered why.

"But only to get away from you," she added.

Lily was silent, eating the sandwich before she spoke. She put it down on the plate and wiped her fingers carefully on her napkin. "You won't get away," she said. "We'd better have another drink."

It was not until years afterwards that Maggie realized that this was not a vengeful or nasty remark, but only the sad truth. The full distasteful physical horror of the whole mess did not strike her until later, and then it was too late.

That night, in her own room, she heard a souped-up car go charging invisible in the street beyond the hedges; and she thought: there are people alive in this world. Why don't I know them?

It did not occur to her that Lily was as uncomfortable as she was. They boarded it up by shopping together. They saw little of Charles. Even so she was frightened at her own decision. When she got a postcard from Luke she tore it up and threw it in the waste-paper basket. Then she took out the pieces and it was like looking at something valuable but taken for granted, that one does not know one is fond of until someone else has smashed it. She wrote him a letter and tore it up. She emptied the waste-paper basket down the laundry shoot.

They were married from the house in town. She had dreaded it so much, now she was committed to it, that it came more quickly than she had believed possible. And almost as a relief.

The last night of her freedom she got out her own car, that was the only private world she had, and took a drive through the dusty campus. In her freshman year, at the beginning, during rush week, she had been pledged—that had been taken for granted—but not very eagerly. Chiefly because she had not wanted to join a sorority at all, but also because she had wanted to annoy Lily, she had joined the wrong sorority, not a fatally wrong one, but one that was wrong enough. Lily had been angry.

"Why haven't you made any useful friends?" she had demanded, and it was true, Maggie hadn't. The scorn in Lily's voice had hurt.

She had preferred to learn the hard way with a funny professor in the history department who had halitosis and suffered from a nostalgia for Budapest. He had been dismissed later for liberal tendencies. She had tried the usual boys, too, but she had felt safer with the faculty, at least the younger members of it. And none of it mattered. It was only for an hour or two. And then she was alone again. As for Luke, Luke was only a toy that she was too old to play with, so her mother had put it away. It didn't matter. It would have broken, anyway. Toys always did.

She drove out beyond the lake and up into the hills, past the couples in the dark and silent parked cars, and got out and let the wind whip her skirt as she stood on the hill. You could not see much because of the perpetual heat haze, but she could sense grizzled mountains in the distance and the barrier hills of the city to the north, with a pink neon glow behind them. She knew almost no one there. Only Charles. But alone on a hilltop, in the open country, was one place Charles would never get. He did not think it worth getting. So she was glad she had the car. The car would help.

She went back to Atherton, pleased, in a way, that it was her last night there. It seemed proper she should be married from her father's house and not from her mother's, even for a marriage such as this one.

Lily drove her up to town. The car was piled with luggage. There was not much to say. At least the house, when they got there, would be a familiar place.

It wasn't. Even Lily was somewhat taken aback. Charles had had the decorators in and nothing was where it belonged and nothing was the same. That was the first real shock she had, and the next came right afterwards. Charles was in the living-room, fussing with the flowers, which he shouldn't have been doing. She saw at a glance that everything in the room, most of it new, was arranged exactly and immutably, as though he had a blue-print of it all, down to the ashtrays, perpetually in his head. Some imperceptible movement of Lily's made Maggie realize that she had not seen the two of them together since the whole miserable engagement had commenced; and now, as she stood between them, for she had gone into the room first, she saw that she *was* between them; and that, just as they were doing now, they could exchange a glance over her head that even if they made each other uncomfortable now, she was not tall enough to intercept. She looked at them both and rushed upstairs, and a strange maid helped her dress. Charles had hired the servants, too.

They left her alone. The only thing they needed her for was the wedding itself. And she wondered what they were talking about downstairs. But when Lily came out in the hall and called up to her—was she afraid to come up?—and she came to the top of the stairs, she thought her mother looked strained and white and old, perhaps because she was trying to pretend it was a gala occasion and a good reason for a cry.

It was all pretty brutal. Maggie took some phenobarbital. She had to take something and a bride doesn't drink. It occurred to her that the only reason they were going through with the wedding was so Lily and

Charles, in different places, could read the same guest list in the same papers the next morning, with the same mental reservations about the names. She herself did not know who half the people were. Charles and Lily had arranged the wedding. Though there were to be people there she had known at college, the attendance had been arranged between their parents and Lily.

The car was waiting at the door, a hired limousine. Charles would go separately. Foster was the best man.

Lily watched her as she floated down the stairs, holding up her skirt, for that was the only way to move in that ancestral dress, and Maggie wondered if she looked like a fresh-faced eager bride, as they would say next day, or like a rather third-rate actress elevated to the rank of Trilby to other men's means.

Suddenly she thought: suppose it isn't Charles, but someone else. She thought of the professor with an affection for Budapest. She put him aside. She thought of Luke and the tropical warmth of Puerto Rico, or a lot of sailors on shore leave, lurching slim-hipped through unfamiliar streets. She put them all aside. No, she had to pretend she was drifting down to some cinematic ideal, though she could not give the illusion any features. She could only remember how some things had once felt at night, things that had nothing to do with her daytime life, or this white dress, or anything she would probably spend the rest of her life doing; but by the time she had reached the car she had concentrated an imaginary blond with a drawling voice, wide shoulders and beefsteak hands, completely selfish, but at least clean. Someone as unlike Charles as escape could make him.

She did manage to get through the wedding without

looking at his beard and the reception by smiling at everything and pretending to be in a daze; but soon enough she would be alone with him. It did not occur to her then that he did not want to be alone with her, either. She smiled nicely for the photographer as she cut the cake. Half-way up the stairs, because the photographer expected it, she threw the wedding bouquet, which was heavy and Victorian, down at the stupid gaping faces instead of into an ashcan; and she was very, very glad she was not a virgin. At least she had had something. Then she turned and ran up the stairs so she shouldn't see Lily following her. For Lily had to speak to her for a minute or two. It was the customary, the obligatory thing that had to be done.

When Lily did come in Maggie was buttoning up the front of a pale brown jersey dress that had about umpteen shiny, slippery buttons. She was also looking angrily at herself in the mirror. She had taken two more quarter grain phenobarbital, but they did not help. Nor did Lily try to. Lily leaned against the door.

"Well, that's over," she said.

"Yes." Maggie went on with the buttons, determined not to cry.

"I'm sorry," said Lily.

"It's over now," said Maggie. "And I don't suppose you're that sorry."

Lily leaned more heavily against the door and somehow her fat had recently got out of hand. She watched her daughter, and when Maggie turned to pick up her coat she saw that she was still watching.

"I wish you hadn't said that," said Lily drily. Her voice was oddly flat.

"There's nothing else to say." Maggie threw on the coat.

"No," said Lily. "I suppose not." She stood aside as Maggie went towards the door, but did not follow her through it. And Maggie did not want to see her mother cry.

They went to Del Monte for five agonizing days. Charles seemed in some secretive way to enjoy them. They did not stay at the hotel but at the lodge over the golf links, though Charles did not play golf. They had a corner room where the light woke her up too early. When she found out that he did not play golf she played it herself, and that made him mad. "I don't play golf," he said tartly at the bar, when she suggested it. But the second day she went out he was there and played well, considering there was a bad offshore wind. So she stopped playing golf. It was a pity because she had a good style and she liked the salt spray and the water slapping at the rocks in small coves between the holes.

That left them riding, so they went riding. Charles rode well, though with a mechanical alertness and sense of form. He did not so much ride as practise equitation in a yellow suede vest and a knobbly tweed sports coat like an illustration in a manual of the English style. She went riding in jeans and a black and white checked shirt, and it occurred to her that she had never seen a book on riding that had photographs western style. Also her saddle creaked. Riding gave her an excuse to soak in privacy in a big, foamy, scented tub. He watched her like a hawk to see if she made mistakes of any kind, but he couldn't very well watch her with the bathroom door closed and locked. Why did he expect her to be gauche?

So they went riding, usually not along the coast but through those well-swept, clinical, somehow German-looking woods around the hotel. They were attractive woods. She watched him ride ahead of her, at a careless gallop, and wondered how she would feel if he hit his head on a lower limb and fell off and cracked his skull, but he didn't. He ducked for low limbs with a regular, well-practised rhythm. He was also annoyed. When they got back to the lodge he wanted to hide her.

"For God's sake go upstairs and change," he said, looking her over. "This isn't a dude ranch."

She was perfectly aware that it wasn't, so she went into the bar and had a drink. He did not follow her. When she went upstairs her jodhpurs had been taken out and laid on the bed, with no comment. She did not see him until dinner-time. She thought it over and when they rode she went on wearing jeans. They stopped riding.

He had made a fuss about the room. He was furious about it, though she couldn't see why, and he wasn't pretty when he was angry. He was then dangerous in the way that someone hysterical is dangerous. He had asked for a corner room and they had given him one. But apparently it was not the right corner. He wanted the one on the south side. He got the one on the south side. She could not see that it made any difference.

He went to bed with her only twice and it was not pleasant. He had a Brooks Bros. body. A Brooks Bros. suit is all very well, but a Brooks Bros. body is not. It requires the clothes. She had to pretend that he was someone else, someone wiry and muscular and masculine and hot. He was none of those things. He was thin and deliberate and thorough, and he paid no attention to her at all. He was willing to kiss her in public, but in bed he simply didn't bother. And he had that slippery, oleaginous, sweaty, somehow artificial skin that does not seem to cover flesh so much as some kind of wooden machinery, like an eighteenth-century wooden clock that expanded in damp weather and so stuck.

Most people at least changed, or became excited, or dived down an animal tunnel, in the midst of things, but he did not change at all. He might just as well have been wearing his clothes. He went to bed with her the first night and the next morning. And that, quite simply, was the end of it. He got no satisfaction out of it. He didn't even bother to close his eyes. It was vegetable and obscene, and his flesh always glistened with that tepid sweat that made her want to take a shower immediately afterwards. In the morning she did, but could not get rid of an elusive rhubarb smell that also seemed a part of him. She wondered what it was and realized it was the sticky, glutinous smell of freshly sliced okra in a pot, before you add water. She turned the shower full on.

He seemed quite content; though it had been such a failure, as she twisted away from his beard, that she would have expected him to be angry. She thought in some obscure way he was getting even, though she could not figure out how or for what. She visualized suddenly, what she never had before, that he had gone to bed with Lily. She wished that she had not visualized that.

But next morning when she woke up he was actually whistling in the shower. She took her chance and dressing rapidly went down to breakfast alone. By the time he came down she was ready for him. She looked at the disembowelled grapefruit in its melting ice crater and felt such contempt for him that she could face him cheerfully. After breakfast he took her to Marsh's, without bothering to say where they were going, as though he had the complete five days planned out in his head and this was what he had planned to do on the fourth day. He picked out a jade pendant and made her wear it. She agreed that it was lovely.

"But", she said, "it doesn't suit me. It's for an older woman." She didn't want a souvenir of these five days.

"I know," he said. "We'll take it." And he made her wear it, too, though she never wore it once they had returned from Del Monte. She put it in a drawer when they got back and forgot about it, nor did he ever inquire about it.

The thing she really hated was the march of the fish. She could not stand that.

Usually they had dinner early. She came down first and went into the long salon that faced the sea, for on the ground floor the lodge was a series of interconnecting rooms on the sea side. The largest and the darkest was this one. At one end were the closed doors to the dining-room. There was a feudal-size fireplace and sofas. The room was about fifty feet long and dreary, though it was supposed to be cosy, for it was only effective at night, with the firelight, and at eight it was still evening.

At about ten to eight the guests would begin to gather. The hotel had a permanent series of elderly Jewesses of great gravity and port. They lurched down the length of the room like ungainly sea mammals, followed by their paid companions, scurrying like pilot fish; and through the years they had so timed their progress that they would reach the doors just as two flunkies appeared to fold them back, giving what was designed, no doubt, to be a magical glimpse of the bright dining-room beyond, with its Hawaiian plants and crystal chandeliers. It was the timing that bothered Maggie, for at about seven minutes to eight, perhaps because he walked faster than the Jewesses, being younger, Charles would appear, wearing brown as did the displaced dowagers, and as he approached her she knew that she would rise, at six to eight, as he had planned, to meet him, and that, allowing the dowagers to enter first, they in turn would enter the dining-room, for all she knew, at 8.01.30. She hated that. She felt that he was building a machine around her. And she was quite right: he was.

On the fifth day they left. He had business in town, or so he said. He was more likely bored with it. They motored up. But she could still remember the dowagers and the futility of that corner bedroom.

Their life went on. He watched her, but he left her alone. In two years she got to learn why. It was his way of softening her up for those few times when he needed her to help him entertain, or wished to be seen out with her. He was good at softening. He knew that if she was alone long enough she would be glad to see almost anyone. He was quite right: she was.

She had no friends. She couldn't go out and pick up casuals and strays; and anyone they did meet who liked her he nipped neatly and efficiently, one way or another, in the bud. Even Lily avoided them. Whether and when he saw Lily or not she did not know. She did not want to know. Mostly she sat alone in that awful house, or used the car, or went shopping. She had a few outside acquaintances, but only a few, left over from college and re-animated by the wedding, but he did not exactly encourage a cosy social life, and he made it clear he didn't think much of her friends. Well, maybe she didn't think much of them herself; but they were the only friends she had, and after he had been scathing to them once or twice, she saw less of them. She knew the trouble: he did not find them useful. Maybe Lily had been right about the wrong sorority business after all, if this was what a marriage was.

She developed a routine. She would decide to do something on Thursday, any crazy thing, like getting creamed spinach in wax canisters for the cook, at a restaurant that specialized in creamed spinach in wax canisters. But then she would go over and do it on Wednesday, even though that meant keeping it in the icebox overnight, because she didn't have anything else to do on Wednesday and she happened to be down town. She always had shops send packages, too: it meant that she could have the pleasure of having them come late and phoning up the shop or some damn thing like that.

She needn't have worried about the bed side of it. It wasn't a personal marriage and she saw that she had known that it wouldn't be. It wasn't really any marriage at all.

She could have moved out and got a job as a clerk in a store, except that she didn't have any experience or know what a clerk in a store exactly did. The phonograph collection got pretty large, but music did not interest him. He was quite content. But sometimes, when they did have guests, he watched her so closely that she could have screamed. She didn't. If she had he would only have groomed her for the looney bin.

In her own right she had just enough money, in a legacy from an uncle that Lily couldn't touch, to pay for the upkeep of her car and things like that. She didn't even go away for week-ends, because she was too dispirited, and besides, she was learning to be afraid of him. She could not do anything about it, but she thought it best to keep a sharp eye on what he was doing. She found herself eavesdropping. There was something about Charles that evoked eavesdropping.

He was a very clever man.

She got to taking too much phenobarbital and broke down. Charles whisked her off to a doctor of his own choosing, and besides, what could she tell a doctor or what could a doctor do? The thing she liked best was either to take a drive by herself and so get free for a while; or else to wander through Chinatown or North Beach, to watch the living people she could not touch or speak to, except over the counters of shops.

In North Beach she found the damndest monument, just an obelisk, with a big plaque on it stating that it was to be opened for the benefit of posterity in 1964. Sometimes at night she realized that in 1964 she would be thirty-nine and wondered what was in the obelisk. Did it, like Joanna Southcott's chest to be opened only in time of England's peril, in the presence of thirty-nine bishops, contain revolvers, or had some eccentric put his personal possessions there?

Often, alone in her room, she wondered whether or

not Charles was in his room. She could frequently tell, for the atmosphere in the house then became thicker. She looked round her room in which he had chosen everything including, she perceived, herself.

Then, one week-end, by accident, she found out what it was that he and Lily had done. She had not said anything. She put the papers back. She waited a week, watching him. She had torn them into shreds in anger and then returned them to the drawer. When she at last looked at the drawer again they were gone, but he did not mention them. He went away that week-end, and the more she thought about what he had done the angrier she became. She got into her car and drove up to Bolinas after him.

She did not tell Luke about that part of it. She bit her lip and stopped talking. She rolled towards Luke and buried her head on his shoulder and felt his hands stroking her hair and could not help crying.

"You don't know," she said. "Sometimes I would wake up every night, for nights on end, dreaming that someone was there to keep me warm or love me a little, and there wasn't anybody. I tried to pretend there was, but you can't go on pretending forever. Sometimes you can't sleep alone. Sometimes you can't pretend."

"Yes, I know." He let her cry and she did not cry for long. She did not need to cry now. He hoped she would not need to again. She had not loved him in the past and perhaps he had not loved her then, either. It was not necessary to say so. They loved each other now.

Maggie sat up. "She could ruin us," she said.

"Not any more."

"She tried. She told me about it."

"Not here," he reassured her. "I don't think she wants to any more. And besides, I'm not up here. I'm down south." He realized that was not what she meant. "What are you talking about?"

"Nothing." Her voice was muffled against his chest. "She was pretty threatening about Charles."

"It doesn't matter now. We'll get you out of this somehow and start over again. Or maybe just start."

"Can we?"

"You bet we can," he said. "We'd better get dressed and go back." He released her and looked around the arena, which was much darker now without the moon, and faintly disturbing. It might have meant something to her once, but it didn't have to mean anything to her any more. It was the past she had to get away from. She'd never had a chance to live in the present. And when he touched her, he thought maybe he could bring it off after all. He certainly knew he had to. He had wakened up alone like that in the middle of the night sometimes himself, and he thought he began to know what marriage was for: it was to save you from the middle of the night.

He helped her dress and they went back to the house.

It was still dark upstairs, but someone had turned on the hall light. They walked across the gravel towards the door. Once inside she turned to him pleadingly.

"No," he said. "Go upstairs." She looked at him. He smiled at her and, taking her arm, he led her up the stairs in the dim light of one wall bracket. Very artistically arranged, he thought, but nobody stopped them. They turned down the corridor towards Maggie's room, the door of which was open, and a night light burning, again artistically. He pursed his lips. Maggie looked at him questioningly.

The door to Lily's room opened behind them. He pushed Maggie through her door and turned around. Lily was standing in the pool of light from her room. She had not even undressed.

"Oh," she said. "Luke. It's so late."

"That's all right. I'm staying."

She glanced beyond him, but Maggie had gone into her room. "Nothing's made up," she said. "I'd better wake Ethel." She looked at him with a curiously dead face and put her hand up to her forehead, to push back her hair. She seemed faintly puzzled.

"You needn't bother," he said. He went into Maggie's room and shut the door behind him. He knew she wouldn't follow him. They did not have to bother with Lily any more, but an object lesson did no harm.

XVI

It was funny about power, thought Luke. It moves in a world where nothing but itself exists. Even the wealthy can only hear dim echoes of public opinion, no matter how hard they listen; and the powerful hear not at all. They are protected by an isthmus; and then the sea breaks through and floods them all. The sea recedes; somebody steals the abandoned brick for new foundations, in another valley, where the isthmus seems firmer.

It is like this city, he thought, looking at the sullen surface of the bay. It looks firm. But when they wanted to expand it they threw all the immediate past into the water—old brigantines, round cheeses, Conestoga wagons, crates of disused machinery, a few dead bodies, and God knows what else besides, to push the water out. Then they build on top of such foundations, but the ground settles a little more every year and the water will flood back in time. San Francisco was a vertical place and top heavy. It might fall over at any time. Or maybe it would just rot.

He considered the breakfast-room. It was supported by four old posts twenty feet high. Cut them through and the whole damn back of the house would tumble down into the slums.

Yet the view, if anybody ever looked at the view from this room, was beautiful. Despite the view he had no desire to live in this house or any like it. Once he had had, when he was shut out of it, but now he did not want to live in any of their houses. He did not think that they did either.

He was waiting for Maggie to come downstairs and the breakfast-room was at least cheerful. They had all driven up for the inquest and they were all on edge. Even Senator Ford had come.

Luke had stayed at Atherton for several days. He had been there this morning. He had got downstairs first, rising early, when the house was deep in shadows mixed with that singularly cheerless steel grey morning light. Wandering through the house was like wandering through a furniture warehouse. He had gone into the library, as the one bearable room that looked lived in, but had then gone through the french windows for a stroll round the lawn. There were no flowers in the garden, only flowering shrubs. They were easy to take care of and Lily obviously had no domestic skills. The dew was heavy on the grass. Looking back he could see his own footsteps walking rapidly away from the house. The air was full of waiting, but he heard no birds. Morning in the suburbs came differently, heralded by a garage door sliding up into the roof, the chirruping of the milkman's bottles, or the bellow of a generator pumping heat through a distant room.

When it was eight he went back to the breakfast-room and heard Ethel in the kitchen. He went to the chair at the head of the table that was clearly Lily's and reaching under it with his foot pressed the buzzer. He did not want to see any of them without something on his stomach. Ethel brought in coffee, tomato juice, grapefruit juice, fried bacon, and scrambled eggs. The first morning he had stayed she had served a woman's bird breakfast, but had changed soon enough. He looked at the hot bacon, the half-drained fat still bubbling on its lean, in a silver platter, and decided that this was what Ethel must have cooked for Charles. It was clearly a country breakfast, suburban style.

It was also well cooked.

What he was trying to get round was the necessity of seeing Lily. Lily had fallen apart and stuck herself together again, but not very well, and it was uncomfortable for all of them. She seemed to have grown heavier. He heard her coming. He looked up and smiled reassuringly.

"Well, this is it," he said.

She had made a special effort this morning, but he could see the grains of powder on her face. She did not look as though she had slept. She had brought down her bag and her coat and her car keys, as though she didn't want to go upstairs again, and these she laid on the buffet. The coat caught on the edge for a moment and then, the fur allowing no purchase, slid slowly and then more rapidly off the polished wood and landed on the floor with a soft, animal plop. She left it where it was. He started to retrieve it.

"Oh, let it stay," she said. She reached under the table and pressed the buzzer more firmly than he had done. "We may as well have some more coffee," she said.

"It's still hot."

She shrugged. "It won't do Ethel any harm to make some more. She's nothing else to do."

Ethel stuck her head through the door, saw Lily, disappeared and came back with a fresh pot already made, a tight smile of triumph on her face. They had gone through that routine for four mornings now. The tight smile had no effect. Lily drank four cups of coffee in a row. She pretended he was not there. It was just as well. It was what he wanted to pretend himself.

Maggie came in last. "Hello, dear," said Lily amiably, not meaning a word of it. She had developed a dry knack of looking at them as though they had no clothes on and were lying in the same bed. She didn't really mean anything by it: it was done involuntarily.

Maggie said good morning a little too cheerfully and slid sideways into her chair, scooping up her skirt. She was wearing black, as was Lily, and she, too, had brought her bag and hat downstairs. She placed the former on the table at her right, away from Lily. Her dress was too smart. It obviously had not been bought specially for the occasion. It did not give the right post-mortem touch of grief, but instead merely looked well tailored. She glanced at Luke and then reached for the jug of tomato juice. He watched her pour it neatly into her glass.

Maggie had changed. She had taken on the life that Lily had lost. But it would not do for her to appear too self-confident. Maybe she was awake for the first time in her life, for her aliveness had that special, self-enchanted quality that kittens and young puppies possess, even on the concrete floor of a pound. She reached out and touched his knee under the table. Lily stared at them both and then poured herself another cup of coffee, watching it soak through the heavy mound of sugar at the bottom of her cup. She seemed both subdued and anxious.

"All I ask", she said wearily, "is that you behave yourselves." It was a fragment of disapproval that had somehow lost its edge, but he could hear her honing it. Neither of them answered. Lily looked as though she was expecting something worse. He thought it was a pity about her. She must have been a nice woman once. She had the remains of a nice face.

The wisps of an old quarrel hovered in the air, like ashes, and somebody had to damp them down for a while. He did not think they would ever dry out and blow away. He realized they were all watching the clock, and having dawdled behind their food, were now rushing towards the half-hour. He dabbled at his mouth with the napkin, folded it in his lap, unfolded it hastily, and put it crumpled on the table. Lily had watched all this attentively. He looked up and caught her eye. She looked relieved. It meant he was leaving. She shifted to watch Maggie, but Maggie's napkin had dropped to the floor and had not been recovered.

"Well, we'd better go," said Luke, after this comedy. He got up and they all followed suit. He picked Lily's coat off the floor and held it, while she went into the pantry to say good-bye to Ethel. She had to have somebody to say good-bye to. Then, in a clump, they moved through the empty living-room. There was a screech of brakes on the gravel and the doorbell rang. They stopped where they were. Lily out in front, by the sofa, and Luke and Maggie behind, but apart. The slip covers had a pattern of blue and black artichokes in flower. For some reason he found blue and black artichokes annoying. They all listened to Ethel grumble. They even heard her say, "Oh, it's you."

Senator Ford came into the room. He looked testy and sardonic, which was his customary party manner. The three of them shifted position slightly.

"Morning, Lily," he said, as though it made no difference that he had not been in the house for several years. He had a trick he liked of unexpectedly picking up where other people left off. "Thought I'd drive Luke to the inquest."

Lily merely stared.

"You're looking fine," he said drily. He glanced behind her at Maggie and Luke, and summed that up. He had a battered shapeless felt hat on his head that only gave him an unsightlier Hapsburg jaw than he possessed. Luke wondered if he still had his own teeth—he must have had, for they were crooked and nicotine stained. He talked, though, as though he had a loose denture.

"Luke was coming with us," said Lily. "I thought he might drive. I'm so tired." So she didn't want to be alone with Maggie, Luke concluded, for it was her habit to do the driving whether she was tired or not.

Senator Ford grimaced. "Maggie has a licence," he said. He gave the room a cursory glance and marched back towards the hall. Ethel had left the front door open, and he noticed that. "Thoughtful of her," he commented without any particular malice that you could put your finger on.

Lily shrugged and followed him without a word. They all clumped under the *porte-cochère*, for the morning was cold and misty, before they separated to their cars. Ford had a battered old grey Plymouth with one front fender missing and bashed-in headlights. The chrome had been stripped away for metalwork was not among his interests. He got into his car and waited for Luke. Luke squeezed Maggie's hand reassuringly and walked round to the far door of the Plymouth. Ford started first, but Lily's Cadillac soon passed them, horn honking impatiently. Ford grinned at her. The upholstery of his front seat was ripped and the seat was too far forward so that Ford's long legs stuck up into the steering wheel. He was a fussy but careless driver. He drove as though he momently expected the dashboard to explode.

"What gave you this idea?" asked Luke.

Ford was humming discordantly to himself. He stopped. "Oh, I don't know. Loving kindness, I guess."

"I'll bet."

Ford watched Lily's car receding ahead of them. "They've impanelled a grand jury for this thing," he said. "It might just be misguided family pride, on the other hand it might be sticky. I thought I'd take a look."

"Oh."

"Grand juries", said Ford, "are always irritable, autodidactic, and smug. The women love it: it gives them a sense of importance and it gives them a chance to be seen. What more does any woman want? It does not give them brains." He chuckled. "What did you do to Lily? She looks as though she'd lost her last pup."

"She has."

"That won't do her any harm," said Ford. He started humming again. He wouldn't drive on the Bayshore Freeway to town, because every time he picked up a paper he saw that someone had been killed on it; so they puttered up through the suburbs, among the heavy traffic, the neon signs, and the eucalyptus trees which, considering the way he drove, were even more dangerous than the Bayshore. This route was maddeningly slow. Luke was anxious, for he did not want Lily and Maggie to be together for too long. Ford cursed all the stop signs. He also gazed moodily through the windshield.

"Used to be open country twenty years ago and now look at it. You could make the city in forty minutes in those days and now it takes over an hour," he said. "That's what Lily always forgot, you know: that anybody could build up around her, people she didn't even know, people none of us ever knew. She might guess wrong about them sometimes. Like she did about Charles. Even that house, she can't hang on to it forever, and I never knew why she hung on to it at all. It's too big for her. Things get smaller. Have you pumped Lily yet?"

"Sort of."

"I can imagine," said Ford. "Well, you don't know her. I do. I've got something at the back of my mind I might use. If I have to. They're both lying."

"What do you mean by that?"

"I mean that they are," said Ford. "And you're no fool. You know it, too. It might be a good idea if one of them told the truth a little bit, just for our peace of mind. That is, if Maggie and you are serious, and you look serious."

"Maggie's all right."

"But you don't believe she's told you quite everything, do you?"

Luke was silent.

"That's what I thought," said Ford. He hit a traffic-free space and put his foot down on the gas. The car gave a vertical leap and gathered speed, though not very much speed. "It's like bringing in a well," he said. "Sometimes you have to go down a long way to get water. Or a long way back. And sometimes you have to soup it up and wait for the explosion."

"There isn't going to be any explosion."

"Somebody knows something," said Ford. "I've got a hunch we'll find out who one of these days. That might be inconvenient. In a way I wish Maggie had done the bastard in. It would make it a pleasure to get her out of it."

"Maybe she did."

"She didn't," said Ford. "Not that I care. And not that you should care either. Do you?"

"No, not really."

"Now you're lying." Ford seemed pleased. "The trouble with you is, you're all too young." Having said which he concentrated on getting into town.

They got there about half an hour after Lily, but though the Cadillac stood outside the house, Lily was not there. Nor would Ford come in. "I'll meet you at the courthouse," he said. "Don't feel like seeing what Charles did to the old place." He drove off, looking determined but very old, probably to sit alone in the Pacific Union Club over his lunch. Luke went into the house.

Lily had certainly been there. He could not think of anyone else who could have filled the living-room with that many flowers. The effect was the opposite of cheerful. It looked like a funeral, or rather like a living-room after the coffin has been carried out and the flowers have wilted a little. He knew what she had done. She never did anything herself. She had simply phoned up the florists and told them to send over a roomful, and here they were, jammed into every available vase, about ten of them, untouched by human hand. They were mostly blue delphiniums of an expensive length, and larkspur in appendix shades, so that the whole room was in a morbid purple and blue condition. The smell was overpowering. It was the stench of pollen.

It worried him that neither Lily nor Maggie seemed to be about, but he did not want to go searching for either of them. There was a mess of newspapers on the coffee table. He picked up the phone to call his hotel but it was dead. Probably Lily had had it disconnected, because of the reporters.

The case had drifted back to the inside pages, which was some consolation. Another few days and Charles would be way back, in the funeral announcements, and then the matter would not interest anyone any longer. If everything went smoothly, that was. He prayed that everything did go smoothly. Maybe Lily's influence was good for something after all.

The inquest was not until two-thirty. He wandered restlessly through the house and went into the library. The shades were down and at first he did not notice Maggie sitting at the chair behind the desk. She wasn't doing anything. She was just sitting there. He pulled up the blinds and saw that a handkerchief was tightly squeezed into a sodden mass in her hand. He looked at her closely. But she had not slipped. For better or for worse, she was alive now.

"Oh, Luke," she said.

"You shouldn't be in here."

"Can we ever get out from under?" she asked. "Can we?" She looked at her handkerchief, uncurling her hand, and then dropped it into the waste-paper basket.

"Things should go okay," he said. "They can't prove a thing."

"That's not what I mean." He knew it wasn't.

"We can try," he said. He was worried about her, so he spoke too sharply. He went over and leaned against her, burying his face in her hair, and she took his hand. "We've got to, I guess."

"He planned everything so well," she said. "If you only knew how well. I think he even planned this, sometimes."

He looked at his watch. "It's a quarter to two," he told her. "You'd better go upstairs and pull yourself together. I'll wait down here."

FOR REASONS HE DID NOT ALTOgether understand the inquest was to be held in the City Hall. Senator Ford and Lily were going to meet them there, so he drove over with Maggie, in her old convertible. He had never driven it himself before, and that also marked a change. She seemed to take it for granted that he would drive. She had longer legs than he, so he had to push the seat forward. At the stop signs he reached over and held her hand, on the seat, trying to pump courage into her, though he didn't feel too confident himself. It seemed to work. He didn't care who saw them.

"Thanks," she said, the first time he did it, but then her hand became smaller, warmer, and more confiding. He hoped she trusted him: she had too; but it was like bringing up a child in five days all the same. And until he knew whatever it was she hadn't told him yet, he would never be sure of anything.

The Civic Centre was far out, built on once cheap, flat land, in a section of town that had refused to boom, and that was mostly shanties and cheap lodgings and a derelict skyscraper or two. Maybe city halls everywhere are surrounded like state capitols, by the cheaper, shoddier, more furtive kinds of vice: they seem to attract it.

It was not a cheerful part of town and he had trouble parking the car. He thought he found a place close, but a traffic cop waved him on. A tall gangly one very new and efficient in striped breeches and black leather. So they had to walk the whole length of the square, a distance of about a thousand yards. The buildings were in different styles and had the inhuman, malignant atmosphere of all buildings that are not lived in at night. The complex, never finished, had been constructed with an idea of solemn grandeur, but it was only a *beaux-arts* copy of reality and all the details were wrong. The Federal Building was the newest, the civic auditorium the oldest, and the two forms of ostentation did not jibe. It was a sad, spittle-stained place, whose flower-beds and low pressure fountains did nothing to help, and whose brickwork was hard to walk on. The usual flea-bitten bums were collected on the library steps, the dirty pigeons clamoured in the air around some bread an old woman was throwing out for them, and the city hall was dingy. It had fallen down in the earthquake and the original armatures had been suited to the replacement, with the result that it looked not like a new building, but like a reconstructed ruin, ready at any moment to topple in on itself. Seagulls roared over its golden dome, screeching pelagic on the air.

Even in sunlight the square never looked right, and to-day was overcast. He took Maggie's arm and walked up the stairs, carrying his brief-case on his outer side. He was walking a trifle too rapidly for her.

The downstairs into which they entered was gloomy and the day had only made it the gloomier. They went to the rotunda. He had forgotten that, an Irish politician having recently died, they had allowed him to lie in state there. He felt Maggie's fingers tighten on his arm.

As in most *beaux-arts* buildings, the proportions were farcical. What should have been a large and airy place, soaring up through the balconies of the floors to the dome, merely looked like the bottom of a chute; and the stone, despite being touched up with peacock blue and gilt, was filthy with fifty years of grime. There were no spittoons, but the marble floor was stained with spilth. The grand stairs that looked as though, there not being enough room, they had been forced to back up, came down behind the catafalque, which was high and draped with a Bear Flag. Flags also stood at the corners. The memorial wreaths and floral offerings rose in a jumble up against the coffin, each flower marcelled into place, like a lacquered wig. There were four guards on duty, two from the State Guard and two from the Police Department, but they looked neither symbolic nor solemn. The whole arrangement looked as though it had been flung down from an upper story. Men with briefcases walked back and forth across the floor, ignoring it. Its ceremony had been held yesterday and this was the tired aftermath.

They skirted the catafalque, as he held Maggie's hand, and went up the stairs. When they reached the top and turned off into a side corridor she sighed with relief.

"It's okay," he said. "It won't take more than an hour and a half. You won't even be called, at least, I don't think so. Everyone's on your side this time." He pushed open the doors and went into the hearing room.

Lily and Senator Ford were already there. They glanced at the aisle as they heard the doors open and

Luke nodded to them. Lily was strained. He went down to join them, slipping into the row with Maggie, but keeping Maggie on his other side, away from Lily and next to Ford. Ford watched this manœuvre and gave him an amiable, amused nod. But he did not look amused. So there they sat, one big happy family, stricken with grief and public responsibility.

It was all most politely done. They were all nice, well-bred, honourable people who, if they didn't know each other, had at least heard of one another's husbands and schools. They owned property, so they wished no bother. They did not want to see Lily and Maggie, particularly Lily, however. There were seven women on the jury, all in good, enormous hats, and all looking prosperous and faintly but honourably puzzled, full of curiosity and an underpaid determination to do their civic duty. The men were another matter. Luke did not think, off-hand, that they had much to worry about, so he relaxed. The coroner, though, was an efficient man with a bald spot at the back of his head. Luke watched the witnesses. So did Ford. These included the highway patrolmen, which gave the women on the jury some pleasure, since they turned out to be handsome ones; the local sheriff; and Foster, who had to testify to Charles's lack of financial or emotional strain.

The testimony was magnificently suborned.

"In your opinion did the deceased drink heavily?"

Foster hesitated, glancing at Lily and Maggie. "He drank a good deal," he said slowly.

"How much?"

"He could hold his liquor."

Wrong answer, thought Luke. Apparently the coroner

thought the same thing. Ford reached across Maggie. "Friend of mine," he explained. "Used to work for Jerome." He meant the coroner.

The coroner frowned. "Did you ever see him so drunk that he lost control of himself?"

Again Foster looked at Maggie. "I've seen him pass out," he said. "He would sit there and then he would sort of just keel over."

The coroner dismissed Foster and called a Dr. James. Luke didn't know him from Adam. Neither, apparently, did Maggie. She looked surprised. James was Charles's doctor, it seemed.

"Did the deceased have any physical peculiarities?"

His blood pressure was a trifle high. He drank a good deal. He was otherwise in good health.

"Anything else?"

Dr. James thought it over. Luke saw pass over his face a look of startled comprehension mixed with ethical confusion. The doctor hesitated. It seemed to Luke that Ford was waiting.

"He had bad depth perception," said the doctor unwillingly.

Ford relaxed.

"What do you mean by that?"

"He had one far-sighted and one near-sighted eye and they did not co-ordinate properly without glasses."

"What did that mean?"

"It meant that for driving and precision work he was supposed to wear glasses. Otherwise he was apt to misjudge the length and height and placement of objects."

Dr. James had been attending Mr. Shannon for a number of years, had he not?

Yes, he had.

Had, in his opinion, this condition been worsening?

He had not attended Mr. Shannon for two years. Mr. Shannon had had an operation on his left eye ten years before, to bring the muscles into alignment. Another operation might eventually be necessary, depending upon whether or not the muscles slackened.

Had they slackened?

It was difficult to tell. When people with that imperfection grew overtired or had too much to drink, they sometimes forgot where things were, or forgot to correct for the displacement of their vision, and then minor accidents sometimes happened.

"Thank you."

Very neat and tidy, thought Luke. He knew about that operation. It had nothing to do with far- or long-sighted eyesight, or its worsening. He glanced at the jury.

He felt Maggie tighten her fingers on his arm and turned to see her looking across the empty seats. There was a woman on the other side of the room. She was, or looked to be, about sixty, with a round, well made-up face and a head of tight white curls. She was clutching a cane. The only unusual thing about her was that she had in her lap a small chocolate-brown Siamese cat.

"What is it?" he asked.

"The cat," said Maggie. "It's Charles's cat." She looked terrified. The woman nodded towards them and smiled.

"Ever seen her before?"

Maggie shook her head, staring at the cat.

"Mrs. Shannon," called the coroner, and she looked

to the front of the court again. Luke watched her as she rose and went to the witness-box. She moved a little too fast, spasmodically, which bothered him. He glanced rapidly at Ford and saw that Ford had also noticed the woman.

Luke kept his eyes on Maggie. She seemed hesitant, but she was doing all right. She was pale.

They only wanted to ask her routine questions. And then the coroner sighed and straightened up.

"Was your husband a meticulous man?" he asked.

"Very. He liked everything to be exactly where it was first put. He didn't like anything moved. Not even an ashtray."

"Would you call him domestic?"

Maggie half smiled. "No," she said. "He let the servants do all that."

"Who instructed them?"

"We both did."

"That will be all, Mrs. Shannon." Sorry to bother you, and other appropriate remarks. Without looking either at the coroner or the jury, and with her eyes down, Maggie came back to her seat. Luke made room for her and then turned round. But she was not looking at him. She was looking beyond him.

"She's gone," she said. Her voice was barely audible.

Luke got up and told Ford he would be back in a minute for the sake of appearances. Then he walked slowly to the door, a man on his way to the lavatory; and when he was in the corridor sprinted down the hall as fast as he could run. When he reached the elevators they were on their way down. The elevators ran through an open wire cage. He could see the right one just coming to rest on the bottom floor. There was no point in trying to follow.

He walked slowly back to the courtroom. For a woman with a cane she had got out damn fast. Unless she had only come to be seen. And who had let her bring a cat into the courtroom?

When he got back everyone was standing up, jabbering away, and Maggie, Lily and Ford stood in an uncertain group. Though he was stooped Ford was taller than any of them. Luke went down the aisle to them.

"Well?" he asked.

Ford shrugged. He was keeping an eye on Maggie and seemed to turn her over to Luke now. "Death by misadventure," he said. "All very tricky and medical. But the case could be reopened if more evidence turned up."

Lily wandered up the aisle, apparently eager to get away from them. Perhaps she was disappointed in the verdict. They watched her go out through the swinging doors alone.

"She had Charles's cat," said Maggie. She began to shiver.

Ford glanced at her sharply. "Let's get her out of here," he said. "Fast." They went out into the corridor, one on either side of her. Lily was ahead of them. They both talked over Maggie's head.

"Did you recognize her?" asked Luke.

"No," said Maggie. "I never saw her. But Luke, if she had the cat. . . ."

"Don't think about it," said Luke. "Ford?"

"I've seen her. I think Charles knew her once. I don't know who she is."

They went down in the elevator and got out in the hall. Mercifully the elevator debouched at the side and not near the catafalque. Ford and Luke got Maggie outside, still following Lily. There was a cabstand below the main steps and Ford blinked at it in the sudden light. Then he hailed a cab, rushed Maggie down to it, and shoved her in.

"It's okay, kid," he said. "Everything will be okay. But we've got some talking to do. Go home and take an aspirin or something. We'll be along later." He seemed amazingly energetic. He slammed the cab door on her. Luke had a glimpse of her white, scared face; and then Ford took his arm and galloped after Lily.

She had just reached her car and was unlocking the door.

"That's fine. We'll all get in," said Ford.

"You have your own car."

"Shut up, Lily." He piled into the car. "We've got some talking to do."

Lily put both hands on the steering wheel. She was wearing grey suede gloves. "Not now," she said. "Do you think I enjoyed that farce?"

"Who was she?"

"Who was who?"

"You know," said Ford.

"I don't know," said Lily. "I've never seen her."

"She had Charles's cat."

"I know." Lily looked stubborn.

"Then you know what that means. . . ."

"It doesn't mean anything. Charles is dead," said Lily. She looked in the rear-view mirror. "We don't want to attract attention."

Ford leaned forward and put his hands on the back of the front seat. His grip was surprisingly strong. "Lily," he said, "what did you and Charles really do to Jerome?" His voice was soft. "What did Maggie find out?"

Lily squirmed round in the seat. Her face was livid, but she looked scared stiff. "Get out of this car," she said. "Get out or I'll call the police." She jammed her hand down on the horn and pressed it as hard as she could. The noise was deafening. Luke leaned over and pulled her hand away. She hit him on the side of the face, scratching him with the edge of those diamond rings.

Ford leaned back and looked at her. His eyes were small, tight, and angry; and his face was rubbery. "He was my best friend, Lily," he said. "I went to Napa yesterday."

Lily was breathing hard. Suddenly, appallingly, she began to sob. It was much worse than that night in the house, when she had screamed, for it was low and controlled and trapped.

"Charles made me," she said. "I didn't want to."

"No, he didn't," said Ford quietly. "He didn't have to. How did Maggie find out?"

"I don't know. Charles kept the papers. I gave him money." She broke off.

"What did you really do?" asked Ford again. But Lily just stared at him. "Very well," he said. "It doesn't matter. There's plenty of time. There's all the rest of your life."

"Let go of me," said Lily quietly. Luke did so and she closed her eyes.

"She'll tell me some time," said Ford. "You'd better go, boy. Give me her car keys first."

Luke pulled out the ignition keys and handed them to Ford, who put them in his pocket and sat judicially in the rear seat. Luke got out and closed the door.

"It's all right, Lily," said Ford. "I can wait. But you're going to tell me just the same. I'm going to save the girl. I'm going to do it because that's the last thing you want."

Luke saw them sitting there, behind glass, the one in front, the other behind with the keys. He walked away.

XVIII

She thought she knew everything about Jerome when she married him; and she was amused that it had been so easy to do so. He wasn't what girls of her own age, but then she didn't know many girls of her own age, would have called a good catch. He was a better catch than that, for not only was he wealthy, he was important; and except for an old aunt who died a couple of years later, there were no relatives to bother her.

It was exactly what she had wanted. Her parents did not have much money. They lived on earned income, though there was always enough of it. And at finishing school, which she had hated, when they found out about the earned income they had snubbed her. She made up her mind early, watching them, what she wanted to do; and she was always smiling and polite. Her day would come.

Then she brought it off, she could put them where they belonged: not yet, because Jerome was older than she and not handsome, but later, when money and power would count for more than romance.

In those days Jerome had still helped to run, once he had completely run, the North California political machine; and though that meant that he had to mix a lot with the Irish, his family had been there as long as anybody else's family; and she had seen, with him, the insides of more houses and dining-rooms than she had seen before, and had faced the girls on equal terms in the powder-room, or upstairs before the men came up. She enjoyed that. She had always thought that that was all she wanted.

Her father was dead and her mother approved of her. Her mother at last had something to talk about while she played whist. She now got the real inside dope.

Then her mother died in the same hotel she had lived in for ten years. It was the longest she had ever spent in one hotel, but after her husband died she could not bring herself any longer to move. She did think of taking a trip to Mexico, but when the war came she decided that that would have been disloyal.

Lily did not miss her. Of course Jerome was much older than she was. His friends were older, for the most part, even than he was. In a way that pleased her. She felt more secure with older men and they made a lot of fuss over her. But Jerome refused to cultivate the young, and that meant that, as time went on and his associates died off, he would lose his grip on the party machine. The trouble with them was that they had no sense of continuity. They wanted absolute power in their lifetime but they were content to let it go at that. But Lily would have to outlive them. She did her best about that, but Jerome simply did not like younger people. Some of the younger people did not know who the Barnes were.

What she did not know was what was wrong with him. Neither did he. When it began to show up he moved down to the Atherton place and secluded himself there. He would not listen to her advice. He never did. He told her it was incommunicable and to shut up.

"But you can't shut me up down there," she said. "You'll lose everything."

He had looked at her very quietly. He had just got back from the clinic and he knew what was ahead of him. "You married me for one thing and you got another," he said. "You simply made a mistake, that's all."

"But I'm a young woman."

He smiled. "Not so young," he said. "And I'm an old man. You'll just have to make the best of it." He had gone out of the room and up the stairs to dress for dinner. She looked after him, hoping that he would never come down. She never forgave him for speaking to her like that. It was the only thing of the sort he ever had said to her and she knew it was true. That was what made it so unforgivable.

He did not come down very often. He stopped talking too. He saved his words for Maggie. He was fond of Maggie. It was he who insisted that she be sent away to school. And he did that quietly, too. One day, she hoped that it would not be too long, he would not be able to speak at all.

She spent ten years that way in Atherton. Their friends melted away. They were his friends, not hers, and he didn't seem to want to see them. She put up with Senator Ford, and then even he stopped coming round. She hated card games. She hated everything she had that she had always wanted. She could remember the first time the dining-room table had been set for only two. Even so Jerome had not come down to dinner. He refused to see her.

On the way to the dining-room, that first time of dinner alone, she had seen Ethel going upstairs with a tray. Ethel was younger then. They did not talk very much, but she saw that Ethel knew why Jerome did not wish to come downstairs. She wasn't going to justify herself to the servant, but she had to talk to someone. She said she would take the tray upstairs herself.

Jerome was sitting propped up in bed, surrounded by newspapers. He did not say anything to her and she did not say anything to him. She was going to, but instead she put the tray down on the table beside the bed.

"I wish you would come down," she said, after looking at him. "It isn't pleasant for me to eat alone."

He stirred slightly in the bed, looking at her foggily. "I know," he said happily. He got gaga sometimes, but not often. She went downstairs and ate alone.

When Ford got her to give the parties Jerome seemed to enjoy it. He would lie in bed waiting. The night of the first one, when she was trying to put on her ear clips and wondering if they didn't perhaps make her ears look too large, Ethel came in and said he wanted to speak to her. She frowned into her mirror, wondering if she really did still look pretty and wishing there was someone to tell her she was. Jerome was the only person who ever did and she did not care for the way he said it. And she saw, in the mirror, that Ethel had caught the look of irritation on her face. Ethel could be trusted, but she couldn't be fooled. That was what made her unfireable. She has a sinecure for life, thought Lily, just like me, and how she must hate it. With a nervous giggle she got up and went down the corridor to Jerome's room.

She could look down at the hall as she crossed the landing. The house had that special party feeling, not for a lot of stiff old codgers, but for people that might be full of suspense and hope and laughter. Older people didn't have a social laugh. They only laughed with each other in a conspiracy, as something socially proper to do, timing it right. She went into Jerome's room and closed the door.

"You look lovely", he said, "as usual. You're thirty-nine, aren't you?"

She could feel her happy smile beginning to fade. She did not see why deliberately he had to be difficult.

"Oh, well," he said, "Ford will tell me all about it." He played fretfully with the coverlet. She wondered suddenly if he *had* to stay in bed.

"I'm not old," she said. "I don't have some filthy disease."

"Oh, well, you didn't inherit much, did you?" he said. She did not like the way he was so gentle with her. Or the way he always watched her, sceptically, as though looking beyond her.

"I was just wondering who would be first and when," he told her unexpectedly. "I don't suppose I'll ever know. You won't find them very interesting, I'm afraid. Young men never are."

He was right. He was always right. She didn't. It was so tricky to tell how far gone he was. He had his sharp moments even now. She asked about his disease, cautiously, here and there, and she read up in various books which she bought and hid in the library behind the *Biographia Americana*, but she found out very little. Sometimes fast and sometimes slow, she repeated to herself. Paresis was locomotor ataxia. Locomotor ataxia was paresis.

When she said she needed the power of attorney he gave it to her without hesitation. Yet there was something in those yellowing hands that was not weak, but only resigned. After she had it, she sometimes let people stay on and come upstairs, for after a party the emptiness of the rooms downstairs depressed her.

"You'd better take care of yourself," he said one night. It was one of his better weeks and there were flowers in his room.

"What do you mean by that?" she asked sharply.

"Nothing," he said, "just your hair." She was wearing it shorter, because that made her look younger, and though she hadn't had it dyed she had had it rinsed. Nowadays she washed it three times a week.

Ethel came in with a tray. Lily slipped out of the room while she had a chance and went down to the garage. She had an appointment at eight. *She* went to *them* now, drawing up before their houses, or entering a restaurant alone, while the waiter smiled, or sitting well back in a corner, waiting for them and trying to be both self-possessed and cheerful.

But then she had met Charles and she saw things differently for once. She didn't want Jerome in the house any more. He got to bother her. No matter what she did she was always aware of him in his bedroom, waiting for her to go in and talk to him before she went downstairs. And once, in the library, when one morning she was going through the monthly accounts and had her glasses on, she looked up and saw him standing in the doorway in an old green paisley wrapper. She took her glasses off at once. He had caught her in a moment of complete self-absorption. It wasn't often that anybody ever did that.

"It's a fine day," he said. "You should be outside." She watched him and saw that he was not really very weak. He was only bed-weak and sometimes confused. But he had the sickroom smell to him, despite cologne and everything that Ethel could do.

The first time Charles stayed the night they were halfway up the stairs when Ethel came out of Jerome's room and without looking at them, though she must have heard them, went down the corridor towards the servants' stairs.

Charles gave Lily a swift glance.

"It's my husband," she said. "He isn't well." They had gone on up the stairs, but she had not felt quite so happy.

Charles sometimes seemed bothered about Jerome.

"Is he really dotty?" he would ask, with the special well-dressed contempt with which he wore the clothes, and the opinions, that she had bought him.

Even so, maybe Lily would not have gone through with it if she had ever believed she had a firm grip over Charles. She had to have Charles. She did not need Jerome. And then she discovered that Maggie wrote to her father. She never got to see the letters. She believed he burned them. But he wrote answers to them and there was no telling how much he knew or might say to Maggie.

"Give them to me," she said to Ethel one day, catching her with the outgoing mail. His handwriting was shady and ran uphill, a series of pale blue spiders, uneven as the handwriting of an epileptic, with the same pulsating systole and diastole of the size of the letters, even though all his letters were shaped the same way. Ethel gave them to her, but she did not open them. She was still too in awe of Jerome to do that. Instead she looked at them and dropped them down the mail shoot on the corner. It gave her something to do, to take a little walk to the box.

During the summer Jerome became disturbed. There didn't seem to be any particular cause. He had long clear periods, but they always seemed to upset him. And Maggie had not written for some time. Lily wished she would write to him, if it would shut him up. Nor could Lily make her do so. She saw as little of Maggie as she could manage.

One evening Lily and Charles had been up to the opera and had then driven down to Atherton, stopping off on the way for a few drinks. They got back to the house at about one-thirty. The lights were on downstairs as well as upstairs. Lily ran up the steps of the house and into the hall. Ethel was leaning over the banisters, looking crazy. Her hair was all awry.

"Oh, madam," she called. "Something's all wrong." She had been crying and behind her they could hear the racket of things being thrown about. It sounded as though it came from Lily's room.

Jerome appeared. He was carrying the top of one of her side tables, with the legs off. It was poorly glued at any time and always came off in damp weather. She looked up at him. He was tall, slim, and grey, but he did not seem hysterical. He was calm, though his speech was thick.

"What have you done with Maggie's letters?" he shouted. It surprised her that even though he mumbled she knew clearly what he was talking about.

"Nothing," she said. It had never occurred to her to touch them. Jerome's eyes strayed to Charles who was standing behind her, watching.

"Get your lover out of here," Jerome said. "It isn't his house. It's my house."

"Jerome," she called. She wished there was someone to back her up. She was really scared of him now. Perhaps she had gone too far. He had grown much thinner and under his gown his thin legs stuck out pale white and trembling.

"Get him out," shouted Jerome. "I've had enough of this." He gripped the rail and then, taking the table top, dashed it down to the hall. It was light and sailed at a curve through the air, smashed into the mirror over the commode and brought down a vase in the clatter of glass.

"It's too late," screamed Jerome. "It's too late. I'm too old."

"Okay," said Charles behind her. He swept past her and bounded up the stairs, two at a time, grabbed Jerome, pushed him into his room, pulled the door to, and locked it. Jerome did not pound on the door, but just before Charles got to him Lily had seen his face. It was the only time in her life that she had ever seen him scared.

Charles came downstairs, took her arm, and led her into the library. They had to brush past Ethel, who stared at them stupidly. Charles poured Lily a drink and then himself one, swallowed his neat, and taking out the bedroom door key, which was rusty and elementary, played with it in his hand. Then he threw it down on the coffee table, where it clinked and slid sideways over the glass top of the table towards a cigarette box, where it stopped. He shoved his hands into his pockets.

"Why don't you commit him?" he asked coldly.

"I couldn't do that."

"Why not? You've got complete power of attorney (she realized she should never have told him that); and he's not good for anything. He only clutters the place up."

"But Maggie. . . ."

"She's under age. She couldn't do anything," he said curtly. He frowned and kicked a log in the fireplace. She could still remember, now, the way he had kicked that log, with a special, slow, accurately aimed shoe, pushing it firmly down until the log broke in a shower of sparks. It only took him a second. She thought he might singe his trouser cuff but he didn't. "We could be alone," he said. "You run the whole thing anyhow."

"No," she said. For some reason the idea frightened her. "Not yet."

He looked at her scornfully. "Why wait?" She had got to know and dread that look. "You've got what you want. Why not keep it?"

"Is it as simple as that, Charles?" she asked wonderingly.

"That's up to you," he said. He made it as clear as that. Charles or Jerome. He set his not quite empty glass down on the table and handed her his key. "I'd better not stay," he said. "I'll go round to the hotel in Palo Alto. Phone me first thing to-morrow." There was no warmth in his voice or expression.

She did not see him to the door. She went right to bed. Of course she did not sleep, at least not until five. When she woke up it was eight and Ethel was knocking on her door. She called "Come in" and Ethel slipped into the room.

"He can't talk," she said.

"Can't or won't?"

"I don't know. Shall I clean up the hall?"

"No," said Lily. "Leave it the way it is." She waited until Ethel went out and then phoned the hotel. Charles had already left. Somehow she had known he would not be there. She sat in bed, thinking, and then rang through to Jerome's doctor. She got his wife and she could hear children squalling in the background. Doctors who marry before they graduate have a hard pull of it. This doctor was young, he had only recently set up practice, and she knew he would be able to get right over. Charles had found him for her. The previous doctor had not pleased Charles at all.

The doctor was at the house by eight-forty-five. He was even shaved and eager. She watched him come up the hall stairs. She told him everything. On the landing, so that he could not help but observe the state of the hall, she paused for a minute, bracing herself to go into Jerome's room.

She need not have worried. Jerome did not say a word. He only stared at them. He was still trembling. When he opened his mouth he merely mumbled, which was a relief. Pretty sure that he would not and could not speak, she went out into the hall and waited for the doctor.

When he came out she asked what had happened, as though she did not know what had happened. She moved down the stairs ahead of him, terribly afraid that Jerome had not really lost his voice after all.

"He's had a severe shock."

"But his speech?"

"It's hard to tell. Has it been getting worse?"

"Yes," she said promptly.

The doctor did not look happy. He refused to catch her eye. "He could be kept here," he said. "That girl takes pretty good care of him (Ethel was sixty). . . ." He let his voice trail off anxiously. He seemed embarrassed and eager to leave. She noted that he was both young and handsome. That always surprised her about him. Charles did not usually like to know handsome men.

When the door had closed behind him she locked herself up in the library, watching the clock. She knew Charles would phone sometime, but she did not know when. Fortunately Maggie was away at school, in Coronado. It was a good school and as far away as possible. It was only the beginning of the term.

She would have to tell Maggie something of course. She began to phrase tactful letters in her head. She needn't have bothered. When she was told Maggie just looked at her mother quietly and asked no questions at all.

Charles did not ring until eight-thirty that night.

"Well?" he demanded.

"I had the doctor come."

"I know that," he said. "I rang him up last night.

There's a small private sanatorium near Napa: they understand these things. It would have to be done eventually, anyhow."

She held the receiver away from her ear. "I can't do it, Charles."

"Yes, you can." And under that soft, emotional, confiding vibrato was something else that was dangerous. "You want to, don't you?"

"I don't know. Yes. . . ."

"I'll take care of it," he said. "You'd better come up to town to-morrow, to the office."

She went up to town. She had no will left of her own.

It was easy and swift. He made it swift. His name was on the commitment papers. He was her lawyer now. They had talked Foster into handing over the administration of the estate to him, in return for Charles's contribution to the firm. Or hers.

Then they hired a private ambulance and two attendants, who came down from the home. It cost like fury. The earlier in the morning it was done the less fuss there would be, so she was dressed and waiting by eight. Ethel served breakfast, but seemed morose. Then she went up to dress the old man. It had been agreed that it would be better to tell him nothing. There was no point in having any extra trouble.

Alone in the breakfast-room Lily went over to the windows and stared out at the shrubs towards the trees beyond. She noticed that there was dew on everything. It lingered a long time under these trees.

Charles arrived in a black chesterfield rather tightly fitted and with, in that morning light, an oddly pale and almost pock-marked face. They found they did not have much to say to each other. His eyes had that special hardness they always had when he was bringing something off.

They both heard wheels on the drive and went through the living-room towards the hall. Charles let the attendants in and they went right up the stairs, grumbling to each other. Their white tunics smelled of carbolic and starch. Charles and Lily followed. Charles even took her arm.

When they opened the bedroom door Jerome was sitting in the armchair with a bundle of letters in his lap, in the cold early sunlight. He looked up, saw the men, and made a grab for the left post of the four-poster bed. The letters cascaded to the floor together with some photographs. The attendants glanced briefly at each other.

"No," shouted Jerome. "No." His voice was disused but completely distinct. Lily drew back behind the night table in the corner. Charles stooped and picked up the letters and photos and flung them on the bed. They were faded snapshots of Maggie at various ages. Lily did not even have to look at them to know that. Ethel watched, memorizing everything. Lily watched her and Jerome glanced at her, too. His hands were white at the knuckles and he braced himself against the bed. But he was too weak: the attendants pried him lose as easily as a trained diver can loosen an abalone from a rock without so much as splintering the shell.

Jerome straightened up. He looked straight at Lily. "I didn't think you'd dare," he said clearly. She saw with displeasure that Ethel had not shaved him. The stubble was a faint mixture of nicotine-coloured yellow and wiry white. She closed her eyes.

Charles took her arm and they went down the stairs after the attendants. Jerome did not speak again. He did turn to look at the house as though it had fallen down around him. Charles and Lily went outside, got into the Cadillac, and followed the ambulance up to the city, across the bridge, and all the way to the hills. Napa was in the wine country to the north. It produced very good wine.

The sanatorium was pleasant and well secluded, a series of bungalows set in a small wood, with an underbrush of bright orange manzanita trees contorted in half shadow and open sun. The general effect was horrible.

Lily waited in the car while Charles took care of the details. She hated sitting there alone. But when she saw him come out of the office bungalow, talking to the superintendent, a plump, red-faced man with heavy glasses and a bald head, the two of them blinking matter of factly in the sun, she wished that she would never have to see Charles again. She did not want him to touch her. She knew that in some way he had tricked her. She was right: he had.

For it was odd about Jerome. With Jerome in the house she had had something to bargain with. She had not realized that at the time, but Charles had. And now she had nothing to bargain with at all.

That left her Maggie. Maggie was fifteen then. She was a nervous child, easily scared. Maggie was no problem. Maggie never dared to say a word.

With power of attorney and full control now, she should have had everything. Yet somehow she had nothing at all. She stopped seeing Charles. She consented to everything he wanted. She never stopped thinking about him night or day.

And now it was over. She stared through the windshield at a street she didn't even know the name of, near the City Hall.

Senator Ford got out of the car and left her. He had heard enough. He went back to the City Hall, phoned Luke at his hotel, and came out again. As he stood on the steps of the building on the square side he saw, on the big expanse of brick paving, a little boy playing a deliberate game. He chose a pigeon and followed it round and round in circles. The pigeon would walk faster, shake its feathers, glance round him, and then fly off in a low despondent circle into the shrubs. At last an old woman with a basket of bread shooed the boy away.

Ford shifted his gaze. In one of the public flower-beds another old woman was digging up tulip bulbs and putting them in a sack. Her manner was anything but furtive. When Ford looked back the little boy was walking round the pigeons again, but farther away. The old woman was glowering at him: angels of retribution have no sex and very little power, and neither do small boys, public tribunals, or very old men. He went off alone to eat his lunch.

They held the funeral the next day. It was May 2nd, the feast-day of St. Mary the Egyptian, but outside of the church, and of Charles, who had had a taste for hagiography, but was dead, nobody remembered that.

Lily had set the machinery in motion days before. No doubt she would have preferred something less formal now, but once she had started it up the machinery rolled over her. She let it roll. Luke did not have that attitude. He was not indifferent. They had no enemies left but the real one, who was unknown, and there was nothing he could think to do. He did not see why either he or Maggie should have to pay for other people's pasts, and yet that was what they were doing. It was what, so far, they had always done. Only Lily had got off scot-free. Lily had done better than either of them. Lily had had to pay only for her own past.

Somewhere in the back of his mind he was afraid, not of what Ford had told him, or what he thought of it, but of something else. He knew perfectly well of what. When you cleaned out an abscess you had to clean out all of it and let it drain. There was some of the infection remaining, that would suppurate still. He didn't know where or what, but he knew it was there. It was something they could not yet supersede.

He phoned Maggie, but only to reassure her. He needed time alone. He went up to the "Top of the Mark" and had a few drinks and then he went to bed. But first he looked out over the city. He thought instead of Los Angeles. San Francisco was one small tight city, but Los Angeles was a series of towns. It was still possible, down there, to take your pick. People in a unified city like San Francisco think it is themselves who count, but they are wrong. Only the city counts. Like a fire, a city, once it has caught on, needs only fuel and a prevailing wind. Human breath no longer helps it.

Which, he supposed, was why he had never liked San Francisco. Its beauty by night was only electricity; and a thousand men hanging by leather straps in mid-air, against poles, automatically repairing frayed wires and then being replaced by other men, who were younger, did not alter the fact that the wires remained. The people who went on fanning the fire blew themselves away. The fire burned on without them.

All a man could do was to gather his own kindling and set the match. When the fire got too hot you moved away, you didn't jump into it. And home was a nice cool place like a cave or a bedroom, more likely a bedroom, for a bedroom had a door you could lock. And you walked through the city jangling the keys in your pocket, the only reminder you had that you had any private existence at all. Even then, ten to one, when you got home and unlocked the door there wasn't anybody there, but just an unmade bed left over from the night before.

Perhaps that phase was over now. He hoped so. You can never know all the odds, but if you're going to play at all you have to use your own chips. That left him Maggie.

He went to sleep and woke up early. People usually don't like to remember how they feel in the morning. He woke up and could sense his body lying in the bed. It was heavier than it used to be. It was thickening into maturity. Idly he visualized the gymnasium he would go to for six months to keep fit, if he had the time; and the gym instructor in canvas shoes and a woolly T-shirt, looking faintly supercilious with the sadism of the overmuscular, who are getting themselves hunched to give you the works for your own good. It would take about six months. He would start in about a week. If he had the time.

It was a three-quarter bed. He forgot about the wooly T-shirt and the gymnasium smell. Not quite awake he rolled over on his left side and played with the pillow, pretending Maggie was there, and running his hands caressingly up and down over the sheet, the mattress underneath bumpy and uneven. The hotel advertised an air-foam mattress in every room, but apparently this room was the exception.

He realized suddenly that he had a heavy body odour that had permeated the bed and was faintly unpleasant. He forced himself to get up and take a shower. He was pleasantly conscious of himself in the shower. Looking down he seemed longer, if not taller, than he was, and he wasn't in half the bad shape he thought he was in the mornings, waking flaccid in his bed, with his belly against the sheets.

He was hairy. He soaped all the hairs, playing up the lather against his brown skin; and he knew perfectly well what he was thinking about. The idea made him happy and cheerful, so he began to whistle. Then he got out of the shower and shaved with great care, knicking himself twice in the process. Standing naked at the washbowl he looked into the mirror and made faces at himself, pretending he was somebody else, and even tried a sort of half-sensual swoon. Then, feeling slightly abashed, he threw all his dirty clothes into the laundry basket, got dressed, and went down to breakfast. He hadn't put on a dark suit, he hadn't brought a dark suit, and he didn't care. It wasn't his town or his funeral. He felt about seventeen years old.

It was time to get married, anyway. He was on his way up. Marriage was the right thing to do now. But if you had luck, sometimes you even got to marry not only the right person, but the preferable one as well. His luck seemed to be holding out.

He finished his breakfast. He tipped the waiter. He brushed off his coat flaps. He put on his hat and he walked jauntily out into the street, feeling exactly like a full page colour illustration in the *Saturday Evening Post*, for those ads showed him just exactly what he wanted to be and how he wanted to feel, and this morning that was exactly how he felt. Los Angeles had many advantages. Taken right, it made everybody six inches taller and a good deal younger in the jaw; and a theatrical tailor also helped. As a couple, he thought, they should really be a wow.

He did not notice the city at all. What he saw was a portable bar, the good hot sun, and both of them beside the swimming pool, with guests. And why not? Life may as well look like the pictures once in a while: it lends the illusion a pleasant air of verisimilitude.

By the time he was in a cab he had sobered down. He knew one dream from another very well and made no mistakes about which was whose. It wasn't time for his own yet.

He peered anxiously out of the window, glad he would be leaving soon. The trouble with these people was that they thought that the dream and the reality were the same thing. The confusion was instructive. They could keep their city and their pride.

When he halted in front of the Barnes-Shannon house, paying off the driver, he thought he could quite well understand how Maggie clung to her car. It was the sort of house from which you wanted a ready get-away; and he would be glad when he saw the last of it. People had stopped living in it decades ago. It had the hotel smell.

Maggie was waiting for him in the library. There was some sunlight to-day, so she had opened the windows. A breeze through the room made it seem dustier than ever. She had opened the doors, too, as though to clear out the house, and the room was cold. She did not seem to mind. She was sitting, alert and waiting, on the sofa, smoking a cigarette and looking self-possessed. He was glad of that. It was as though she were catching up with lost time.

"Lily went down early," she said. "She's changed, Luke. I can't make it out."

"I know." He shoved his hands in his pockets and looked round the room, the way you look round a hotel room before leaving it, to see if you have forgotten anything. It looked about as impersonal as a hotel room and he wondered if Lily would sell the house or just board it up. It wasn't a room to settle back and be comfortable in. To try that out he sat down on the sofa beside her, took her hand, leaned his head back and put his feet up on the coffee table, looking thoughtfully at his shoes. They were well polished.

"It's like going to a play," she said.

He frowned. "Well. Maybe." He didn't want to talk to her now. He thought she was too keyed up. Yet he might as well know the truth some time, now that it didn't matter. It didn't matter. That was the way truth was: by the time you found it out it very seldom did.

He looked at his watch. "We'd better go," he said, and leaned over to kiss her. She drew away and glanced towards the door.

"Not here," she said. He stood up, disappointed, but she was quite right. Not there.

They went through the house to the garage and she got out her car. She felt like driving this morning and she drove with an efficient, self-satisfied self-confidence. But she was also biting one of her nails.

"What's wrong?"

"Is it really over?" she asked.

"I don't know. I should think so. Anyhow, we'll go away."

"That's what I mean. Can we? I mean, it's a scandal and you're a lawyer."

"People forget," he said, but it was what had been at the back of his mind and he knew it. "We'll go away."

"To Los Angeles?" She watched him briefly.

"Yes," he said, but it made him thoughtful. "Yes. Where else would we go?" He glanced at her out of the sides of his eyes and realized he should have sounded more cheerful. It was the side of it he hadn't wanted to face.

"I don't want to trap anybody," she said. "I never did."

"We can talk about it later," he said warily.

"Yes." There was an acuity in her tone he was not expecting. "But we have to think about it now."

He watched the traffic.

The funeral parlour was in a valley between hills, or what had been a valley once. Now it was built up with hotels and a garage. She parked the car. The car was blue. Most of the cars parked along the street on that side were black. She had been driving bare-handed, but now she slipped into her gloves as though they afforded her some sort of protection. Infections from the dead could be dangerous.

He got out and held the door open for her and they walked towards the building. The reception hall was soundproof, finished in mocha of the shade of a Siamese cat. Lily was sitting on a round ottoman. She did not notice them. She was wearing a black astrachan coat that was heavy and stiff, and which did not suit her at all. Maggie was wearing a little round black hat. Now she lowered her veil, not like a visor, but like a wire cage. She did this automatically as soon as she saw her mother.

Lily looked like an old woman. She would have been more attractive if she had not always tried to appear young. This morning she had made herself up that way from habit, and it gave her two faces, neither of them flattering or kind. She did not speak to them. She just stood up and led them into the mortuary chapel. They were scarcely a unified family, but they pretended to be one, for the sake of the press, except that the press hadn't bothered to come; and for the sake of their friends, except that they didn't have any.

The chapel, in that plaster Georgian which smart funeral directors seemed to prefer, leaving Tudor and stained glass to fellow-operators with a less expensive clientele, had a heavy, faintly disagreeable odour of vacuumed carpeting and scented air-conditioned air. The coffin was placed on a trestle, head on to the aisle. The three of them sat in one row and listened to a few inappropriate words. It seemed to take a long time. He could see, through her veil, that Maggie had her eyes closed, but Lily watched everything with a chipmunk furtiveness. For her, he supposed, it was the end of something. Or perhaps she was counting the house, for she watched the guests rather than the coffin.

Soon enough they passed up the aisle towards the cars. As he looked back he saw the coffin sinking through the floor on an hydraulic lift. The mourners were clumped in the reception room.

"Get out your handkerchief and play faint," he said to Maggie. "Lily can handle them."

Maggie gave him a startled glance and uncurled her fingers, in which a handkerchief lay already crumpled. He looked down at it. It was stiff and dry. He took her arm and got her outside into the street and the car.

They sat in the car, waiting. One or two streetcars went by, clanging their bells. It was a busy intersection. She did not say anything. She hid behind her veil. He saw the coffin carried out and slid on to the grooves of the hearse. Then everybody, like a theatre crowd leaving a not very good show, got into the other cars and he swung Maggie's out into the procession. The blue car was all too noticeable. It was like one false bead on a string. Once they were away from traffic the cars spaced out. He wondered which one contained Lily. Then, at a stop light, several of them pulled up abreast, and he saw her, two cars over, sitting comfortably alone in the back of one of them, behind the chauffeur. She was powdering her nose.

Then they drove on again. He turned and looked at Maggie.

"How did you find out about Jerome?" he asked.

She lifted her veil and stared at him blankly. Then she left the veil up over the brim of her hat and looked down at her finger-nails.

"I found the commitment papers," she said quietly. "I think now he wanted me to find them. He was very angry."

"Is that why you wanted to kill him?"

"I didn't want to kill him." She was quite matter of fact about it, to his relief. "I wanted to hurt him. What good would killing him do? He must have engineered the whole mess. He wanted me to know it, I think." She watched the cars ahead of them and gave a queer half smile. "It's a pity you don't really trust me."

"I trust you." It was the truth, but trust had nothing to do with belief.

"People make a mystery of things," she said. "I always knew what was wrong with Daddy. I think I always did. Ethel told me. But I loved him. He was the only person I had. The only one. I didn't want to see him if he really had gone. I thought he had gone, you see. And Lily said maybe that . . . well, I might have inherited it. It took me a long time to find out she was lying. I could have found out, I suppose, but I never did. Of course for the marriage I had to have a blood test whether I wanted to or not."

"You went to Napa that Saturday, didn't you?"

She hesitated. "Yes, I did. Oh, Luke, I didn't even recognize him. They gave him good care. They had him in a bungalow. He'd had the same nurse for ten years. A male nurse. He just sat around and he couldn't talk at all. He mumbled like a man with his teeth out, but it didn't make any sense. And he got horribly excited. I had to leave while they quieted him. So at least he remembered me still. And then I talked to the nurse. . . ."

"And?" he asked. The car in front abruptly halted and he had to draw up with a jerk.

She looked away from him. "He's only been that way for three years. Before that he was more or less normal," she said. "He was my father. I could have had him all that time." She toyed with her gloves. "They all live in little imitation houses up there, with lawns and window-boxes and everything. Each place has a sort of living-room and a bedroom with a bath. There were stacks and stacks of magazines in the living-room, old ones. The *National Geographic*, and *Look*, and *Life*, and *Colliers*, and *Ken*. *Ken* isn't even published any more. They said he used to read a lot. Now he tears the pictures out. He hides them under the bed."

"Oh," he said. He thought of Lily in the car ahead, calmly powdering her nose.

"I didn't go back to San Francisco at all," she said. "I drove round and round the hills until it was late and then I went right to Bolinas. I guess I wasn't thinking very clearly."

"Ford went up there, too," he said. "To Napa, I mean."

She looked at the cars ahead. They seemed to fascinate her as they wound through the suburbs towards the hills.

"I wouldn't be Lily", she said, "for anything in this world. But I don't want to see her ever again either."

He looked at her with grateful surprise. She carried it so calmly and so well.

On the south San Francisco was bounded by a high and complex mountain, but the mountain did not extend all the way across the peninsula. Beyond the gap so made the cemeteries had been laid out, pushing up the mountain and over the sprawling, rolling hills that eventually led to the sea.

This place, because of the configuration of the ground, was usually foggy and damp, so it had once been farming land. There were still one or two farms abutting on the cemeteries. Mostly they raised poultry. Originally, also, there had been an Italian shanty town here. And everywhere the Italians go they plant cypress trees. Long after they have moved on the solitary green flames of their trees lick up into the sky. There was also the city of Colma. It was still more or less a shanty town where gangsters hung out and the cheaper sorts of vice found a refuge, and where nobody looked very happy. The stoneyards were full of spun sugar angels brought over from Italy, some with the crating still around them. There were florist shops and one or two garden nurseries under the eucalyptus trees. Surely the eucalyptus is one of the noisiest and most restless of trees. The effect of all this was of a mortuary jumble shop. From the rise of ground they could see the competing cemeteries; the one with a lake and a columbarium resembling the Tombs in New York; the one with floral clocks and emblems; the one with the white ducks and Swiss chalet; and several that had no special advantage. They could also see the rows of cheap marble stones crowded together beyond the landscaping of the more expensive private tombs, so that the whole area was like a living suburb, with rich avenues in the middle, the ground growing less valuable farther out and imposing structures on the corners. To make matters worse it was not a foggy or overcast day, but one of those gusty days when clouds alternate with the sun in a concerted guerilla attack, so that just when the sun seemed to help it was wiped off by a wet shadow and the sun came out somewhere elusively else, and not where one was at all.

Charles, he remembered, was to be buried in the Barnes vault. There was to be only a short service. If masses were to be said for his soul, they would be said somewhere else. That duty, he suspected, was now what Lily had left to do. It made him uneasy to think of such masses being said. He had fallen away himself and his faith never went any deeper than the momentary anxiety of prayer when liquor failed. He preferred to think that the dead were permanently dead.

If anything will happen, he thought, it will happen now. Get him in the ground and we'll be safe. The clouds had passed over the sun. It gave him sudden discomfort. Certainty failed and he was ill at ease.

The short procession turned uncertainly down the ridge and into the grounds of one of the cemeteries, ornamented in a false Scots baronial style, with miniature buildings that looked like toys. They had pink roofs. The sward, though not immemorial, was certainly a smooth Gaelic green, and the flowers in their beds looked stiffly metallic.

They passed through the gate lodge and up among the trees, planted too close together and somehow dwarfed, to give the impression of a wood. The cypresses here were planted not by immigrant Italians but by the holding company. They were less slim, of a paler green, and much less tall.

It was a long zigzag up the hill and over it to where, just on the other side, the ground rolled down into what had once been a gully where the grass was softer and spongy underfoot. Small vaults were scattered under the trees, in imitation of Greek temples, or even less compromising than that. The Barnes vault was of the same size as the rest, but somewhat older. They had previously been buried in Pioneer Park and had been moved farther into the country as the city grew. The cypresses here were of a darker hue and the roof of the building was of cuprous tile. It was about the size of a large doll's house in a back yard, and one of its gilt gates stood open.

The cars parked below and the mourners started up the hill to where a priest awaited them. Because of the incline of the hill, it took a while to get the coffin up. Lily, slightly apart from the others, twitched her fingers impatiently. Luke saw her doing it. He took Maggie's arm and they trudged up the hill, also standing slightly apart, but Lily on the opposite side of the group. She looked at them both with a mixture of impatience and apprehension. The sun came out briefly.

There were only about twelve people and Luke wondered who they were. They were too well dressed to have been hired for show. Foster was there, of course. He moved closer to Lily. The others he did not know. For the appearance of things he, too, moved closer to Lily, pulling Maggie with him. The distance between them was publicly obvious, even so.

He did not hear what the priest said. He did not attempt to listen. Perhaps the priest did not concentrate either, but Lily followed every gesture. She was facing the vault and seemed to be watching the open door. Maggie did not look at it. She looked down the slope.

Family vaults, thought Luke, were a mistake. They were so seldom ever completed, even by Medici. Dynasties are soon over and in America they only last a generation.

There was some awkwardness about the coffin. After the prayer, and it was short, was over, the pallbearers stooped to lift it. They were union men. The priest impatiently yanked open the other gilt gate. Since it was rusty he looked at his hands afterwards. The pallbearers edged into the vault whose entrance was not quite wide enough to admit them head on.

Luke felt Maggie tug at his arm.

"Over there," she whispered.

He looked to the left of the tomb and saw the woman who had been at the trial. She was standing slightly up the hill, leaning on her cane, her hand partially covered by the paws of a fox stole. Her face was white, especially as she was wearing dark lipstick, and her head was bare. In her other hand she held the cat. She held it too tightly and it snarled. It had, he noticed, only one fang, and that gave it the look of always drooling. Against the fox fur, because of the colour, it was scarcely noticeable, but as the sun emerged again there was a reflection from the lavender eyes.

Luke did not stir. And as she saw that she had at last been seen, the woman eased her cane and half smiled. Maggie's pressure on his arm was hurting him. With a nod the woman turned and, poking her cane ahead of her, moved into the trees.

"Well," said Luke. "Now we know." He looked around him and then loosened Maggie's fingers and took her arm. As he did so he caught a glimpse of Lily. For some reason she also nodded.

"But who is she?" Maggie's voice was half lost in the noise of the vault doors closing.

"Come on," he said. "She wants us to follow her."

Above them, hidden in the trees, he heard a car motor turning over.

"No," said Maggie. "I'm afraid."

"We have to find out some time," he said. "It may as well be now."

He walked down the hillside to their car. So, unfortunately, did the others. Snarled in the cars he thought he had lost her. But he had not lost her. She was idling ahead and he could see what she had done with the cat. She had put it on the rear shelf of the car and it was sitting there, looking out of the wide-angle window at them. Then the car pulled ahead.

Maggie sat far over to her side of the car and did not speak. It was just as well. He did not want to speak himself. They followed the car all the way to town. Sometimes it pulled far ahead, but they never lost it. It did not want to be lost. He did not want to catch up with it either.

It did not stop in town. It swept down to the approach of the Bay Bridge and up on to the ramps. He followed it. There was not much traffic and he kept the car to a steady forty-five. Far ahead of them and over the slightly rising surface of the bridge highway, like the camber of the earth, he could see the other car. Then it vanished into the Yerba Buena tunnel. The weather was better up here, but moist, so that everything was sharply etched. He slowed down. He did not want to catch up with her at the tollhouse on the other side.

They came out of the tunnel, leaving the city behind them. Maggie involuntarily turned to look at it. It rose white and dirty from its fret of wharves, in an untidy jumble over its hills, with almost nowhere a touch of green. And yet from across the water it gleamed like a magic city. They ran into a military convoy, headed for Yerba Buena and its military establishment. It did not impede them. The woman ahead never looked back, but she slowed down a little while he paid the toll to the uniformed guard. They went through the flat suburbs and began to climb the hills.

It was a steep, twisting climb and they came out above the houses on the ridge route, in different air. The car ahead drew into a garage. He stopped Maggie's car and looked for a moment at the view.

The whole bay and city spread out before them. They could look into the city and see the other, bright red bridge, and, on the far side of it, Mount Tamalpais, yellow and green. On the other side of that was Bolinas.

"You'd better stay in the car," he said. Maggie nodded. It occurred to him that from up here you could see everything, and clearly, precisely because this part of the region was above the rest. Only spectators would live here.

He put his hand on the door handle. "Luke," she said.

"Uh?"

"Please kiss me."

"I'm coming right back," he said. He looked each way to see if the road was empty. It was.

"Please." He leaned over and kissed her and let his arm slide round her. He could feel that she was shaking. There was nothing he could do about that. He was almost shaking himself. But he was glad he had touched her. It reminded him of certain important things. He flicked on the radio.

"I'll try not to be long. Have a cigarette and listen to some music."

He got out of the car and walked the short distance to the woman's house, and when he looked back she was watching him. He heard the radio, warming up, as it became audible. She reached over quickly and turned it down. He waved and went to the front door.

The house was older than the other houses on the way up and had a vacant lot next door to it, on the car side. The ground fell steeply away. Like so many California houses built on that sort of ground, it would have the living-room on the top floor. The house was shabby. The wood was oiled, not painted, but even so it was sun-blistered and splintering at the joins. There was no garden but only a blank wall facing the road. There was a card under the bell. The script was cursive. It said Marie O'Neill. Well, at least we know her name, he thought, and rang the bell.

HE WAS NOT KEPT WAITING LONG. Clearly she was expecting him and she answered the door herself. He had not been prepared for that. He stood on the threshold looking at her.

"You're the lawyer," she said. Her voice was noncommittal. She stepped aside to make way for him with a sort of mock politeness.

With a glance down the street towards Maggie he entered and the woman shut the door behind him. She gave him a cursory, half-disapproving glance, as though she thought he was not much, and walked ahead of him, planting her cane firmly on the rugs. They were old rugs, worn and frayed, but very good ones. The whole house somehow had a patched-up look.

She went ahead of him into the living-room. It was a long room with two panelled walls and two walls of glass that gave on an open slat balcony. Even though it was flooded with light and had that magisterial view, it was still an oddly chaotic and dishevelled room. There was a piano, closed and locked, and a couple of worn-out sofas before the fireplace, near a wing chair, in which she sat. She allowed him to look round the room.

On either side of the fireplace, which apparently she had just had time to light, were crowded bookcases, but the books did not look particularly recent. On one wall hung a frayed but gorgeous Spanish ecclesiastical cope, and by it some etchings by John Marin of Venetian palaces all falling over in their lagoons in the scratchy technique of fifty years ago. The pictures were mostly line engravings. There was an undusted desk. It was the sort of room where everything was once of the best quality, stylelessly, and nothing is ever replaced and, though it gets chipped or cracked, is never broken.

"I call it home," she said drily. "Sit down."

He sat. The sofa was too big for him. She leaned forward from her chair. "There's a decanter beside you," she said. "You'd better have a drink."

Watching her he unstoppered the decanter, which was unwashed cut crystal, and poured himself one. It was sherry and he poured too much. He detested sherry, though this was good.

"Well," he said, after a sip. "Who are you?"

"My name is on the bell, I suppose you read it. The O'Neills are a little older than the Barnes." She shrugged. "The only difference being, I suppose, that the insurance company wouldn't pay up after the Fire."

"What's that got to do with it?"

"Nothing. Only an irony. But you're too young for irony."

She smiled and he saw that she was unexpectedly beautiful, with a distinction Lily lacked, but though her face was delicate, she did not look soft. It made him marvel at the consistency of women, that she was so well made-up and yet so old. Probably not even that white hair that lay in a row of curls all pointing the same way across her forehead, to lower it, was all rooted in her head. He wondered for whom all that care was expended, not realizing that women dress for themselves.

"I know all about you, you know," she said, as though saying: "Make yourself at home." He was sure of it. He was not surprised. Los Angeles had taught him that as you move up through the social pyramid the number of people who knew each other grows smaller and smaller until, presumably, at the top, wreathed in clouds, like a public monument to a god unknown, is somebody who knows everybody but whom nobody ever meets. There were also women like this, who are nobody but who know everybody. You see them sitting patiently at parties, sometimes with their legs crossed, not talking very much, with no obvious power, but always listening. They were usually demons on the telephone. They liked to get their own way.

"I'm sure of it," he said, as drily as she had.

"That's the girl out in the car, isn't it?"

"Yes." He looked at her warily. By the sherry was a dish of biscuits, an old maid's hospitality, and he took one. He was too much at his ease in this room. Perhaps it was the off-hand way she had welcomed him, as though he was late for a familiar appointment. Perhaps it was the resemblance the room had, in some way, to Senator Ford's house, a resemblance that was not much altered by an impatient woman's touch, an inefficient attempt to dust and a bowl of badly arranged pale white tulips over by the windows. Looking at her more closely he realized for the first time that she was really extremely angry, but with a restrained, probably permanent anger that squeezed down to find an outlet and found only scorn.

"Why did you want us here?" he asked.

"Us?" She seemed amused at that. "I don't know," she said. "I don't think I've made up my mind yet."

"You waited long enough."

"I thought perhaps it wouldn't be necessary," she said. "I've no desire to see any of you."

"That's frank, anyhow."

Miss Marie shrugged, but he thought that as well as being angry she was also amused, being one of those people who can stand outside themselves without losing their personality. If he had not had so much to lose, he realized, he would have liked her. She had some kind of personal resource that made it easier for her to play the grande dame than it was, for example, for Lily to do so. All the same he remembered Maggie in the car and grew cautious.

"Who are you?" he asked again.

She shifted her cane with amusement. "Not anybody these days," she said. "Ford might remember the family."

"I don't mean that."

"Of course you don't." She eyed him easily and did not seem entirely displeased with what she saw. "You're too young for us. You don't belong here."

"I'm glad I don't."

"Oh." She shrugged. "You're just starting. You belong down there. This isn't your sort of puzzle at all, is it? I shouldn't think it was. It has roots. And you don't have any roots, at least not here."

He did not so much care for that turn of the conversation.

"That's better," she said, seeing his discomfort. "I suppose you think you love the girl?"

"Maybe."

"She looks simple and insipid enough," said Miss Marie. "And probably pleasant. That isn't the point."

"What is?" he asked slowly, watching her.

She looked down at her fingers and waggled them. "I brought Charles up," she said. "I grant you he wasn't commendable. Very few people are, really. But I made him. He probably wouldn't admit it. He preferred to use people and then forget them. But somehow I don't think he found it so easy to forget me. I didn't let him." She smiled firmly.

"I enjoyed both comedies. The inquest was so well done. Ford always did have a certain cleverness of that wire-pulling sort. And the funeral was about what one would expect. But I don't like to see brains put away in a box. Not my brains. They were my brains."

"Charles was clever."

"Oh, yes, he was clever. But he wasn't intelligent. He was only shrewd. It took me a long time to find that out. A long time. I met him when he was fourteen, you see. I have never married. I never wanted children. But when you get to be my age and something you have made is destroyed you don't like it. Nobody ever forgives you for smashing the best china."

"And so?"

"I thought perhaps Lily Barnes would take care of that," she went on. "But she didn't. Perhaps I know why. The Smiths were nothing: she's not as clever as she thinks. She has a very special kind of stupidity."

He let her talk. What interested him was not her anger or her contempt, but the calm with which she spoke, even though she was angry, even though she had no part in all this, but was some judge of a secret court, elected late in life, who enters the courtroom for the first time.

There was no clock in her living-room and no movement. There was not even a mirror. Time must pass slowly here, he thought, sifting down like dust on a table of unanswered letters. It was not that these people were too old; but they were old in another way that did not have anything to do with years. And the young can only live in their own world. The air is too thin for them to breathe in any other.

"I met him by accident," she said, "if Charles ever did anything by accident. Perhaps he picked me out in advance...."

He did not comment. He had almost finished his sherry and he did not want any more. Despite all the windows the room was shadowy. He supposed it was cheerful only at night. He eyed the woman's cane.

"You were at the Bolinas house," he asked, "weren't you?"

"Yes."

"What was in the picture frame?"

"Nothing of any importance," she said hesitatingly. Her eyes lit up for a moment with something like mischief, as though she had read his mind. "No, she didn't kill him," she said. "She didn't have the time. The point is that she meant to. And suppose I said that she had? That's what I've been wondering. Suppose I did say that."

"It would prove nothing."

"But I don't want to prove anything," she said. She seemed suddenly sad and wistful. She was one of those old women who have kept their sex in a fragile, porcelain, contrived way that is none the less genuine for showing art. She had avoided that confluence of the sexes that makes the elderly as merciless and malicious as eunuchs. It meant also that she had retained her feminine logic. And of feminine logic he was afraid. Its conclusions were always as unpredictable as its methods were untraceable. A boyish woman like Maggie, already slightly old-fashioned, and so clearly of the 1930's, though born out of place in that sequence of time, but with some understanding of men; or a woman as domineering as Lily and with as openly tortuous a dishonest mind, was elementary and comprehensible. Women like Miss Marie were more difficult. Their other side of the fence was never left unmended and ran down the years to the original Adamic property line.

"I haven't made up my mind," she said suddenly. "I wanted to see you first."

"You've seen me."

She frowned slightly. "What are you going to do with the girl?"

"Marry her," he said, the first time he had admitted that even to himself. Apparently that showed.

"You aren't certain, are you?" she asked. Again she smiled and stretched out in the chair, leaning her head on one elbow and watching him. "I still know some people," she told him. "And you are a lawyer. It's amazing how soon people forget scandals like this, but they don't really forget them. They save them up for when they may be needed. And then, with a little reminding or a word here or there . . . well, a good many careers have been finished that way and you are not really very well established yet. Also I understand the girl can be difficult and odd. Which is another fulcrum, in a way."

"That's over with."

"Is it? Are you sure?"

"Quite sure," he said, but his eyes were a little wider and he wondered if he was. Suddenly he wanted to leave. He did not want to hear any more about his own doubts. He started to rise.

"I mean what I say," she said. "She took away something that belonged to me."

"Nobody belongs to anybody."

"I want someone punished."

"And so what do you think you will do?"

"I think I'll let you think about it yourself," she said. "Come back and see me to-morrow."

"You can't play with people. Charles tried that."

"I think it depends on the game," she said. She frowned and stood up. "I think you'd better go. It isn't very easy to keep my temper, you know. And I don't even dislike you. Or the silly girl. Or any of the whole lot of you. But sometimes one wants to even up the score, I think." She stood with a slight effort, slightly swaying, leaning on her cane, and looked around the room. "It's hard to tell whether you've got a spine or not," she said. She smiled again, but only to herself.

"Suppose I don't come back?" he asked.

"You'll come back," And he knew she was right.

He turned and walked out of the room and down the hall, and there lingered for a moment, not wanting to open the door. But he knew she was watching him sardonically, so he opened it and let himself out of the house.

He needed to think. Whether he had a spine or not he did not know either. He was ambitious. He didn't want a finished career. That would have been worse than an unfinished life. He did not want to be turned back, now that he had climbed, but he did not want to be alone, either. Perhaps he was capable only of that special kind of love that is always grateful for receiving what it needs when it needs it, like the love of a dog. And Miss O'Neill knew that. He wished he had not met her, for it left him knowing it, too.

He faced up the empty road and saw the car waiting. Maggie had her face turned towards the bay and was watching it. Then she saw him and honked the horn. He forced himself to wave at her and smile, wanting to do that, but feeling a little smaller than his own gesture. He walked swiftly towards the car, without a backward glance, and got in. They were both smiling, long after their real smiles had faded.

"Let's go for a drive," she said, obscurely tactful, and he looked at her gratefully. A drive was what he needed. He headed the car uphill, away from the house, up over the crest to the secure woods on the other side, where the city was no longer visible. He told her all about it.

"Oh," she said, "I see." She glanced at him sideways, around her falling blonde hair, and withdrew into herself at the same time.

"I have to go back to-morrow."

"We're leaving to-morrow."

"We can stop on the way," he said. "Was there anything good on the radio?"

She smiled nervously. "I was planning what we'd do down there," she said. "What kind of house we'd have and everything. Perhaps that was bad luck to do."

"No," he said heavily. "It wasn't bad luck."

He would marry her, but he did not want to marry her because he had to. People marry each other, but they marry their social roles, too. He wouldn't give much for their chances together if he was just a Spanish-Mexican failure. It was not that she would mind, but that he would. It is all very well to lose the world for love, but not so wise to get lost in it for the same reason. Some people have to have both. Some people do not dare to fail.

Could the woman ruin him? He knew she could. Anybody could ruin him. He didn't have foundations. He only had props. He wanted to stop the car and get out and run, and was ashamed of himself because he wanted to, which only made him want to run the more.

He put on the brakes and swung the car off the road, under those everlasting eucalyptus trees. He knew it didn't matter what he said to Miss Marie to-morrow. What mattered was what he thought about to-night. And she knew it, too. He didn't want her to win, for a secret personal defeat can never be rectified. It ruins us for good.

"What is it?" asked Maggie.

He switched off the ignition and groped towards her. "Oh, come here," he said. "Come here."

XXII

NOR DID MISS MARIE HAVE ANY easier time of it. She, too, was locked up with her own thoughts, a little too dry to fight green memory.

She had been pretty as a girl, but too intelligent to make a marriage; and, at the same time, not quite eminent or rich enough to achieve the proper social marriage possible despite intelligence. Her father was a successful seed and grain merchant who put all his money into real estate and who owned a house half-way up Nob Hill, though the family was not particularly social. Even so, in those days, perhaps because of her deportment, she had known most of the more interesting of the better families, but always the older members of them rather than the younger. At the time of the earthquake and the Fire she had been staying in the country with friends. She was twenty-five and already over-ripe. She was a safe guest to ask anywhere, for she presented no danger either to the sons or the daughters of a family, and she left her father at home.

The earthquake began during the very early morning. They could see the first fires starting up in the sky over the mountain. She drove in the next day, in a barouche. She managed to get to the Van Ness approach to Nob

Hill, but there she had to abandon the carriage. The crowd was thin. The panic was over on her street. A few people were wandering about searching for things left behind among the façades of the houses fallen to the ground. There was still a lot of dust in the air, and though the fires were not visible by day, you could hear the city burning with a soft rush of omnivorous flame. There was something aimless about the wanderers. They were like the pickers of an unprofitable crop. They moved as such workers do, through fields of silence.

Her house was just below the crest of the rise, near the site of what is now the unfinished cathedral. She reached the top and looked at it. She just looked. The whole front had collapsed into the street. All the decorations had been shaken off the walls of what rooms remained. It was to look into the front parlour of a doll's house. The pictures were still on the walls. They rose and fell in gusts of tricky wind. A bedstead projected from the upstairs rubble. And that was all.

She walked on towards the shell of the Fairmont Hotel, an unoccupied lamasery without windows, and from there she could look down on the city burning. Ruin had not even made it unrecognizable. She knew each street so well.

She walked down the hill. Her own carriage had been wrecked by a sudden cave in, but another one came by and picked her up. They went out from town to Twin Peaks. They had put up tents there. The emergency organization was impromptu but efficient. It was even possible to procure water. She met several people she knew. Some of them pitched in and helped and some did not. She was given a bed and was not uncomfortable.

For five days, at night, it was impossible not to see the city burning, and as it burned some ruined buildings and towers became more gauntly prominent than others, until you thought you would never be able to forget them.

A few days later they excavated her father from the rubble. He had suffocated to death. Six months later the insurance company, a Swiss concern, bankrupted by claims, announced that it would pay only to the letter "m".

Friends were very kind. She managed to secure a teaching position in the public schools as did one or two of her friends, all old women now, or dead. You did not need a teaching certificate in those days and some of her father's friends were on the Board of Education. They stayed on it and she stayed on as a teacher. She enjoyed teaching. It was just that her past had been completely removed, as though by surgery. She had had to start life again with only the clothes she stood in.

Then, as she did every year, she took her vacation in Santa Barbara, about 1935. She had arthritis, which the climate helped, and she found the town agreeable. She was in her fifties. She would be retiring soon. She did not know what she would do once she had retired. Every day she went down to the beach, planted a deck chair and a sun umbrella, and either read or knitted or else simply watched the ocean or the people.

She soon noticed one boy who came every day and who also watched the people. He was thin and weedy, with impossibly white skin and champagne shoulders. She supposed he was in his early 'teens. Physically he was unformed. His movements were jerky and she knew that he was unsure of himself. But he was teaching himself to swim, and about his efforts in that direction there was a mathematical precision and certainty. His application was ferocious. He was overstraining himself. She wondered why.

She did not really go to Santa Barbara, but to Carpenteria, a small beach resort twenty miles south of it. She went there in preference to Santa Barbara because she was no longer smart and it never had been, which she found restful. It was a small, random, and almost empty town, a few cottages and houses scattered over an unfinished real estate development, grass in its streets. An arroyo led down to the sea between yellow cliffs. The beach was humpbacked, but of fine white sand. There were tourist cabins on it and one of these she rented, for she liked the sea smell and the sea sound of the night. It was not a place where younger people came, so he must live there, she thought.

She watched him for several mornings and realized with amusement that he had spotted her and wanted to speak. That made preliminaries unnecessary. She watched him come out of the sea with his too thin and not attractive body, and waited until he walked up the beach. He was puffing hard and his face was purple. Each day he crossed the beach closer to her chair.

"You don't have to be so hard on yourself," she said, as though they had talked before and been over the whole problem. She liked talking to people. But outside of school she seldom got the chance any more. "You shouldn't. You might strain yourself."

"You have to learn properly," he said. "It's important."

"Is swimming so important?"

"It's something I *can* learn," he said.

"But why do something you obviously hate?" She smiled up at him. "How old are you?"

"Thirteen." He had a lumpy, shapeless, cuttlefish kind of jaw and he hadn't yet learned how to lie very well. He hadn't yet learned that you have yourself to believe that which you want other people to believe about you. She knew he was older than that and wondered if it was only vanity or something else that made him conceal the truth.

They went on talking about why he wanted to learn things. It wasn't knowledge he wanted. She suspected it was equality. He was ugly and he was clearly poor, but he had deceptively large brown eyes and a very bad temper. The temper, she thought, for she was already thinking about it, would have to go. She found she preferred to watch him in the water. In the water he looked more helpless and more malleable. Three days later she asked him to lunch. She had got tired of eating alone.

The chief glory of Carpenteria in those days was a forty-foot and heavily mature avocado tree. She gave him avocados. They were not the polished, bright green, smooth skinned kind like Fabergé jewels. Those were rare in those days. These had coarse purple skins, they were large, and they had an overipe, often fibrous, pustulent yellow fruit. She served them sliced in half, with paprika and lemon juice.

He did not know how to eat them and he did not like them, but he pretended that he did know how and that he did like them. The third time he came to lunch he had clearly persuaded himself that he did like them and had added them to his list of foods which carry social prestige in the eating. She watched this process with lively amusement. That left him green olives, sweetbreads, Rocky Mountain oysters, seagull eggs, pompano, pheasant, grouse, venison and, when he was old enough, caviar. She was sure that he would persuade himself that he liked them all, and she had an impulse to try him out on abalone, wienerschnitzel and German wine soups. She was vastly amused and in some way fascinated. He was so patently learning and so patently afraid to show that he was. The eagerness was pathetic, but the effect on her was curiously appealing. She began to wonder who he was and what would become of him. His knowledge of some things was rather frightening. She looked forward to seeing him every day.

Then she told him she wanted to send him to a good school. She had gathered that his family was not much, though physically he seemed well-bred enough.

"They don't understand," he said. He looked up hopefully. "I could run away." He seemed to take it for granted that she would take care of him.

"I'm afraid that wouldn't do," she said. "Perhaps I'd better speak to your parents."

"No," he said.

"Why on earth not? You're very clever. You shouldn't be lost. You could make anything of yourself.'

"Yes," he said, "I know."

"Do you know?" At that stage his assurance still amused her. But she had hurt him and he wandered away thoughtfully. Next morning he appeared at the cottage with a bag. She was taken aback. She sent him packing. And then, as she thought it over, she went up to the post office and asked a few questions. They looked at her oddly, but yes, they knew.

She left the post office, squinted in the sun, frowned, and followed directions. He was an orphan living with his married sister. Beyond the town was a long, narrow, ill-tended farm of bad yellow earth. It was an artichoke crop that had been allowed to go to seed. The tall, desiccated plants straggled up out of the baked earth, each topped by brittle purple blossoms. There was a board shack. The sister was not much and the husband was worse, but the house was clean and respectable. There was even a cat under the stove. To her surprise it was an expensive and well-tended Siamese cat. She made her proposal.

The husband was relieved but the sister remained suspicious. She was an oversexed but washed-out looking woman. They didn't seem much to care. They had an enormous unpaid bill at the local grocery store. At any rate it seemed enormous to them. She paid it, so in a way she bought Charles for ninety-seven dollars and eighty-three cents. Then she went home. The next day he appeared with his bag, looking pale. He looked as though he had given up something he had not wanted to give up. He also looked determined.

"You shouldn't have done that," he said. He was not exactly angry. He was scared. "I didn't want you to know about them."

"Somebody always knows these things," she said. "What does it matter?" But she saw that to him it mattered very much, and that he would never forget that she knew where he came from. Considering what she was doing that was perhaps just as well.

She cut short her vacation, took him back to San Francisco, scrubbed him up, bought him some clothes, and packed him off to the Jesuits. She thought somehow that the Jesuits were the appropriate choice. They always liked to know exactly what things were worth without actually asking the price and he had that sort of mind himself.

She enjoyed teaching people things. She did not enjoy it very much as a profession, for she found her raw material somewhat dull. Most of her students were not interested in the things she really had to teach. Charles was different. She did not have to teach him. She only had to show him. And so from the back of her mind she pulled out all the disused but not entirely worthless knowledge she possessed and she began to wake up. He came to her house twice a week. She began to look forward to that. Nothing was ever said about these sessions, but it gave her pleasure to be useful. They went through wines and table manners and forks. She even got out the Georgian oyster forks and what other silver had been salvaged from the house in 1906, after the looters had got through with it. Sometimes in junk stores she had seen things that she had seen before in other people's houses.

Life with the boy was like pretending to be elegant again. And talk had to go with it, so she talked about the old families and their scandals, and she could see him memorizing everything. It was nice to watch knowledge like that being packed away securely and so not lost.

Between them they had a lot of fun, she thought, despite that cold eye with which he watched everything all the time. It was a pity he could not relax, but then the autodidact never could. It was his one obvious flaw, she believed. She found out soon enough that there were others.

As soon as he went to college he began to change. He kept people curiously in separate compartments. He had no friends. He should have made some, but he did not. She thought that was also a fault. He said he did not need them. The college—and he had got a scholarship to Stanford, again through her older friends—was the better of the two available, but it was fifty miles away. She missed him when he did not come to see her and he did not encourage her to go down to see him.

"It would look odd," he said, embarrassed yet angry.

She was hurt. "What if it does?"

"You don't understand," he said.

She was beginning to understand very well. People like Charles could never be taught that while most people have to do the correct things, really correct people can do anything they feel like. That saddened her. It was the missing extra half-inch that would always cut him down to size.

He came to see her less and less. The house was empty without him, though he did sometimes stay the weekend. He was less tractable than before. She would catch him watching her, speculatively. She told him, because he asked and had been agreeable for once, everything she knew about Senator Ford.

"He's on his way down," he said.

She had a vision of people in his mind, arranged on a graph of influence, riding always against their will, in banked elevators of prestige. She didn't like it. She could not see her own name on the graph and did not want to. But when he asked her about Lily Barnes he was more cautious about it, so she knew that Lily was important to him. She began to watch him.

Then, one day, she saw him with Lily in town and she knew instantly what the situation there was. She drew back, not wanting to be seen, and spent an unwilling half-hour hiding herself in Gump's, a reasonably diverting dry goods store. She felt suddenly shabby and let down, and the downstairs table furnishing glitter of the shop together with the social titter of male clerks did nothing to make her feel any better.

Seeing him outside herself, and away from herself, with another woman, that air of watchfulness of his, that had once seemed bright and amusing, was more clearly opportunism. She wondered how anybody could be taken in by it. Yet Lily had looked happy. Well, it had made her happy, too, if she confessed the truth of the matter. She began to understand Charles's secrecy. It had the secret in it that his charm only worked on one person at a time and he knew that. It gave her an idea.

He did not see her for a month and that made her angry. There was no reason for his being so obvious about casting her off. Nor was she to be cast off that easily. He might do as he pleased with other people, but she was determined that he should not do so with her, if only out of a sense of the fitness of things.

One thing he would not do was that he would not allow her to telephone him at college. She did not telephone him at college. She was angry. She telephoned him at the Barnes house. The maid answered, laid down the phone, and Miss Marie could hear voices in the background. When he came to the phone he was clearly rattled. Good, she thought, and was deceptively sweet. She asked him to come to see her. He had always wanted to meet the Sterns, for theirs was another house he had not entered and which he felt it was important for him to enter, even though they were Jewish. She said she had arranged it for Saturday. She knew that would work. He was still envious of houses he had not been in.

She hung up. She knew he would come, not so much because of the Sterns as because she had frightened him by phoning the Barnes house. And he did come. She even knew he would come early to embarrass her by catching her before she had dressed, so she dressed at six-thirty. Then, quite contentedly she settled down to wait.

She did not intend to feel any of the emotions that a cast-off woman feels. She did not feel them, really. She tried to, but could not quite manage it, because she understood him too well. However, she had spent eight years teaching him everything she knew and she did not intend to let him forget it. She pursed her lips and drank a glass of sherry and waited. The trouble was that she was fond of him. That one loves a well-trained dog does not necessarily make it lovable. It does not even have to be lovable to be loved. On the other hand one is not pleased when it begins to run away, or prefers the neighbours' house down the street, the neighbours who never had to housebreak it and therefore feel it is cute. And one doesn't much like the neighbours down the street either. They only just moved in. They don't belong to the neighbourhood.

He came early, as she had expected. He had taken a taxi up the hill. That must have made him angry for she never gave him money. Lily, she supposed, did.

"You're almost a stranger," she said, when she answered the door. Then she turned her back on him and marched into the living-room, letting him follow her.

"You shouldn't be so open about it," she told him, when she had poured him some sherry.

"Open about what?"

"About dropping old friends." She settled back in her chair. She saw he was wearing a new suit, better cut than she had seen him wear before. He was learning about luxury, she thought, and also thought how he must hate to do so, for she knew instinctively how he was learning. You can always tell when people have just been to bed with each other and she had seen him with Lily in town, after all. No doubt he felt a young man on his way up has to do many things that bore him. He had already grown his beard. He hid behind it. He had even learned how to control his temper. He had not yet learned how to control his eyes.

"You didn't pick me," he said slowly. "I picked you."

She knew exactly what he meant and she snorted. "You didn't have much choice in those days," she said. "And perhaps even so you made the wrong one. I know a lot about you, Charles."

His eyes contracted slightly and she was pleased with what she had said, though it made her feel curiously tired. Really, it was not worth the bother. His sister had died two years before and he had been relieved when he found out. He found out because she told him and she had found out because the brother-in-law had asked her to pay for the funeral, which she had not done. That left his brother-in-law and she supposed a few people in Carpenteria who wouldn't remember him now, with his beard. It had never before occurred to her that men grew beards to avoid their own pasts as well as their own selves. She thought for an instant of the bearded nineteenth century and saw that beards, looked at that way, explained a good deal. "You won't do anything," he said.

"I don't have to." She had said enough and did not want to pursue the subject. She rose. "We'd better go. We're due at the Sterns'."

He was sulky. "I don't want to meet the Sterns," he said. "They're Jewish."

She blinked. It sounded so silly coming from him. Lily, she supposed, must be anti-Semitic. She looked at him contemptuously and he got up and put on his coat.

She greatly enjoyed seeing the Sterns again. She had known that they would not like him and they did not. Like so many Jewish families they were most themselves as a group. Charles tried to charm Mrs. Stern, but her daughter was also there, watching from the side. Charles's charm was based upon a curious felinity that worked well with middle-aged women and some businessmen, but confronted with the young and androgenous charm of a Jewish family, where the men are nothing until they are fifty, and the women everything until then, and where it is impossible to tell who is the most important member of a family because it is the family itself that is important, Charles was at a loss. They thought he was young, brash, silly and perhaps also stuck up and rude. She was very pleased. She had made him his first enemies. It was about time he acquired a few enemies and she was delighted when he realized that something had gone wrong. It gave him someone else to avoid and that was the only way to hedge him in.

It was the only malicious thing she had ever really done and she had enjoyed doing it thoroughly.

She had challenged him and she wondered how he would solve the problem. He could not get rid of her and she knew too much. For a while, after the evening at the Sterns, he avoided her, for she had taught him a well-needed lesson. She had taught him how much he still had to learn and so had forced him back to that mental Carpenteria that drove him forward through life, away from it. She wanted to know what would happen next. She had begun to enjoy following the folds of that oddly crumpled mind. She wanted to know how he would solve the problem.

He solved it by making her his confidant. He told her everything that he had done that he knew she would not want to hear. He had turned her to some use after all, for everybody has to talk to someone or else keep a diary, and no doubt he thought she was safer than a diary. Like so many autodidacts he would retain all his life a terror of the written word.

She got to be pleased with her new role. She derived a certain pleasure from comparing what he was making himself into with what he had been, long ago, on that beach. She had given him the opportunity. And in a way it was a luxury to be insulted, when no one had ever dared to do so before.

But she did not like it when he told her dirty jokes about what he did with Lily. That was going too far. It showed an essential lack of respect for decorum and for the sexes which she could not admire. He had no respect for men, for women, or for himself. He had only ambition and pride of place, which is no real personal pride at all, but a surrogate personality that protects the inferior from being hurt. All the same, she could hurt him, she knew, if she wanted to. She did not want to any more. She did not care. When he wormed his way in with Foster at the law firm, she did however ask him what he was going to do next. After all, he could not climb much higher in his own particular world. To go anywhere else he would have to level out.

"Marry the daughter," he said.

She was a Catholic and he was a Catholic, and though that made no difference to him, or at bottom to her, life had other rules and regulations that were even more stringent and binding. He had caught her out this time. He had genuinely upset her. She did not like the idea at all.

"Nobody's going to know," he said.

"The daughter is."

"The daughter doesn't count. Nobody cares what she thinks. She can be managed."

"Then why marry her?"

He shrugged. "Why not? It seems appropriate somehow. You could come to the wedding."

"Thank you. I don't enjoy farce."

"I do," he said simply.

Telling her everything seemed to give him great pleasure. But he did not tell her about the marriage. Perhaps he did not know very much about it. He did tell her about the return to the same room at Del Monte though. He thought that was a huge joke. Or did he? She could not be quite sure. It seemed to her that sometimes he was tired of his jokes, or perhaps that was her imagination. Or perhaps he had at last gone too far, even for himself. She knew he had been found drunk, once, not in public, but in one of the better hotels. He must have blanked out completely. He had insisted on taking all his clothes off. He had laughed the matter away, but he had seemed worried when she brought it up. And then he had bought the house at Bolinas, no doubt to drink in, privately.

So something, she knew, had gone wrong. It could not have done anything else. He had got what he wanted; and anything else he wanted he could not get. He had not the public personality for political office. Certain people would never have him. There was nowhere else for him to climb.

And Bolinas, she thought meditatively, was not unlike Carpenteria in a different place. The same arroyo cut between similar cliffs to the sea, though the sea up here was more dangerous than it was down there. The beach had the same hump to it, the cliffs the same yellow colour. It was a neglected place, with few visitors, and those not of the first rank. There were even surrounding farms which, if they did not grow artichokes, at least had a good crop of thistles; and the two plants were of the same family. She gathered he went to Bolinas rather a lot, to drink himself silly. Maybe he had tired of it all at last.

The thought of that made her sorry in a way she could not define. So she had driven up there on impulse, perhaps out of some past tenderness for what he might have been. She had stood in the hall of his house and heard all about Jerome.

She had not known about Jerome. That was one of the things he had not told her. She turned round and went out instantly, around the side, to the garage. With Jerome he had gone too far. Jerome was someone she had known as a child. Jerome was part of her own life.

And then when the girl had run out she had gone back in, because of what she had heard. It had never occurred to her before that he would or could touch any part of her world. It had never occurred to her that he would dare. She wanted to have it out with him. She went into the living-room and found him there. She was considerably shaken. The cat came in from the kitchen. She had not known about the cat, either, but she remembered now that there had been a cat in that shack at Carpenteria. It was something else that he had never mentioned. It was obviously spoiled and well taken care of. It was loved and incapable of love, as he had been. Siamese cats are, once they are out of the kitten stage. It stood in the doorway, watching Charles. On an impulse she could not explain, though she hated it on sight, she scooped it up and took it away with her. It scratched her badly before it settled down. She did not like to see animals ill-treated. Perhaps somebody hated it even more than she did.

She had also taken the photograph. She had found it while searching for something to wrap the cat in, to prevent its scratching.

So that was that.

She got up wearily now and went out to the kitchen to feed the cat. She kept it locked up in the kitchen which was at the other end of the house. It would not eat while she was in the same room, so she had to go out again. She moved round restlessly. She did not know what she felt. She did not blame the girl. She did not blame anybody. She did not really want to see anybody punished. He was better dead. But she had found him, and she had brought him up, and she had taught him all he knew. He was all she had. It was not fitting or fair that nothing of all that should be left to her. Someone, somewhere, should have to pay for that. She did not see why it should have had to be, ultimately, Jerome, a man of her own age and stock.

Certainly she did not want to wind up feeding a sinuous brown cat. She wanted to reach out and touch someone. She wanted something back. But she was not stupid. She could not have it back. It was gone for good. It never was.

XXIII

Luke had a bad night. He could not sleep and he had nightmares. He had left Maggie and gone to his own room. He was faintly ashamed of his own weakness. They were staying at the house in town.

He thought about Los Angeles. He did not like his apartment there. He did not like his life there. He did not like to live alone. He had never found anybody with whom he could live. He did like his office. He could see it clearly.

The firm was not an old firm. It had been in business ten years. It specialized in criminal law and the flashier forms of divorce. The business was actually based on the histrionic talents of the senior partner, a squat ugly man who went to the gym twice a week and who had carefully greyed hair. Luke handled race cases, when they came up, and he seemed likely to be popular. He was getting good at it. The offices were finished in cross-sawn cedar and everything else was greyed to match. The lettering on the doors was in a square modern face, carved out of wood and even all the way round. The designing consultant had done a good job. Luke's own office, though small, was restful and soothing. There was a portable bar and a television set, and he and the senior partner shared the same toilet and shower, though the senior partner had a dressing-room and Luke did not. The other two partners, on the other hand, did not have a shower. He did not have his own secretary, he shared a secretary with the other two partners, but she had, for the past year, put flowers on his desk, even when she did not put flowers on theirs. That is, she put flowers on their desks when she remembered to, but he never had to worry about there being flowers on his desk at all. He liked flowers.

He had not dropped his Mexican friends. He liked them and liked to get away with them, but recently he had not had much time. He had bought a new convertible a year before and was looking forward to turning it in on a newer one. He had not thought about buying a house because he didn't need one, but if he had thought about it he could have swung it easily enough. He did not go to the gym, he was not that old yet, but he did go out to the beach on week-ends, both to swim and to do some muscle building, but only if he went out with some of his Mexican friends who had a passion for that sort of thing. He was careful not to overdo it. Too many muscles would not suit him and he had other ways of evening up the social score.

Swimming kept him in trim: he liked to swim far out. He liked being envied, he liked being admired, he liked his having climbed out of the Mexican ghetto; and he was proud of that, without pushing the issue at any time. But he did not like to think of ever having to go back down into it. He could not go back down into it.

There was also Maggie. She was awake now and alive. She was older. He felt slightly ashamed of himself for the game he had played with her and with himself when they were younger. He had not known the score then. There was pride in having her know him as he had been and as he was. The difference was perceptible, and if she loved him now he was pleased, for it meant she loved, as he did, what he had made himself. He liked to keep the score. He didn't mind being remembered for what he had been, even if some of his past gaucheries now made him wince. There had probably been plenty of them. They came back to him sometimes. He didn't know whether she was in love with him. Nobody can ever really know that, except in bed, for a little while. But he did know she was in love with his body, and he had a good body, and he couldn't think of any better place to begin.

He got up and saw it was 4 a.m. He went down the corridor and into her room. The curtains were not drawn and he stood in the doorway, watching her. She was curled up on one side and her body, under the covers, made a long young line that was vulnerable and nice. Besides she hated it here as much as he did. She didn't belong here either. And that was something worth knowing. It helped.

She stirred and he quickly let himself out of the room and stood at the balustrade, looking down into the crypt of the hall. "Oh, hell," he said. "Oh, hell." But he knew he had made up his mind. It made him feel the sturdier for having done so. He went back to his room, flexed his back muscles, because they ached, and lay down on the bed without pulling the covers over him. He smoked a cigarette contentedly, enjoying the luxury of having won out over his own fears about his future. He had taken on a dare. And he supposed it was that young and vulnerable curve of her body under the bedclothes that had made him do it. That was what he had had to see. Deliberately he pitched the cigarette into a corner of the room, and rolling over on his stomach, went blissfully to sleep.

He woke up at eight, but he did not feel tired. He showered and shaved, in that illogical order, and went into Maggie's room to wake her up. When she was awake he went downstairs without even bothering to notice the house any more, said hello to the maid, went through to the garage, got Maggie's car out and drove it round to the front of the house.

Lily's car was already parked there. When he saw it he stopped and whistled. He did not see her. He was making his second trip down the stairs with Maggie's bags when he saw her. She was coming out of the living-room, pulling on her gloves, and she was not wearing black. He stopped and put the bags down half-way up the stairs.

"You're both going," she said.

"Yes."

"Isn't that a little soon?" But her voice conveyed no emotion. It was only something for her to say.

"No," he said. "I don't think so." He glanced down at her with momentary compunction. "What about you?"

"About me?" She smiled to herself, but not at him. "I'm going back to Atherton," she said. "I'll shut this place up."

"Why not sell it?"

"No, I won't sell it." She shrugged her shoulders. "I'll leave that to you. You'll probably enjoy selling it."

"I'm sorry you feel that way." He meant it.

"I don't think I feel any way." She glanced up the staircase. She clearly wanted to avoid seeing Maggie. She had been sneaking out of the house, almost as though it were no longer hers. "Oh, go away," she snapped, "and have done with it." She blinked rapidly and went out the door. He waited on the stairs until he heard her car start up. In some way he felt sorry. She was alone now. She had lost both husband and lover. Nobody should be alone. It was not compassion he felt, but sympathy.

Maggie came out of her room. She was only half dressed and she was in her stockinged feet.

"Hurry up," he said. "We're going."

"Was that Lily?"

"Yes." He crooked back his neck to look up at her. "I ordered breakfast unless you'd rather go right now."

She hesitated. "I'd rather go." She looked at him as though not quite believing that he was there.

"O.K.," he said. "I'll tell the maid not to bother. I'll wait in the car."

He went outside. It was sunny for once, though some fog was still caught among the buildings on the hills. As usual there was nobody out in the street. Pretty soon she came out carrying a handcase. She smiled at him, looking up and down the street, and got into the car. It was amazing how many times they had both looked up and down that street, and he wondered what for, for it was always deserted. There had just been the fear that maybe one morning it wouldn't be.

She did not say much, but she watched which way he was going. At the top of Nob Hill he eased the car down past a clanking trolley, diving into the financial district. When he took the road that led to the Bay Bridge rather than the road that led over the sluices of the factory district towards Los Angeles, she let out her breath with a long sigh. Neither of them looked back at the city, but she didn't look towards the Berkeley hills either. The day was too clear. It made the hills appear too close.

"I'm sorry, honey," he said, "but I have to go back to see her."

"She won't really do anything, will she?"

He noticed she seemed to take it for granted that she could if she wanted to, the way children always believe their elders can punish them, until they are themselves past a certain age.

"I don't know," he said. "It's hard to tell." He thought she might as well know the chances. "She might be able to make it unpleasant for us."

"Do you care?" she asked slowly, not looking at him.

"We both care, and you know it. But I don't care that much."

"But, Luke, are you sure you can afford to take the chance?"

"Are you?"

"Yes." Her hand fiddled with the knob on her window. "Yes, I am."

He laughed. "I'm not going to send you away," he said. "Not ever. But it's different down there. Have you thought of that?"

"I hope it is," she said fervently.

They were on the approach to the bridge, and since there wasn't any traffic coming their way he speeded up and got to the other side as fast as he could. "It's early," he said. "I thought we'd go to Planters' Dock for breakfast. We may as well have a drink on it." He wound through the traffic. They had bored a tunnel through the mountains, to connect the valleys beyond with the bay. On the other side of the bore was Planters' Dock. It was a night place, but he thought they could get some scrambled eggs there and a highball or something.

It was a big fake South Sea Island set on top of a hill. The hill had been dotted with plaster copies of Easter Island statues whose flat faces leered down towards the highway at an artistic tilt. At night they were lit up with green and orange floods. He turned up the private roadway. He thought she might as well get the true Los Angeles feeling, for it was a very Los Angeles kind of a place; and he could use a little of it himself. They even got their ham and eggs and coffee and two rum highballs apiece, with a lot of garbage in them, very artistically done. It was quite a change from the sort of places they had gone to in the old days, and if the windows had not been tinted or the area built up recently the view would have been magnificent. It was all very restful.

"Are we running away?" she asked.

"You bet we are," he said. "Straight home."

They went back to the car and he climbed up to the ridge road by the back way, past an artificial lake and a carefully preserved wilderness area that contained a perfectly preserved golf course. It gave him a pleasant feeling that everything was under control to drive that way, through trees.

They reached the house soon enough and there was no

question this time whether or not she would stay in the car. She stayed. He was running things now.

The house, if anything, looked shabbier than it had the day before. He rang the bell.

She was waiting for him, as before. When she opened the door she was holding the cat. He looked at it blankly. It was not a nice cat. It looked thoroughly ill-natured and uncomfortable, for she was holding it by its middle, so that both ends sagged down, and it twisted its face up to him and yowled. She dropped the cat and it ran from the room. She watched it run rather thoughtfully. Wordlessly she made way for him to come in and shut the door behind him. He went ahead of her into the living room, as before. Neither of them sat down.

"Well?" he asked. He jangled the keys in his pockets and then stopped when he realized it annoyed her.

"I don't know," she said. She looked at him with some complex emotion that did not have a name. It had a great many things in it, but defeat was the main one, mixed with a certain aged bewilderment. "Somebody should pay for this."

"It seems to me quite a lot of people already have," he said. "They had it coming, too." He shoved his hands into his pockets, slightly ashamed of himself for feeling self-satisfied and proud about having taken a decision against what might be his own advantage. Maybe in his case the melodrama was built in. If it was, he was not sorry.

"I should tell you," he said. "I'm going to marry her anyway. Maybe you can make it difficult, the way you say, but I've made up my mind."

"I haven't made up mine," she said, and he saw that it

was not a threat, but only that she felt alone and did not know what to do.

"He had it coming," he said. "You know that."

"I know that. I didn't until . . . well, Jerome was someone I knew. Once, a long time ago. He shouldn't have touched Jerome."

"He didn't care one way or the other."

"I know," she said. "I suppose I knew it all along."

He hesitated. "That puts you one up on Lily," he said. Suddenly he put out his hand. "Good-bye," he said. She looked at him from a great distance, and then took his hand, but without smiling. She watched his face instead.

"Some day make up your mind," he said. He didn't want to defeat her. He wanted to leave her the comfort of a threat. "There's a statute of limitations, even on libel."

She played up to him gratefully. "Not on gossip," she said. "And in ten years perhaps love does not mean very much."

"It matters now." He wished he could stop and sit down and talk to her, but he had met her at the wrong time in the wrong way. Yet there was something beguiling about her. She was someone he should have known, rather than Ford, and at the same age as Charles had. But she had wanted Charles.

He turned round at the door. "What was in the picture frame?" he asked.

She did not answer at first and he thought she had forgotten him. "Nothing," she said at last. "Just a picture. Nothing that meant anything at all."

He thought he understood. He said good-bye again and left. She did not show him out and he had not expected her to do so. At the end of the hall he turned around and she was still standing in her living-room, looking not at him, but through the window, at the strange modern city across the water, that was not the city she remembered or that any of them any longer knew. As quietly as he could he let himself out of the house.

So he did not see her go over to the desk. By the time she went over to the desk he was half-way down the hill. She slid open one of the drawers, the sort of cluttered drawer that accumulates discarded odds and ends, and took out the photograph. It was an old photograph, faded and brown, of a woman of perhaps fifty, leaning on a cane, wearing a big straw hat, gazing confidently into the camera with beside her a young boy. He was long and gangly and about fourteen, and he looked into the camera, too, but with an eager, almost anxious face. They were both smiling, but in different ways. In the background was the beach and some surf. She looked at it and then she put it back in the drawer and turned the key.

There were other pictures in the drawer as well, even more faded, but she never looked at those. One of them was of a young girl of oh, say fifty years ago, with her hair tied in a bow, a pensive finger to her cheek, and with a sweet, confiding face. It had faded badly, but the smile remained.

It was merciful, she thought, that he did not know that each to their generation, they were all the same people, at different ages, in a different milieu; that they became each other; that in two generations his seed would be spilt for a Charles, a Lily and a Jerome, endlessly; he could save only himself. But who was merciful to her? She was the older one, whose wisdom died. She had inherited only herself, and that was not enough. For her the wheel stopped spinning like a prayer wheel on a mountain, cracked with cold.

THE QUICKEST WAY TO TAKE THE road for the south was to cross the bay once more and drive down the Bayshore Highway that paralleled it. It was a big six lane highway with overpasses, underpasses, clover-leafs, safety lights, and a high accident rate. The region was proud of it. But using it involved passing through Atherton, fortunately not the secluded part where Lily lived—it by-passed that—but the new, recently developed area of smaller, jerry-built homes. Maggie looked the other way.

The sun was bright. "Look in the glove compartment," he said. The glove compartment was really a drawer, and he had put his sun-glasses in it that morning. Sun-glasses, when you put them on, help you to pretend that you're really living in a private world. Sun-glasses help to cut the glare.

"Thanks, honey," he said, when she slid them over his nose. He squinted at the drawer. "There's an extra pair if you want them. They help."

She reached in the drawer and took them out and put them on. It made them look like any couple, driving anywhere. And maybe, just for once, that was what they were. All the same he knew he would feel better after they had got far enough south to hit the first indigenous palm trees. People are better off where they belong.

Ischia—Roma—Atherton
15th July 1953
9th May 1954